River of Dust

River of Dust

—

Virginia Pye

UNBRIDLED
BOOKS

Unbridled Books

First paperback edition, 2014
Unbridled Books trade paperback ISBN 978-1-60953-103-4

Library of Congress Cataloging-in-Publication Data

Pye, Virginia.
River of dust : a novel / by Virginia Pye.
p. cm.
ISBN 978-1-60953-093-8
1. Americans—China—Fiction. 2. Missionaries—China—Fiction. 3. Kidnapping—Fiction. 4. Nomads—Mongolia—Fiction. 5. Retribution—Fiction. I. Title.
PS3616.Y44R58 2013
813'.6—dc23
2012039098

1 3 5 7 9 10 8 6 4 2

Book Design by SH • CV

First Printing

For John,

Eva, and Daniel

In or about December 1910, human character changed. I am not saying that one went out, as one might into a garden, and there saw that a rose had flowered, or that a hen had laid an egg. The change was not sudden and definite like that. But a change there was, nevertheless. . . . All human relations have shifted—those between masters and servants, husbands and wives, parents and children. And when human relations change there is at the same time a change in religion, conduct, politics, and literature.

—Virginia Woolf,

"Mr. Bennett and Mrs. Brown,"

Collected Essays

Northwestern China
1910

One

The Reverend loomed over the barren plain. He stared at the blank horizon as if in search of something, although to Grace's eyes, nothing of significance was out there. Sunset burned his silhouette into a vast and gaudy sky. Standing tall in his long coat on the porch above his wife and son, he appeared to be a giant—grand and otherworldly. Perhaps this was how the Chinese saw him, she thought. Her husband spread his arms toward the blazing clouds and shadowed flatlands as if to say that all this was now in the Lord's embrace. The breeze shifted, and billows of smoke circled their way. Grace watched the Reverend's outline waft and shimmer. She would not have been surprised if his body had gone up in flames right there before her eyes, ignited in a holy conflagration with only a pile of ash left behind to mark his time on this earth. Grace shook the strange notion from her mind, although she wondered how so good a man could appear so sinister in such glorious light.

As he started down the porch steps, Grace roused their sleeping child from beside her on the seat of the buckboard. "We're here," she whispered. "Our sweet vacation home."

The boy opened his pale blue eyes and blinked. How would it

appear to someone so young? Grace wondered. Desolate or full of potential—she could not know. The Reverend lifted the boy from her arms and swung him high on his shoulders, Wesley's favorite perch. He rubbed his cheeks and surveyed the endless plain.

"If you look closely, you can see all the way to the Great Wall," the Reverend said. "And beyond it, the Ming Tombs and the enormous sand statues of Buddha that defy all belief. Then come the tribal provinces and the vast Gobi Desert that stretches on and on, further than you can imagine. I have seen it all, and I promise to take you there someday."

Wesley squinted into the slanting sun.

"That would be marvelous," Grace said. She slipped her hand into her husband's to step down from the wagon, and they proceeded on the rutted road.

"I am afraid that you will find the countryside here far from marvelous," the Reverend said. "It is too dry and forlorn to be called pretty. I hope, though, that it will grow on you. In the fall and spring, the light turns a most remarkable bruised shade at the end of day when the mourning doves return to roost in the willow trees."

"You are waxing poetic again, Reverend."

"Forgive my enthusiasm for boulders and scrub brush."

"There's no need to convince me. I have all faith that you have chosen well for our respite." Then, as they arrived at a narrow stream with a tree hanging over it, Grace took a seat on a rock and added, "I can see that this willow alone is reason for a visit."

The Reverend reached a hand toward her hair and patted it kindly. "Your forbearance is remarkable in someone so young. In all ways, you suit your name."

Grace blushed, which she knew was quite ridiculous. He was her husband and father of her child. Still, it was hard not to think of him as her master in matters of the soul, which were the only matters of consequence. Even after marriage, she continued to call him Reverend as she always had, and he never dissuaded her. That only seemed right.

"Don't you find this spot spectacularly Chinese?" the Reverend asked as he set Wesley down near the stream and took his hand. "It is as if we have stepped into an idyll depicted in brushwork. The setting warrants such artistry precisely because it is so lacking. The way they attribute beauty to bare rocks and ravines and rain clouds is really quite strange."

"But suppose I had not liked it here in the countryside?" Grace asked as the breeze made playful havoc with strands of light brown hair fallen from her bun.

The Reverend glanced across at the cottage he had built over the previous months with the help of his Chinese manservant, Ahcho. "I suppose then we would simply turn around and ride back to town and let the desert do whatever it liked with our little home."

"That's too sad to consider." She looked across at the charming structure that rose up surprisingly from the barren landscape.

"The desert winds would turn it to rubble in short order. You know how a corncrib or an outbuilding on our plains back home will tilt and then tumble if left uncared for?" he asked. "I believe the winds carried all the way from the Gobi can be at least as insidious. The weather has no mind or care for us."

She pushed the dusty soil with the toe of her laced boot. "But surely our cottage is better made than that?"

"You have far too much faith in me, my dear."

He looked down at her, and although she knew he was teasing, his face hardly showed it. Grace felt the breeze and breathed in the mossy air by the stream. She admired the tendrils of willow swaying in the trickling water and wondered if she could have been happier than on this day in June, here with her accomplished husband, healthy young son, and another child on the way. The Reverend bent and accepted a stone handed to him by their boy. A routine transaction and yet it made Grace marvel at her remarkable good fortune in this most unfortunate land.

Wesley stood straight, a miniature version of his upright father, and pointed to a cow in the field across the dirt path. The animal chewed at the brittle grass, oblivious to the watchers who wondered at its strong appearance and appetite.

"Odd, I didn't notice that creature before," the Reverend said. "I don't see how I could have missed it all those times we worked at building the cottage. It must have been left more recently."

"Perhaps someone will return for it soon." Grace stood and slapped the infernal dust from her skirt. Fine yellow silt wafted out from the folds of linen. They called it loess, this loamy soil that blew in from the distant Gobi. She would ask Ahcho to buy a better broom in Fenchow-fu and bring it with them the next time they visited the vacation home. She followed the Reverend and Wesley across to where the cow grazed.

"Quite surprising to see such a healthy animal in these lean times," the Reverend remarked. "No ribs showing. Any farmer would want to keep a close eye on this one. I cannot imagine who left it here unfettered."

She thought she heard an uneasy hitch in his voice and tried to judge if the Reverend was merely registering a general complaint about human profligacy or a more specific concern. When he noticed her watching him, he smoothed his brow and tried to smile, although his mouth more readily formed a mild grimace.

"Nothing to worry about," he said. "I have brought you to the countryside so that you might let go of all concerns."

As she continued to study him, a humming began in her head: a slight bothersome background murmur that was not altogether a noise but could grow to become one if she was not careful. It was a matter of controlling one's worrisome sensibilities, she reminded herself. She was, quite truly, a cheerful person and always had been.

The Reverend then addressed their son with an insistently joyful tone quite unlike him. "You may pet the cow if you wish." He lifted Wesley, and the boy's hand shot out toward the twitching tail. "Don't grab hold of it, although there is nothing more tempting. Just pat the hide. That's right."

Her husband now fully smiled down at Grace, and her heart ached to think of the effort it caused him to be frivolous for her sake. She stepped closer to his side and touched his jacket sleeve. "Reverend, I know you have brought me here so that our unborn child stays with us this time. I am most grateful."

He froze for a moment before handing her their son. He appeared ready to speak but had lost the words and now was unable to bring himself even to look at her. He stepped away and surveyed the plains.

"It is perfectly all right," she said more softly, for she knew that her words bruised him as if they were stones. "Mai Lin is in the cottage unpacking our things, and the door is shut. She can't possibly hear us. Ahcho has gone off in search of hay for the horse, and our little Wesley is too young to understand." In her arms, as if to prove the point, their son kicked his legs in delight as he patted the cow's back. "There is nothing shameful in it," Grace tried again. "I have heard that back home husbands and wives discuss such matters nowadays."

The Reverend took out his handkerchief and wiped his nose. Then he folded it carefully and returned it to his breast pocket. Yet still, he did not speak.

Instead of dwelling on her disappointment, Grace chose to help free her husband from his own harsh self-judgments, for surely he must have sensed he had fallen short. But how could she expect more of a man so preoccupied with matters of the spirit? She whisked away any unreasonable hopes along with the flies on the back of the cow and began to pet the animal with pretend delight, which was silly given that she had spent enough time on her grandparents' farm to know a work animal for what it was.

The smell of smoke wafted near again. She could see that the Reverend felt some relief that her onslaught had subsided. He appeared happily puzzled by the simple concerns of this world as he searched for the source of the distant fire.

"They must be clearing the fields," he said, rising onto his toes and rocking back again. "Extraordinary how spring brings out the optimist in man, even the poor farmer with no rain in the forecast. I believe the Chinese are even more resilient than my father was in a bad year."

"They have to be," she said, more flatly than intended. "It is their pitiful circumstance."

The truth was that Grace had seen no signs of industriousness on their ride into the countryside from Fenchow-fu. The fields stood fallow as the drought entered its second year. To her, the black cloud that had appeared on the horizon seemed to be rising not from fields as a sign of some farmer's forward-thinking efforts but instead as an indication of trouble in the last hamlet they had passed through. Then again, she was more apt to look for indications of ill luck or sorrow.

He had been right to bring her into the country, away from the town of Fenchow-fu, where, outside the missionary compound, instances of human suffering abounded. The Chinese children to whom she taught kindergarten routinely ate dirt. Many of their parents, good Christians, had not seen proper soap in months. Grace presided over the weekly ablutions where lye and a small strip of cloth were handed out to the long lines that formed before the men's and women's tubs. But how these people survived on so little sustenance remained a mystery to her. They ate nothing more than pale broth and dried meats swarming with flies, stone soup, and mush made from the ragged grasses nearby.

And those were the ones who still had homes. The beggars in the streets sat on their haunches not far from human and animal refuse. They stared at her with eyes scabbed over and unseeing. The smells, dear Lord, even the memory of the smells should have been enough to make them gag, as Grace did suddenly now. The humming in her head started to return, and she felt upset with herself for having brought it on with unpleasant thoughts. She bent forward and tugged at her high lace collar, covering her choking sounds with a cough. But the Reverend clearly recognized her familiar symptoms and appeared at her side in an instant.

He took the child from her and wrapped his long arm around her waist. Grace knew she was showing weakness by leaning into him, but she held on anyway. She looked into the wild red sun dissected by the black horizon. Was it happening again? Her knees buckled slightly as the vibrations in her brain persisted.

She glanced back toward the house and was not surprised to see Mai Lin appear on the front porch. Her amah had an uncanny way of knowing when Grace needed her. She squeezed her husband's arm, and he looked down at her strangely. Had she called out to Mai Lin, was that why her servant had come outside?

Grace swayed as the sunset pulled her gaze toward it. She stared into that bloody ball and saw red in a Chinese chamber pot, red on her linen nightgown. Her knees gave way, but the Reverend kept her upright and held her tight to his side. Twice Mai Lin had come to her in the middle of the night when Grace had needed her most. The old woman had rubbed ointments and herbs into her skin, swinging incense to calm her. Grace had survived, although her two unborn babies had not, but the Reverend was correct. It had all been too much for even a sturdy Midwestern girl.

Grace gripped him now in hopes that his unwavering stance would stop the dizziness in her head and erase the streaks of red behind her shut eyelids. After a long moment, she came to her own rescue with a biblical truth: the thought of being made of her husband's rib seemed right. She opened her eyes and saw that he was Adam surveying his world. And she was but Eve, the lesser one, and grateful for it. She must hold on to that perspective at all costs, although other, perturbingly discordant notions had started to seep into her mind even here in this distant outpost.

Then, far off, from the direction of the smoke, they heard the faint rumble of fast-approaching horses. Two specks came into view, and within a few moments the smudges of motion became riders charging their way across the open plain.

"Nothing to concern ourselves about," the Reverend said to his wife, "Most likely men of trade on their way to market. Perhaps the cow belongs to them."

When the horses came within fifty yards, he could see that the riders were not dressed as was customary for the region, but more like nomads of the borderlands. He had seen their type in his more distant travels toward the Gobi and the Mongolian steppes. They wore sheepskin coats draped heavily over their thick shoulders. Tattered rags stuck out beneath the matted fur, as if they had been on the road for some time and had sampled a piece of attire from every district they had passed through. Smoke smudges darkened their faces, and oily strips of cloth and strings of leather held back their slick black hair. Around their waists and across their chests hung amulets and metal canisters to store snuff and other sinful potions. Long sabers slapped against their legs, and daggers poked from their belts.

The Reverend handed Wesley to Grace, who slipped around behind him as the horses pulled up abruptly in front of them. The two men began shouting. The older one gestured for the younger one to hop down. He did and circled close.

The Reverend squared his shoulders and straightened to his full six foot four inches. He stared hard into the younger man's bearded face and did not move or betray anything but calm. The older man on horseback pointed from the Reverend to the cow and back again.

With an uncustomary chuckle, the Reverend said in English,

"Why, it's only the cow they're after." Then he spoke in a local dialect and asked the men, "Is this your beast, then?"

The men froze, apparently astonished that the white man seemed to know their tongue. The younger man came near again and poked at the Reverend's topcoat with a filthy finger.

"Or perhaps you know to whom it belongs?" Grace asked.

The Reverend grimaced. While he was proud of her ability to pick up the language, he also knew the rogues would not approve of a woman speaking to them directly.

The two men suddenly turned to her and let out a startling cry that echoed on the still plain. The Reverend's jaw tightened as the younger man took his knife from its sheath. Wesley began to whimper, and the Reverend patted his head. The man's dagger began to shadow Grace's chin. The tip of the blade flipped up her lace collar, and she let out a small, involuntary gasp. The young man laughed, and the Reverend had no choice but to step forward and speak more forcefully.

"Gentlemen, we have no claim on that cow. If you have a dispute, it is with the owner. We wish to pass in peace. We are here in the name of the Lord Jesus Christ and intend to follow the exhortation of live and let live. We assume that you will do the same."

The older man's face tightened. "Lord Jesus?" he asked.

The Reverend's eyes grew bright. "Yes, you have heard of him?"

"Lord Jesus, king of the Ghost Men?" the older man asked.

The Reverend turned to Grace. "How remarkable. They know of Him and the Holy Ghost already." He looked to the men, and the edges of his lips rose in a genuine smile.

Surely, the miracle of salvation could cleanse even the filthiest of louts. And the Reverend was fast surmising that louts indeed they were: the smoke smoldering on the horizon seemed irrefutable evidence of what these hooligans had torched along the way.

The older man suddenly began to shout again. He let out a hideous cackle followed by a long, low growl. Staring down into the Reverend's blue eyes, he spat at his chest. The man thrust his saber at the sky. "No Lord Jesus! Death to Lord Jesus!"

He released a stream of sounds the likes of which the Reverend had never heard before. He felt certain the man was the devil incarnate, screaming with every intention of waking the gods—both his and theirs. The Reverend had met with fury and treachery before. He knew that to stand in the face of it, to neither turn one's cheek nor one's back but to straighten the shoulders to face one's fate, was the only way to illustrate the true strength of the Lord. He stared into the man's wild face, ignoring the spit and the curses and the swords.

Grace began to whimper and held tighter to his waist, pressing Wesley against him, too, until the child clung to his father's back like a frightened monkey.

"Please," she said, "let us alone. Take the blasted cow, we don't care. Let us be. Certainly, we have done nothing to harm you."

These words seemed to infuriate the older man beyond all else, and he threw his thick leg down over the horse. He landed with a thud on the ground, his fur boots sending up a cloud of dust. He raised his sword over Grace's head and began chanting in words the Reverend did not understand. Not words so much as sounds, rocking and keening, as if he had experienced a great loss. The older man bowed his head in soulful prayer. After a long, low moan, he looked up and clapped his hands.

The younger man appeared before the Reverend and thrust his hand into the minister's breast pocket. He snatched the white handkerchief neatly folded there. His grimy fingers held it aloft, whipping it in the breeze. The thing unfurled as he waved it in circles, and the older man laughed, although not as maniacally as before. He seemed somehow calmed by the sight of the small white flag on the breeze.

The Reverend was relieved that his wife did not insist on further communication. It was best to remain as neutral as possible. The dangerous men seemed to be releasing their fury, and perhaps that meant they would move on soon. In the meantime, the barbarians appeared positively light-hearted now. As the younger one waved the handkerchief, the two joined arms in a little dance. They each held a corner of the cloth aloft and spun around it like peasants at a festival, two simpletons rejoicing over the harvest. The Reverend managed to pat Grace's arm in feeble encouragement. The older man appeared to be humming to himself. Then, as abruptly as their prancing had begun, it ended. The older man clapped once more, and the younger man let go of his corner of the flimsy fabric and the dance was over.

The older one wiped the Reverend's handkerchief across his own perspiring forehead. He held it out before his face and inspected it. The black initials—J. W. W: John Wesley Watson—hung in the air. The man nodded in confident affirmation, although of what the Reverend could not know. Then the fellow let out a high, happy cry of triumph.

Baffling people, Grace thought as she watched the man stuff the handkerchief into one of his many pouches. As he did so, she noticed something that equally surprised her: hanging from the dirty, embroidered sack was another strip of cloth that appeared to be made of the same fine linen as her husband's handkerchief. Thin and gray from use, the edge of this other piece of fabric looked identical to the one the man's thick hands stuffed inside now.

The Reverend appeared mesmerized by this sight, too, although he did not seem concerned about the coincidence. His face remained steely and firm until Grace noticed the slight twitching of his eyebrow, a tic from his boyhood whenever self-doubt captured him. The older bandit pulled the red string on the pouch. He let out a long, satisfied sound, then looked directly at the Reverend and pointed, his eyes fierce and sure.

The Reverend suddenly whipped around and shouted at Grace. "Go, woman, get inside with Wesley and lock the doors!"

Grace heard her husband's words and wanted to obey, but her arms wouldn't let go of his sleeve. He pried her fingers off and pushed her toward the cottage. With effort, Grace finally began to move.

"Run, Grace, run!" the Reverend yelled again.

Clutching Wesley to her chest, she hurried up the rocky path in the direction of the cottage. She heard Mai Lin screaming to her from the porch. It was a harebrained plan. She could not possibly escape two men on horseback. But Grace tried anyway, her fingers digging into her son's small body to keep him close. As she approached, she called out to Mai Lin to open the door.

"Gentlemen," she heard her husband behind her plead, "take this very fine watch. Sell it for many cows."

The older one shouted orders. Grace turned back, and it wasn't the gold watch she saw held in the air but a sword aloft in the older man's hand and pointed in her direction. The younger man threw himself onto his horse and rode hard toward her. Grace stumbled over the rough ground toward the cottage, but she did not fall.

Mai Lin called, "Here, Mistress, come!"

Behind Grace, the Reverend instructed her to press onward, too. But as she did, she was in such a state of confusion, she could no longer tell who was yelling what, and then it no longer mattered—none of it mattered. She might as well have been standing still, for the young man barely slowed his horse as he swooped down over her. He grabbed Wesley's arm and pulled. The boy held on to her neck for as long as he could. He cried out as his mother and the bandit fought over him. But finally, the barbarian stopped toying with Grace and simply yanked her son away.

She would never forget how easily Wesley was lost to her, as if to show that these men could have done it at any moment all along. They could take whatever they pleased. And what they wanted was not her but the child.

"My son!" she screamed.

The robber turned his horse and rode away across the flat land with her baby in his arms. The older man let out a loud cry, too, as he whipped his horse away. Grace chased after them. She ran until the frantic noise in her ears became unbearable. She tried to press on through it, but finally she bent over to catch her breath and crumpled onto the hard dirt. Her hands gripped her belly, and she squeezed shut her eyes and saw blackness. A quick prayer passed through her mind for the unborn child in her belly. She opened her eyes again and through tears saw the sun blazing on the horizon, that too-red ball of fire and blood. She could not bear to lose another one.

The Reverend ran past her and frantically worked to unhitch their horse from the wagon. "Mai Lin," he shouted, "help her!"

Grace tried to stand but fell again and clawed at the dust that quickly turned her palms yellow. After a few moments, she lay unmoving except by her sobs. Through the dust and tears, she saw Mai Lin hobbling toward her. The old woman bent low, her face alive with worry and indignation.

"Take care of her," the Reverend shouted as he mounted his horse and rode off after the kidnappers, who were becoming smaller and smaller in the red distance.

Two

Mai Lin shook her fists in the air and shouted, "Lord Jesus and the great ancestors rain curses upon them!" She then lifted Grace to stand and helped her up the steps and into the cottage.

It was the first time Grace had walked over the threshold of the new little home built for her by her husband. Her eyes immediately found, over in a corner of the open room, a newly made baby's crib with a toddler-sized bed pressed up beside it. Despite his many duties as head of the mission, the Reverend had clearly spent hours turning the dowels and staining the wood for each charming piece. Such was his love for his children. The infernal humming in Grace's brain grew louder, and she thought she might go mad if it continued. Doc Hemingway had said that she needed rest, and yet how could she find rest in a country that tormented her with loss?

She broke free of Mai Lin's grip and staggered to the child-sized bed. Suddenly on her knees, she bowed before it, her body pressed over the low cornhusk mattress. A cry broke from her throat, and she wailed into the calico quilt.

Then she sat up again and looked about frantically, for what she did not know. She grabbed the boy's pillow that his father had no doubt set there himself. She thrashed it until feathers flew out from the pretty embroidered case. She slammed it down again and again, as a dog shakes a rabbit until it grows limp, all life ravaged. Finally, Grace flopped forward onto the bed and simply wept.

The last of the white feathers fell onto her outstretched arms like surprising snowflakes back home when she woke in early spring to find the milk bottles frosted on the back porch. Black twigs and cherry blossoms littered the sudden whiteness. It was on such days that Grace was glad to be alive in a world where surprising things happened, yet never so surprising as to carry away all hope of something better, of redemption if one simply bowed to the Lord's great plan.

On springtime mornings like those, when the rain had finally stopped, they waded out toward the creek that had been rising for days. From farms upstream floated all manner of tires, cut logs, old boots, and once a bloated cow, swirling in an eddy until it was skewered by the limbs of a fallen tree. The Lord had seen to such disasters, but there was always an escape, a way to survive and even grow stronger in one's faith. There was a lesson to be learned, and then you carried on.

Grace sat again, and her head hung limply in the posture of a supplicant. She knew she appeared to be praying there beside her son's unused bed. But she was not. She was cursing the Lord instead. Above the incessant vibrations in her brain, she cursed Him as she never had before. She would not carry on. She would not survive, especially not in this terrible land that He had created out of fire and brimstone and suffering.

Mai Lin knelt beside Grace and tucked a strong hand under her arm. She helped her stand. As Grace stepped away from the child-sized bed and the crib, she did not look back but tipped her head to see past the curtains and out the window as wild strands of pink and purple slid down the sky. Soon a gray stillness would spread. With nightfall, a frightening moonscape would appear, cold and lifeless and full of peril. Her husband was out there in that lonely land in pursuit of their beloved son.

Mai Lin hobbled forward on her miserably deformed feet and helped Grace sit on the adult bed in the far corner of the open room. Grace leaned against the pillows, almost calm now, although the dizziness and agitation in her brain remained a quiet refrain. Even in her grief, she noticed the touches the Reverend had added to please her: the coat hooks beside the door, a handsome cabinet to hold pans and plates, a fine celadon pot on the mantel and calico curtains he must have sent for from back home to separate the bedrooms from the living area.

With a long intake of air, studded by staccato sobs, Grace swung her legs around so she might lie down. But in that instant, she felt wetness between her legs. She sprang up from the bed in alarm. She pawed at her long linen skirt and tried with trembling hands to yank it off. She had no words to say to Mai Lin, but somehow the woman understood.

Mai Lin worked with gnarled fingers on the ivory buttons that ran down the back of the delicately made garment. Then she undid the endless buttons that confined Grace into her high-collared shirt and pulled it off her. Grace stood in only a simple petticoat and looked down and saw what she feared most.

She fell back onto the bed. Red pooled on her white slip, red rose up from her broken heart and filled her mind. She shut her eyes and felt water fill her ears, but then she knew better: not water but blood. Blood streamed around her, tossing her about and spinning her in its own ill luck, like that cow in the eddy that had been stopped only by a limb like a spear. The robber had raised his sword high in the air before he had raced forward to steal her son. Grace would have given anything for him to ride toward only her and plunge his blade into her heart. Perhaps he had. Perhaps that explained the oozing wetness that now surrounded her on all sides. She felt Mai Lin blot between her legs and place her healing hands upon Grace's stomach, but she knew it would do no good. Yes, the robbers had pierced her and were taking away her life's blood.

The old woman bustled around the bed, but Grace no longer cared. The vibrations in her mind were terribly loud now, and she knew the blood poured forth. Soon she would lie on a bed made only of blood. Mai Lin pulled potions, creams, tinctures, and lumps of incense from the many pouches and sacks that hung on leather strings around her waist and neck. Grace was dimly aware of her grinding something with a mortar and pestle on the bedside table. Within moments, the bitter, sickly-sweet smell of incense wrapped itself around Grace's faint head. Mai Lin whispered soft and mysterious words over her as she had in the middle of the night two times before. Grace did not know the meaning of the chants. She did not hear the word Jesus, nor did she care to. This fact surprised Grace with such force that she let out a cackle, a most unladylike sound the likes of which usually issued forth only from her old amah.

"Death to Lord Jesus!" Grace shouted feebly. "That was what the robbers said, and I say it now, too. Death to the Lord!"

But the instant she repeated it, she feared she would be punished, struck down utterly and forever. She heard thunder raging in the distance and felt certain that a lightning storm would come this way. In a blinding flash of light, she, Mai Lin, and the cottage would be reduced to a smoldering pile of ashes. That was what she deserved. That was what she wanted. It was she, not her husband, who would be carried upward in a holy conflagration.

Three

Night fires gleamed in the distance, and smoke clung to the horizon, blurring the far-off mountains in a blanket of dark haze. The Reverend pressed on in the direction of the smoke, although the robbers might easily have slipped into one of the ravines or outcroppings that bordered the dirt road. In this maddening countryside there were too many possibilities, as many directions as travelers. It occurred to him that at this very moment the bandits may have been watching him from a rocky hilltop, laughing at his efforts. Or they might have turned away, no longer interested in the father who rode on and on forever in search of his son. For the Reverend understood that he would not stop his journey until Wesley was found.

The old horse was not meant for such swift travel, but the Reverend paid it little heed. He had not ridden bareback since he was a boy on the farm. It did not matter. Nothing mattered except going onward. Off to his right he saw a fire burning, and further ahead on the left a hamlet appeared—a cluster of buildings made of yellow brick, though in the dark they resembled nothing more than dark outlines. He had passed this cluster of derelict buildings before but assumed they were empty and no longer in use. Now from this ghost town came a dim light that the Reverend headed toward.

He let himself wonder what he would do if the bandits were holed up inside. He had no weapon. No sword or gun, not even a rock to hurl or a stick to swing. The Reverend bore nothing except his fury, height, and stature as a Man of God in a land of infidels. That would have to be enough. As he grew closer, he let the horse slow and then come to a stop. He swung down off the sweat-soaked back and kept hold of the reins. He could at least use the element of surprise to his advantage. He would come out of the black night to frighten the devils.

He passed through a broken wooden gate whose fence had long since fallen away. The moon came out from behind a cloud, and he saw the lay of the courtyard: a barn on one side, its roof staved in; a shed on the other, with no door or windowpanes and only darkness inside; and there, before him, an old inn with the windows boarded over. A light shone dimly through chinks in the brick near the back of the building.

The Reverend ducked behind the edge of the barn and tied his horse to a leaning post. He strode across the courtyard with his traveling coat billowing. A rough board with a knot of rope for a handle served as a door to the inn. On the wood were scrawled careless Chinese characters that the Reverend could not decipher. He couldn't be troubled about the meaning of the words, nor did he care to unravel the mysteries of this decrepit place. He merely wanted the Lord to lead him to his son. Faith, not knowledge, would guide him.

In his hand the knot of rope felt prickly and unwelcoming, but he twisted it and pushed open the door. He, who had been called a giant by even the friendliest of Chinese, now ducked below the lintel. He stepped over the threshold, placed both boots firmly on the sunken dirt floor, and rose up to his full height, impersonating Goliath as best as he could.

The Reverend thrust out his chest, pulled back his shoulders, and glared with as much menace as he could muster into a smoky, dimly lit room. His top wave of reddish hair grazed a low wooden beam. It took a moment for his eyes to adjust to the smoke. His lungs, which were never strong even in the best of settings, began to constrict in his chest. He hoped he would not cough and spoil the full effect of his pose, for he intended to appear not altogether human but rather a creature from an Amazon tribe, more native than the natives themselves.

An old, gnarled man wrapped in a heavy woolen cape and high fur boots stepped forward from the shadows at the back of the unfurnished room. He was bent so low, the Reverend felt certain he had spent decades behind a plow, although the ropes and pouches he wore around his neck and waist suggested more the life of a nomad or trader.

Perhaps, the Reverend thought, he was the grandfather of the bandits. The Reverend took a step forward, and the man cowered, suggesting he had none of the swagger of the men who had stolen his son. No doubt this fellow was instead the patriarch of a sorry, lost clan that still tried to hold on in this forgotten corner of the western plains.

The man did not speak but looked up at the Reverend with bright and nervous eyes. They regarded one another like animals of different species, although, the Reverend considered, at least animals had an instinct that told them who was predator and who was prey. He wished he had paused to wipe the infernal desert dust from his spectacles before entering, for now the dense clouds billowing from the back of the dark room further narrowed his vision. He was seeing the old man as if through the wrong end of a smudged spyglass.

"Grandfather," the Reverend began in as deep and sonorous a voice as he could muster, "I am here to find my son. He has been stolen, I believe, by the likes of you!"

The older man flinched at his words and seemed to be trembling, but that did not stop him from daring to step forward. He inched closer, reached out a palsied finger, and poked the Reverend none too delicately in the chest. When his touch reached firmness, the man staggered back and let out a frightened yelp.

"Yes, old fellow, I am real, and my mission is most urgent."

The grandfather nodded his head repeatedly in an attempt at understanding.

The Reverend boomed, "Have you, or your family, seen a small boy taken by robbers this very night?"

The old man flinched and sank deeper into his dark cape, clearly still frightened, but finally answered, "No. No boy here."

Although the man did not seem threatening, the Reverend knew to keep a close eye on him. In the seven years since he had come to Shansi Province, he had dealt with all manner of Chinese: the fine and upstanding as well as the tricksters who were more desperate than dangerous. He had also glimpsed the criminal element. Twice, he had come upon a beheading in a market square. Each time, it had become immediately apparent to him that the prisoner and the warlord who had orchestrated the punishment were equally evil barbarians. But the Reverend could not be bothered with such distinctions now. If he was in danger, so be it. His own safety was not what mattered. The boy was all.

The Reverend strode deeper into the room, and as he did so, he heard laughter coming from the dark. Could that be a woman's voice? A girl's? Or, his heart quickened, perhaps it was the high, angelic sound of his son.

"Your family, in the back." The Reverend gestured toward the darkened door. "Have *they* seen something in the past hours?"

The grandfather did not answer but turned and beckoned with the same palsied finger. On his face appeared an unexpected grin. The Reverend heard the laughter again. This time he was certain it belonged to a woman, or perhaps several women. His son's voice was not so cloying or crass. But still, the Reverend ventured further into the place. He followed the outline of the bent man in the wooly cape, more like the back of an animal than any human outline. The Reverend intended to interrogate each and every person he encountered back there. He would gather clues, then leave quickly and press on into the night.

The old man bowed his head humbly and held open the inner door for the Reverend, as if honored to offer tea in a formal parlor. The Reverend ducked low again, and when he lifted his head, he saw the terrible source of the smoke. All manner of miscreants lay about on low mats, puffing on pipes that emitted an awful stench. The Reverend squinted into the smoky den and covered his nose with his hand. An acrid scent seeped into him. This foul place seemed uninhabitable, as if he had entered an underwater world where he was the sole oxygen-loving mammal. He took off his glasses and was about to clean them on his handkerchief when he realized he no longer had it. The bandits had taken it, too. The Reverend chided himself for even a moment's lapse in pursuit of his mission.

"I wish to know if anyone here has seen my boy?" he shouted.

Quiet fell over the room. Even the most delinquent of men sprawled on mats turned their heads toward the Reverend. Several girls in flowery silk robes crowded together and whispered at the sight of him.

The grandfather held up his hand and said something in a rapid dialect that the Reverend could not catch. The ancient fellow clapped his hands and waved them in the air as if conducting a silent concert, and then his message was over. The room buzzed again as the fallen all around him were apparently appeased by whatever had been conveyed. They no longer concerned themselves with the white giant in their midst.

The Reverend shook his head. Extraordinary, he thought, the way evil could be so all-consuming. They had their sinful business to attend to and could not be bothered with anything else. These people would not notice if the Lord Jesus himself walked through the door.

At his elbow appeared two thinly clad ladies, while another stood writhing happily before him. Not ladies, not remotely ladies, the Reverend knew. He was a minister, but he was also an American male who had grown up in a sinful world. After school one time, a classmate had surprised him by handing him a card. Assuming it was an invitation of some sort, the Reverend had flipped the thing over and stared for several long moments at the ample, naked backside of a woman who offered a coy smile over one shoulder and most beckoning eyes. No, the Reverend knew precisely where he stood: at the puerile heart of Sodom and Gomorrah.

He attempted to slip away from the girls and search through the smoke for the grandfather. The ladies surrounded him again, and he could not help but notice that although they were young, they were not children. As their robes fell open, their slight breasts shone in the lantern light. The Reverend did not look away immediately, but when he did, he shook his head vigorously. He must turn from such sights. This was precisely how the devil did his work: by sneaking in under the door of the mind and taking control.

Needing clearer vision now more than ever, he began to undo the buttons on his traveling coat in order to use his shirttail to clean his spectacles. The girls misunderstood his gesture and grabbed his arms and pawed at his traveling coat. They appeared eager to undress him. The Reverend's heart, that involuntary muscle, beat frantically with what he hoped was honest fear rather than prurient desire.

Then their pale hands sneaked into his pockets, and he felt certain he was about to be robbed. But each girl merely held up the object she had found and giggled. Truly, they were hardly older than children. One excitedly examined his small folding knife and simply tossed it back into a side pocket of his coat. Apparently, his throat would not be cut this evening, at least not by these urchins.

Another snatched his thick, compact traveling Bible from his jacket. She flipped through the thin pages crowded with his scrawled commentary. Several sheets of ministerial notes and ideas for future sermons fluttered to the dirt floor. The Reverend snatched them up, stuffed them back into the book, and took the Bible away from her. He returned it to his breast pocket, where it always stayed close to his heart.

Yet another of the young ladies sank a lithe hand into one of his deeper pockets and pulled forth his leather-bound copy of the Romantics. This thick volume, every page of which the Reverend had read and reread, committing many fine lines of poetry to memory, had been given to him upon his graduation from seminary. Here in China, it had proved almost as important a companion as the Lord's good book. Within those poems, the barbaric was tamed; the wild was praised, and yet the language, through its refinement, proved that civilization won out in the end. Whenever his heart was sunk low by the unresponsive Chinese, he turned to wise Wordsworth, swashbuckling Byron, and sublime Keats and knew that faith would abide.

Now this child harlot before him waved the heavy thing in the air and sang a silly song. He grabbed it back from her and placed it out of reach in his other interior breast pocket. At all costs, he would keep these profound and uplifting texts safe from sly pickpockets.

Luckily, the ladies did not go into his other trouser pocket to find the gold watch his father had passed down to him before he had left for Shansi Province. The temptation of that shiny object would surely have been too much for this greedy gang. Instead, one of the girls reached for the spectacles in his hand, and before he knew it, she was swinging them in the air and wearing them herself.

The Reverend grabbed for his glasses, but the girls had him now. Their ranks had swelled, and they pulled him down onto one of the filthy mats, where he fell like Gulliver himself. They swarmed him, and he felt certain they would tie him down with ropes in the manner of the Lilliputians, but it was merely their delicate hands that pawed over him and made him frighteningly weak.

"Please, ladies, please," he shouted. "This must stop!"

And they did stop—such was the force of his voice speaking their tongue. But then one of the younger ones burst into giggles again, and the older ones put on more determined faces than ever. They dove for his shirt buttons. The Reverend pushed them off with some effort and managed to get his boots back upon the dirt floor. He finally snatched his spectacles, put them on, and stood.

He held out his arms in preparation for a further attack, but the girls just looked up at him. Disappointment and even boredom quickly passed over their young faces. Several of them trailed off toward the opium pipes and lamps. Others went to customers who mumbled in the sickly air. Such were their distracted natures and the fickleness of their passions. Sin could be quite desultory at times.

Over in a back corner, the Reverend spotted a group of men he had not noticed before. They sat on their haunches and threw dice against a mud wall. They cursed under their breaths, or sometimes quite loudly, and drank from dark bottles.

This sort of behavior rotted the soul to its very core. The Reverend faced the room and called forth his most effective preaching voice. "You, every one of you, is giving your one and only life over to the Devil," he announced, loud enough he hoped to reach even those most lost in their own ether. "Throw off the mantle of evil and join the pure way of Christ."

The grandfather shuffled forward from a corner of the chamber and reached out a claw to grip the Reverend's arm. Strangely, the Reverend felt almost glad to see him again. He felt he could talk sense to this fellow and perhaps get somewhere. The old man had taken off his wool cape, and, as he stood close, the Reverend was puzzled to notice that he wore a high lace collar, a European or American woman's finely wrought garment with ivory buttons down the neck. As the man inched forward, the Reverend saw on his bent head a thick, crocheted oval. He was mystified at the sight. Could it be an antimacassar?

But then in a flash he understood: the antimacassar and the lace collar had once belonged to the missionary families that had perished in the Boxer Rebellion a decade before. This grandfather standing in front of the Reverend wore loot from the massacre of the American faithful.

"You must leave now," the old man said softly. His voice again surprised the Reverend with its high timbre. "You see, no son here."

"Grandfather," the Reverend began, but then, through some strange intuition, he corrected himself and said, "I mean, Grandmother."

The old woman looked up at him and offered a crooked smile as she squeezed his elbow. Then she took a thin leather rope from around her neck. From it hung a brass coin, though of no denomination that the Reverend had ever seen before. She held the thing up before her, and the Reverend understood that she meant for him to wear it. He hesitated. While he had no intention of taking on the appearance of these types, it did not seem wise to refuse.

"This will help you find your way," the grandmother said.

The Reverend had no idea who these people were, and he was fully convinced that evil ruled their every thought and deed, and yet the old woman's expression seemed somehow convincing. He bowed low, and she placed the necklace over his head.

Then her ancient hands worked at a knot on a strip of cloth that served as a belt around her thick waist. After a moment, she had it off, and he could see that from it hung a small sack embroidered with twin golden dragons.

"And this will help you find your son," she said, holding it up in offering.

The Reverend took the soiled red fabric from her hand and kept it in his open palm. With quick gestures she showed him how to wear it slung over one shoulder and across his breast. He lifted it into that position, and she nodded. The Reverend did as she instructed and strapped the ragged red cloth across his chest, over one shoulder, and down toward his waist so that the pouch with the yellow dragons hung at his hip.

When the Reverend looked up from this complicated business, the room had grown silent. The men who had been gambling in the back stood now and were watching. The girls in their open robes stared with dark eyes. Even the steady, almost comforting murmur of the opium pipes had stopped.

"I remember your people," the grandmother said. "They all died. But you, you come out from the desert. You are the man we have heard rumors of for years." She looked around at the others with gleaming eyes. "This, before us, is the Ghost Man. He is alive!"

"No, you see," the Reverend started to explain, but then he stopped and did not continue. Perhaps, in this instance, it was best to leave them to their ignorant beliefs. He took a small step backward toward the exit, their eyes still steady upon him.

Suddenly, a man lurched out of the darkened corner where the gamblers huddled. He was young and strapping and the only healthy-looking specimen in the place. He pushed past the grandmother, although she pawed at his shoulder with an arthritic claw and shouted for him to stop. He yelled back and shook her off with ease.

As this commotion took place, the door behind the Reverend swung open. He glanced back over his shoulder and was overwhelmed at the sight of his manservant, Ahcho. Never had the Reverend felt so grateful for a familiar face.

"Good God, man, how did you find me?" the Reverend asked.

"I know this place," Ahcho answered.

"You do?" the Reverend asked.

"No, no, not I. Everyone knows it."

The Reverend made a mental note to follow up with Ahcho, his most devoted convert, on this unsettling suggestion. Then he looked back at the grandmother and, in a flash, saw the young gambler raise his hand. A loud noise sounded, followed by a puff of smoke. The Reverend felt a thud against his chest. He stared out at the room and swayed slightly. He prepared to fall, and yet he did not.

"Ghost Man is shot!" someone shouted.

The Reverend watched as the grandmother used her fists to pummel the strapping gambler. "You idiot!" she shouted. "Ghost Man will rain curses on us like never before."

"We will all die!" screeched one of the girls.

"He will haunt us forever!" another shouted.

"But look," someone else pointed, "he does not die."

A frightened screaming and general agitation overtook the room. Ahcho raced toward the young gunman and wrestled him to the ground. The Reverend took the opportunity to study his own chest. As a man of science, he searched for a logical explanation for his survival. In an instant, he understood what had happened. He had read of just such miracles taking place on battlefields for those boys wise enough to carry their Bibles over their hearts.

"Help us, you drunken louts!" the grandmother yelled above it all. "Stop this fool before we are cursed for all eternity."

The young, strapping fellow was too much for Ahcho. The gamblers finally gathered their wits about them and joined the elderly Ahcho in his attempts to subdue the strong gunman. But in the confusion, he managed to yank his hand free. He raised it for a second time and shot again.

The Reverend grasped what had happened by the anguished look on Ahcho's face. He felt a searing heat rise up in his torso as his head grew light and vague. The sight of the red cloth over his chest startled the Reverend as he wondered if it had always been the color of blood. He had forgotten he wore such a strange talisman, but now he noticed that the second bullet had gone right through the fabric, and yet it had not been severed so badly as to fall off him. Like the pouch with the twin golden dragons attached to the red cloth, the Reverend swayed gently. But still, he did not fall.

A great hush filled the room. The people sucked in gasps of air, their hands covering their mouths, their eyes wide and unblinking. Ahcho left the gunman, finally held fast by the other gamblers. He wrapped the Reverend's arm over his shoulder and had him lean into him.

Unable to disguise the desperation in his voice, he said, "Don't worry, Reverend, the Lord Jesus will save you."

"No doubt," the Reverend mumbled. He clenched his teeth and hoped his convert understood that his lack of enthusiasm was no indication his faith was faltering.

Yet his mind was narrowing, his vision closing in. He placed trembling fingers over the second bullet hole, where blood had begun to appear. Using all that was left of his blurred and pain-filled brain, the Reverend pieced together that he must have been turned sideways when the gunman, lying prone on the dirt floor, had fired. The second bullet had risen at an acute angle, grazing his rib until something—something quite impenetrable—had stopped it from bisecting his heart.

The Reverend looked up with wonder in his eyes. If he was going to live, which remained to be seen, he now fully grasped that he would owe his life to poetry and, by extension, to the Lord's great whimsy. There was a lesson in it, one he would exploit for a future sermon should he be allowed to live long enough to give another. As his vision fully darkened and he began to topple, the Reverend managed a final wish: that his son be brought home on just such a tide of good-humored grace.

Four

Ahcho pushed open the screen door and joined Mai Lin on the front porch. She crouched on the top step, chewed betel quid, and spat the juice over the side. They acknowledged each other with customary grunts. He brought out his pipe, struck a match against the rough side of the mud-brick home, and puffed. Smoke wafted into the restless air. Ahcho squinted into the darkness, where the wind rustled under a moonless sky. He was thinking about the boy out there somewhere.

"Your patient is the easy one," Mai Lin started, interrupting any peace Ahcho might have hoped for. "He has merely a gash and a broken rib. Those will heal with little help from you. As always, you're the lucky one."

"It's not so simple as that, and you know it," Ahcho said. "The man has lost his son."

Mai Lin shrugged. "Well, at least the mistress did not lose the baby in her belly. I saved it. No one else could do that. Am I right? You tell me anyone else in these provinces who could have done that?" She did not wait for a reply but carried on. "I will be up all night, giving her remedies and burning incense over her. You know all that must be done. Her female organs are—"

"Enough, woman," Ahcho said wearily. He bit down on the stem of his pipe. He had no intention of listening to a medical report about their mistress. Mai Lin had no sense of propriety.

"Ha, you are still squeamish?"

"Quiet, I said."

Mai Lin let out a long yawn.

Ahcho tried to think of where the kidnappers might have taken the boy. There was little chance that the opium sots from the nearest hamlet had been involved. They existed only in an ineffectual haze, although he did not blame the Reverend for starting his search there. By the Reverend's description, though, Ahcho could tell that the bandits had traveled a great distance to get here. If still alive, the boy was no doubt being taken far away.

Over the past seven years, Ahcho had accompanied the Reverend further than any men from Shansi Province had gone before. They had seen the Mongolian steppes and the great Gobi Desert, about which Ahcho had previously heard only fantastical stories. He admired the Reverend in many ways, but not least because the younger man had shown Ahcho a world he had dreamed of since he was a child. And now, the Reverend's only son was out there in that vast land.

"She kept calling for her boy," Mai Lin's grating voice interrupted again. "So I gave her something to ease her."

"The Master doesn't like you giving her that," he said.

Mai Lin let out a disgusted puff of air. "He should understand by now that I know best. I saved her twice already when she lost the other babies. The man thinks only Jesus can perform miracles. I am better than that long-faced Ghost Man with the straw-colored hair. You have seen the picture of him in the chapel? Why would anyone believe a person with pink skin and watery eyes the color of a summer sky? That Jesus person doesn't even look healthy."

"This is a sacrilege, you know. Besides, you should be careful. Their bodies aren't like ours."

"That is my point. *You* be careful of the Jesus man. He is not one of us." She reached into a pouch, and her fingers reappeared with more betel quid, which she packed into her already full cheek.

Ahcho sucked harder on his pipe and watched the small clouds billow and disappear into the darkness around them. The grasses on all sides swayed. How could the Reverend possibly go back into that unfathomable landscape to rescue his son? The long mission trip that had taken place before the mistress had arrived from America was, without a doubt, the most remarkable experience of Ahcho's life. And yet he knew his tired body could not go forth for months on end like that again. At sixty, he was too old. He shook his head and told himself not to worry. There would be time to consider such options. What was that expression the Reverend liked to use about a cart and a horse?

"I am not the one who needs to keep track of my charge," Mai Lin started again with a chuckle. "You let yours wander off, and look where he ended up. He is a grown man, but I believe he had never seen anything like that before." Mai Lin's laugh scraped at Ahcho's weary heart, but her eyes sparkled with mischief that was hard to resist.

"Yes," he conceded, "the Master was out of his element."

She spat into the bushes. "It's high time he had some fun," she said.

"Woman," Ahcho scolded.

"Aha," she said and pointed at him. "You know what I'm saying."

Ahcho straightened up and knocked on the porch railing with his knuckles. He was too old for such talk. It was not proper. Mai Lin adjusted her skirts around her and spat onto the ground. He sensed that she was too tired to tease him any longer, and he was glad.

"It's strange," she said after a moment, "but the Mistress calls out not just for her son and her other babies who were never born but also for the others, the ones who died long ago."

"What ones who died long ago?"

"You know, the other American children. They never live long in Shansi." She shrugged again and spoke as if this were a fact. "They do not belong here and are simply whisked away."

"What are you saying? Of course they belong here," Ahcho said, puffing on his pipe to calm himself. The woman could agitate a stone in a dry riverbed.

"No, they don't," Mai Lin said almost cheerfully. "Remember the boy who was washed off in the Fen River when it rose too high? He fished like a man without the sense of a man. And that other one who snatched fruit from the market, ate it without washing, and died the next morning. Just like that." She snapped her fingers. "And I am not even mentioning the hordes that came down from the mountains to slaughter all the white babies. You see, they have no business being here in the first place."

Ahcho cleared his throat and spoke as sternly as he could muster, despite his fatigue. "That's enough now. I remember the Boxer time better than anyone, but it is past. And besides, the Lord takes away babies only when he has a better use for them elsewhere, not as a punishment. The Lord is not a foolish old woman like you."

"Suit yourself. I'm just saying there are reasons for such disasters.

The Spirits do not like things to change," Mai Lin said and squirted an arc of juice onto the ground. Ahcho heard it land as always with a splat, and this time it infuriated him.

He raised himself up to his full height, which was considerable for a Chinese man, and stood, steely and unperturbed, just as the Reverend would in a moment like this one. Also like the Reverend, Ahcho had no use for the old superstitions. Thoughts about Spirits were no longer permissible.

He preferred the new ways. Improvements were coming all the time. Although Fenchow-fu was only a small city, it boasted a new road and a hospital that the Reverend had built. Chinese children attended the Christian school with a roof over their heads. The Reverend had even recently proposed that a library be erected, although the province of Shansi possessed only one book, an encyclopedia that the town elders forbade anyone to open in order to preserve it. Ahcho was a chief propagandist of this new wave of progress and prosperity. And although he knew pride was a sin, he hoped it was all right that he was proud to be his master's number-one boy.

He glanced down at Mai Lin, seated on her haunches, her many skirts, ropes, cloth belts, and pouches spread out around her. No one could dispute that she knew everything about birthing and the care of babies. She could also help a patient recover from croup or a sour stomach, and sometimes even more serious illnesses. But as the future took hold, Mai Lin was in danger of becoming a sorry throwback to another time. *She* was the one who had less and less business being here.

"Enough about that," Ahcho said, his full voice returning with confidence. "Tomorrow morning, we will take the Reverend and

Mistress Grace back to Fenchow-fu. I will prepare the wagon so they can lie down on straw in the back. The poor Master, every bump in the road will be agony with his broken rib."

"I will give him something for it."

"He will not take it."

"If he hurts enough, he will," she said, her laugh moist and abundant. Everything about her was that way, and for a brief moment, Ahcho did not let it bother him. He was in charge again and knew what needed to be done.

Then they both looked out at the night. The restless grasses hovered nearby, and the mountains rose, a shadow of a shadow in the distance. To find the boy, they would have to cross over them and then traverse much more.

"Little Wesley boy is out there," Ahcho said. "We must form a search party from the mission and return to the countryside as quickly as we can. The Reverend will not be able to lead it until his rib heals, but Reverend Charles Martin can rally the other ministers. I will help gather our own people. We must send messengers to every warlord in the neighboring provinces. We will try everything, and we will find him." Ahcho spoke with more assurance than he felt, but that was as one must when putting one's faith in the Lord. He had learned this from the Reverend.

Mai Lin let out a long hissing sound.

"What?" he asked, although he did not want to hear it.

"You know better," she said in a singsong voice that teased him. "The Fates have their ways."

Ahcho tapped his pipe on the railing to empty it. Now it was his turn to let out a disgusted sound. "Well, you know nothing," he said with finality. "The Lord Jesus is on our side, and miracles do happen. Just look at the Reverend tonight. Not one but two bullets, and he survived. It is remarkable, and so will be our rescue of the child."

Ahcho was pleased to end the conversation on that clarifying and uplifting note. But as he stepped back into the cottage, he could not help hearing Mai Lin's cackle echoing in the night.

Five

The candle flickered as the Reverend turned in his bed and let out a soft moan. Ahcho was at his side a moment later and adjusted the pillow so it cupped his head properly in the manner that Americans preferred.

The Reverend's eyelids fluttered several times and then opened. A grimace of pain crossed his face. Ahcho held up a newly opened bottle of brandy, its amber liquid glowing. The Revered nodded once, and Ahcho poured a small amount into a glass. He raised it to his master's dry lips, and the Reverend drank. Then the Reverend lifted a finger toward the bottle again. Ahcho was surprised but held it steady as the Reverend took several more long pulls.

His pain must have been considerable, Ahcho thought, to tempt the man so. Not that Ahcho blamed him, but he knew he wouldn't mention this to anyone. Nor would he mention the events of the evening and the sinful setting into which the Reverend had stumbled. He cursed himself already for having told Mai Lin where he had found him. But Ahcho had been in such a panic when he had returned to the cottage with the bleeding man that the tale had flown out of him like a bird flushed from the bushes by a cat.

The Reverend's eyes closed again. Ahcho pushed the cork into the bottle of liquor and placed it upon the shelf with the other supplies. They would need more cotton strips to create a proper sling. And more bandages to keep the wound clean. Perhaps he would purchase another bottle of strong spirits to help with the pain, should it continue. On his way back to the Reverend's bedside, Ahcho paused before his own satchel that he had hung on a hook by the door. With a heavy heart, he reached into the bag and pulled out something wrapped in a cloth. He carried it back to the Reverend.

"Sir?" he whispered.

The Reverend's eye twitched, and his lips pursed ever so slightly.

"The robbers seem to have tossed something onto the ground before leaving," Ahcho said.

The Reverend opened one eye. "Spectacles, please."

Ahcho set down the item, found the glasses, placed them on the Reverend's nose, and carefully bent the soft metal wires around his ears. He dreaded the moment the object came into focus.

"What is it?" the Reverend asked.

Ahcho peeled back the corners of the cloth. "A human skull, sir. It appears to be that of a child."

The Reverend flinched at the word but then asked, "You say you found it on the ground?"

"At the base of the cottage steps where the boy—God protect him—was taken."

The Reverend took the small round thing into his hands and held it up before his eyes, where it glistened in the lamplight. Ahcho could not help but notice that it appeared delicate and refined, like a porcelain vase, although also quietly menacing, like a snake curled upon a sun-drenched rock.

The Reverend's face darkened, and his features shifted. They became tight and firm, all softness draining away. His eyes betrayed little, but Ahcho could sense a realization coming over him like a fog rolling over a mountainside in the morning. It was the same realization that Ahcho had arrived at some hours earlier.

"Dear God," the Reverend said. Then he looked into Ahcho's face and asked in a halting voice, "What have I done?"

Ahcho started to reach for his master's arm to comfort him but stopped with his hand in midair. He swallowed and waited for words to come forth, but none did. The two men looked at one another and understood something of which they could not speak.

Ahcho wondered if he should have simply tossed the skull into the desert grasses and not shown it to the Reverend. But with some consternation, he realized that he still had enough of the old superstitions in him to believe that ignoring it could bring the Fates down upon them all. Ahcho feared he was a weak man and an imperfect Christian, and this was the best he could do.

And yet he also reminded himself about the many Sunday mornings when the Reverend had spoken of Jesus's honesty and forthrightness. In order to obey the Reverend's entreaties to be like the Lord, Ahcho had had no choice but to show his master the skull. He could not hide so important a clue. For while the sight of it might ruin the Reverend, it might also help bring his son back to him.

Ahcho felt relief as he transferred the object from his old and weary hands into those of the Reverend, who was far wiser and bound to know what to do.

"Place it in here," the Reverend said. He pointed to the pouch with the twin golden dragons that the unfortunate madam had given the Reverend earlier that evening.

"You do not intend to wear that filthy peasant thing strapped over you?" Ahcho asked.

"I will carry it with me until dear Wesley is found. It shall be my hair shirt."

Ahcho would have liked to have asked what this shirt of hair was all about, but another wave of pain washed over the Reverend, and he shut his eyes.

Six

In the first days and weeks that followed, as the Reverend regained his strength and his rib healed, his second-in-command, the Reverend Charles Martin, led several unsuccessful search parties into the Shansi Desert and the borderland provinces beyond. The Reverend was most grateful, and yet he could not have been more frustrated. While he waited for his compatriots to return, he wrote passionate letter after letter as he sought help from the Chinese authorities and the local warlords of the region. The American legation in Peking became involved for a time.

A long month later, Doc Hemingway granted permission, and the Reverend was finally able to take over the search. During his period of recuperation, he had devised a plan to visit every village of the mountains and plains. He set out right away. He followed rumors. Someone had seen a startlingly pale child in a market, or on a boat going upriver, or on the back of a Mongol tradesman's horse. The Reverend remained on the road all through that summer. He would return to the compound for a day or two but then quickly saddle up again. As head of the mission, part of his duty was to support and grow the outlying churches, yet everyone soon understood why he was gone so much of the time.

Confined at home through the humid summer months as the child in her belly held on, Grace had her bed turned to face the window. Her nervous condition remained inflamed, and Mai Lin saw to her health with strong potions. Grace could not shake from her rattled mind the feeling of her son being torn from her arms. The panic that had accompanied that moment hovered over her still. It kept her awake at night until Mai Lin arrived at a correct dosage.

When the moon spread a pewter glow over the rocky ground and a breeze from across the plains finally blew in milder, Grace was given respite and reward for her vigilance. The ghosts of her babies came back to her, and she was most grateful for their presence. They hovered just over the windowsill and beamed at her with their sweet, divine faces. Their high, angelic voices sang her to sleep, although a restless sleep it was. In that dreamy state, she listened to her angels of the desert, whom she came to both love and fear. As night wore on, she thrashed about in her bed, waiting for the visions to calm her. Sometimes it took hours for her to no longer reach out and try to snatch her children back. Instead, she would finally let them go and, when morning came, she woke with a pillow wet from tears but with a renewed lightness in her heart. Her children were out there, she was sure of that. It was only a matter of time before she was allowed to hold them again.

It would have been so much easier to simply give up, to lose one's faith; easier to turn against the Lord as she had on the first night after Wesley had been stolen. But from that dark moment, her true self had risen again. There was no denying she was a cheerful Midwestern girl at heart: an American girl, synonymous with optimism. And in so being, she understood that she must endure her greatest punishment.

She must live with the hope, the infernal hope that love could survive even out here where nothing else did. Her son would return to her. She just knew it.

One evening near the end of summer, as Mai Lin prepared Grace's sleeping concoction by the water basin, the Reverend startled them both by rapping on the bedroom door. Mai Lin let him in and stepped aside. He did not seem to notice the old woman. Grace knew he had been terribly preoccupied since Wesley's kidnapping with his travels and attempts to find the boy. But she wished he would be kinder to the one person who had been kindest to her in the aftermath. Given her delicate condition, Grace felt certain that her current pregnancy could not possibly have lasted into the fourth month if it had not been for her skilled amah. The Reverend needed to appreciate that.

He strode into the room with remarkable haste and stopped at her bedside. He rattled as he walked now, the several pouches and bags he had begun to acquire on his summer-long trips making him sound altogether too much like Mai Lin, who wore similar belts of accessories. Grace started at the sight of him bedecked in his amulets but then quickly began to pat down her flyaway hair. She was glad that she had changed into a fresh gown that morning.

"My dear, this won't do," he said abruptly.

She looked down at her hands.

"People are beginning to wonder about us," the Reverend continued. "I would like you to accompany me to chapel tomorrow morning. The natives need our example."

She nodded. Of course she would. He was right. In so many ways, he was right.

"We must carry on, mustn't we?" he asked.

She lifted her chin and attempted a smile.

He pushed aside his long coat and the belts with the pouches hanging down as he sat at the side of her bed. The sack with the twin golden dragons was most handsome and bulged as if it held some sort of orb. She had meant to ask him about its contents, but she had seen him so rarely in the past few months, she did not wish to distract them from more pressing matters.

"My dear," he said, more softly now. He took her pale hands in his own rough, red ones. "I am so sorry. So terribly sorry."

His high, usually erect head bowed, and then suddenly, he fell forward and pressed his face against her breast. The metal of his wire-framed glasses dug into her soft skin, but she did not complain. She placed her hand on his head. She let herself feel the actual touch and texture of his fine, thinning red hair. He was no apparition.

"It isn't your fault," she said. "Please, don't blame yourself."

He groaned as if she had struck him a blow. "But it is, and I do."

She pushed her fingers through his hair more firmly now. Then she touched around his unshaven cheek and rough jaw and lifted his face to hers. "The baby inside me will also help us to heal. This one is going to make it. I know he will."

The Reverend must have seen the doubt in her eyes, or heard the quiver she tried to keep from her voice. He looked at her with a tender expression, and she felt tears rise up behind her eyes. He brought her to him and kissed her on the lips. Grace thought she might faint, she was so happy to be in his embrace again. She had feared she had lost him forever.

But his lips were dry, and they did not press for long against her greedy ones. He pulled back and looked away out the open window.

"I have a sermon to prepare," he said. "You will come with me to chapel tomorrow?"

"Of course I will come with you."

"Bless you, my dear." He turned and began to leave the room. Then he paused and stepped back, closer.

Her heart could not help fluttering with hope that he might bestow upon her another kiss.

But he simply added, "Do not be surprised to see that our ranks have swelled. I seem to have sparked a revival of sorts. Most strange, but positive for our cause, I believe."

She looked at him, waiting for more, but he bent quickly and merely kissed her on the forehead before stepping away.

Seven

Grace cherished the Reverend's firm grip on her elbow as he steered her up the aisle, but she hated the moment when he placed her in her seat in the front pew and moved away. It took all of her self-control not to turn to him before the assembling congregation and beg him to hold her a moment longer. She watched him rise to the platform behind the simple podium. Then she looked down at her lap and ran her fingers over the fine lacework of her dress stretched tightly across her growing belly. She hoped that no one would spot the tears gathering behind her eyes and prayed she could make it through the morning service without causing a stir.

But, quickly enough, she and the other missionaries and the usual Chinese faithful were distracted by a racket at the back of the chapel. Grace turned to see what the disturbance might be. A cart had pulled up out front, and from it climbed more than a dozen men. A second cart followed closely behind, and another after that. While Grace couldn't see all that was happening beyond the open double doors, she gathered that a steady stream of congregants was clamoring toward the little chapel.

She recognized none of the peasants' faces that entered through the door. She heard the rattle of more carts arriving, and the influx continued with no sign of abating. In the seven years that the Reverend had lived in Shansi, the mission had grown slowly and steadily in numbers that were nothing to be ashamed of. But as she glanced up at him now, he must have sensed her eyes upon him, because he glanced back and raised a single eyebrow, as if to say that he, too, wondered what the Lord had wrought.

The service began a full half hour late because the new congregants had to pack themselves into every pew, some sitting on each other's laps. More stood at the back and along the sides. Others filled the central aisle and edged out the door. The faces of those who could not enter pressed against the windows.

Grace peered around for her young lady friends with whom she had lost touch during the recent difficult months. None of the not-yet-wed missionary teachers appeared to be in attendance. The night before, when Grace had pressed Mai Lin to tell her about the changes to the congregation to which the Reverend had referred, her servant had alluded to the fact that the chapel now belonged to the Chinese. Grace surmised that this recent change was the reason the young ladies now stayed in their homes on Sunday morning.

She did spot Mildred Martin, the Reverend Martin's wife, and offered what she hoped was not too desperate a smile. Mildred had been quite dear in the first days after Wesley had been taken, although her visits to Grace's bedside had tapered off in the subsequent weeks of summer and finally stopped altogether. Grace realized that she had hardly noticed, occupied as she had become with her constant vigilance all night and then her need for sleep during the day. But now she looked across at Mildred and yearned for her gentle company. Grace smiled, and Mildred offered pursed lips and a little nod that made the hair on Grace's arms rise.

The Reverend cleared his throat and began to speak. As he did, the new congregants sucked in air, as if amazed that he could converse in their tongue. Why on earth had they come, Grace wondered, if they did not believe they would understand him? Such a daft and mystifying people, she thought.

Her husband's face appeared pale and calm, but rather quickly perspiration appeared on his handsome brow. He seemed to have a difficult time finding his handkerchief in his jacket pockets or in one of those little sacks and pouches that he wore. As his voice began to gain its stride, she found herself wondering what on earth were in all those odd items strung about him. She had noticed that several of the coolies who had come tromping in carried just such amulets in their hands. She hoped to heaven they weren't bringing them all to the Reverend. The man was beginning to look like a great Hawaiian chieftain sporting one too many leis. At such a ridiculous comparison, Grace giggled quietly to herself. Getting out and about seemed to agree with her. She must try to do so more often.

The Reverend's cheeks flushed, and the timbre of his words echoed against the plaster walls that he himself had erected. He was a master builder, a man with a vision in the full stride of life at forty years of age, and here, surrounded by witnesses, it was to God that he spoke with force and purpose and even anger, something she did not recall from his previous sermons. Now, from the simple wooden pulpit, he called out and begged the Lord for mercy.

Grace could not help remembering what a thin reed of a fellow he had been when she had first met him. He could barely raise his voice then to reach the back of the crowd where she and her girlfriends were hanging about. It was in 1903 on the Oberlin College campus in Ohio at a ceremony celebrating the erection of a memorial arch to the recent martyred missionaries of Shansi. As the band played a rousing march and the dedication gained momentum, with speaker after speaker extolling the bravery of the missionaries who had lost their lives in the battle against ignorance and fear in a distant province of a distant land, Grace had left her friends under the trees and drifted toward the front of the crowd. Once there, she had noticed the young Reverend who glanced repeatedly at the papers in his hand as he prepared to take the stage.

When he stepped forward, the young man towered over the dais, inspiring hope in the crowd that this chap would carry them away with his words. But, instead, his voice had faltered, and Grace could plainly hear that he had the uncertain rasp of a humble servant of God with a head cold. His eyes did not blaze yet with purpose, although he vowed to move to China that very year, but instead blinked under eyebrows that twitched unpredictably. Young Grace felt a surprising tenderness toward this man who bowed awkwardly when he finished speaking. Later she would wonder how she could possibly have sensed his power and potential based on that uninspired performance.

As she looked around now at the crowded chapel and her husband's flushed face and heroic stance there above them all, she allowed herself to consider that her direction had changed forever, not only because of the message of sacrifice and endurance that the young Reverend had conveyed on the first day she had met him but because the sun had glinted off his fine spectacles and the hand that held his remarks had trembled most sincerely. There was no doubt in her mind that she had chosen her path well, especially because he had become enamored of her, too, not long after her arrival in Fenchow-fu, and their destiny together had been sealed.

In a surprising magazine that had fallen into her hands during her brief stay in New York prior to her departure for Cathay, Grace had read the rather forward advice that a modern woman must take the reins in matters of the heart. *The Lady's Realm* printed articles not only about how women now had the right to vote in four Western states, whereas it was unheard-of in the rest of the country, but also on how a lady could manage her own honeymoon. The modern woman understood that when she married a gentleman greatly distracted by ambition, she must nonetheless persevere with her own hopes and dreams. Grace was not sure what her own hopes and dreams might be, but she recognized that the Reverend was a man much distracted by ambition.

Indeed, the man before her today bore none of the human frailty and lack of surety of the young man she had first met but instead, was a substantial figure who had achieved a great deal. She rather liked that he appeared now as the Chinese had come to see him—as a bear, a giant, an oversized miracle of a man. Ghost Man, they called him, and she could see why.

Grace reminded herself that as a girl of twenty, she could instead have become a schoolteacher in a one-room schoolhouse on the Midwestern plains, a librarian in the college town, or most certainly a secretary to one of her father's fellow academics on campus. Instead, four years before, she had followed a man in whom she sensed greatness into the desert halfway around the world, and it was here that she now watched him spin his words into blazing gold.

"I, too, am a sinner," the Reverend called out in a fiery voice. "I am one of the fallen."

Grace glanced about and saw that the Chinese sat on the edges of the pews, their whole bodies tilting toward him, their hands clasped and their eyes rapt in attention. The other ministers and their wives shifted uneasily in their seats. The Reverend's sudden urge for self-revelation was not at all the usual approach to their mission. Grace dared to look again at Mildred Martin and swallowed hard as she saw the older woman's jaw go slack and hang partially open. Her husband, Charles Martin, the Reverend's most loyal friend, looked on with an expression that could only be described as horror.

Grace turned back to her husband and widened her beaming expression up at him. Unlike her compatriots, she was proud that on his journeys he seemed to have come to the same stark conclusion that she had in the several months since their disaster: she and the Revered were indeed sinners, and not just in any usual sense. The Martins might still believe themselves to be otherwise, but Grace, and apparently the Reverend as well, knew the truth. The Lord had chosen to reveal their sins by punishing them most thoroughly. They were, without a doubt, as fallen as Adam and Eve on the wretched morning when the Lord had raised His arm and pointed them out of Eden.

"I am lower than the lowliest of beggars on the streets," the Reverend shouted. "I am as blind as the men whose eyes are crusted over with scabs. I am as infirm as those who lie in the streets with limbs hanging torn and useless. I am no better than the poorest of the poor, for my heart is black with sin."

Grace felt a shiver rise up her spine. She feared she might faint, and yet she knew her face glowed with recognition. She understood as never before that she had been guilty of the sin of pride when, as a blithe and naive girl, she had been overly pleased with herself for having married such a man. Several of the other ladies at the mission had been partial to the Reverend as well, but Grace had won out. She had always considered herself blessed. The Lord would spare her any true pain. And yet, decidedly, He had not.

The echoing hum had begun in the back of her mind again, and she felt herself starting to move away from herself, rising up from her seat and looking down over them all. She welcomed these strange sensations that usually accompanied her nightly bedtime odysseys. It was the familiar feeling of being washed over with shame.

The new Chinese Christians all around her rubbed their hands together in delight. No doubt they must have wondered how it had come to pass that a white man who had once stood so tall and upright and clean now hung his head and debased himself before them. If this great man who had built roads and hospitals and schools professed such weaknesses, what did that mean for those who struggled simply to plow their dry fields and place meager food upon their tables?

Grace looked upon their faces and saw a strange sight: she saw hope. She felt she had no business recognizing it in her own current miserable state of loss, but there it was, quite undeniably. Hope lit up their faces, as it did her own.

The Reverend raised his fists at the timbers. He shook his head of shaggy hair. His shirttails came loose as he lifted his enormous arms. The greatcoat wafted, and the talismans and bells tinkled on their ropes. He described the torture he had endured at the hands of the world, and the Chinese let out cries of agreement and shouts of joy. They knew of what he spoke before he even said the words. It reminded

Grace of the sounds she had heard coming from the Negro church at the edge of her Ohio town when her family rode past on a Sunday afternoon. The native faces around her now were alive with both anguish and bliss.

Someone called out from the back of the little chapel, "Speak loudly to the heavens, Ghost Man!"

Reverend Martin in the front row turned instantly and put a finger to his lips to shush them.

"Call out to the Jesus for more miracles," another voice called.

Reverend Martin stood and said, "Quiet now, gentle people."

The Reverend looked over his friend's neatly combed head and shouted to the increasingly restless crowd, "Yes, my friends, we understand one another, do we not? But now, let us pray."

The crowd, which he had worked into a frenzy, would not be calmed with the notion of prayer. They stood and suddenly surged forward and up the aisles. They reached out their hands toward him.

Reverend Martin shouted and waved frantically for them to stop. "That is all for today. Help yourselves to water in the courtyard, and please return for Bible study at four this afternoon."

But the people did not seem to hear. They continued to surge toward the Reverend with outstretched arms. Grace was not surprised to see them clamoring for his attention. She herself had done as much in recent weeks, but with little success.

Now the dizziness and humming in her head became quite forceful. Perhaps Mai Lin's medicines had worn off altogether, Grace thought, and she looked around for her servant with a growing sense of panic. The trick with her potions was to maintain the correct balance, and clearly Grace had gone too long without being administered to. She knew Mai Lin did not care for Sunday services, always a sticking point between her and the Reverend, but Grace was certain she would at least stay nearby when her mistress was in such a weakened state.

The vibrations inside her skull were decidedly pronounced, and Grace shut her eyes. She longed for bed. Then, just when she thought she might faint, the Reverend's voice boomed over the chapel again, and the entire congregation snapped to attention, including his wife.

"Silence!" he bellowed. He pointed at the crowd, his long arms sweeping over them. They stopped where they stood. "The Lord, the greatest Ghost Man of all, wishes you to file out peacefully, get into your carts, and go home to rest on the Sabbath. Tomorrow you will rise, and the crops will have grown."

The crowd let out a hopeful gasp.

"Go now in peace." The Reverend swept his hands through the air, his fingers spread wide like great nets to catch them and pull them into his embrace. "I bless thee, my children. I bless thee."

Grace shut her eyes and tried to feel his blessings rain down upon her. All around, she felt the crowd ebbing back out the door. She kept her eyes pinched shut and waited for her husband's absolving hand upon her arm.

Eight

Grace had come to think of the iron gates of the mission compound as the gates of heaven and herself as one of the Lord's many helpers. It was her job to welcome each new arrival, to set them at ease and oversee their transition into this new world. At night in restless sleep, she watched out her window as figures came toward her. Then, in the morning, she had to shake such visions from her head and try to understand them as but overwrought dreams, although they had appeared so real. But now, in the late-afternoon light of early autumn, she watched as actual people of all ages came plodding into the mission. Every one of them Chinese, yet nonetheless she searched amongst the multitudes of black heads for her towheaded children. They lived for now amongst the masses, but soon Grace would spot them and fly down into the courtyard and bring them home.

Long shadows preceded each person who entered the courtyard as the sun cut across the plains. They walked with heads bent, these tired people, the young as well as the old and infirm. Even the strongest and healthiest amongst them walked with sloped shoulders, hardly lifting their feet from the dusty ground. In their weariness, they all looked alike to Grace, and she thought that was how it was meant to be: all of God's children were identical in the end. She could see that now.

It was a lesson she would never have believed while in America, but now it seemed so obvious. Here in China, the vast numbers of people staggered along day after day, struggling to feed and clothe themselves and their families. Their skinny bodies all appeared to share the same misery. There was no color to them, no liveliness any longer even amongst the young ladies. A girl in America could be quite vivid: Grace and her friends dressed in Easter pastels in springtime, rich reds at Christmas, with ribbons to match in their hair. She searched now for any sign of brightness but saw only the shadows of strangers. All of them were daguerreotypes, tinted brown by the sun, the desert soil, and whatever other dusty matter made up their souls.

The crowd that poured in through the open gate appeared more sizable than usual, and Grace squinted hard to keep track of each new arrival. Their carts and donkeys waited outside the compound, and she rose from her bed to spy over the high wall to search for anyone who might have been left behind on a buckboard or under a bale of hay. It was difficult, but she needed to keep track of them all.

In a flash, and out of the corner of her eye, she thought she saw a pale face down near the ground. Grace swore she spotted small hands holding fast to a woman's filthy black skirt. Could it be a blond child, her child?

Grace called sharply to Mai Lin. The old woman sat, as she always did, on a spindly chair in the corner of Grace's bedchamber. Her hair looked wilder than ever, and her little clublike feet—squeezed into brocaded shoes no bigger than Grace's small clenched fist—were hitched up on the rungs as if she were some sort of monkey. Despite

Mai Lin's unfortunate appearance, Grace felt such warmth toward her. She wasn't sure why, but she did.

"Dear Mai Lin," Grace said breathlessly, "the day has come! Dress me quickly, please. I have seen my son."

Mai Lin rose, and as she came forward, Grace noticed something she had not before.

"I have been remiss," she said as she lifted a brush from her dressing table and combed her hair for the first time in weeks. "I have never asked you, Mai Lin: are you in great pain? You hobble from the feet-binding of your childhood. I wonder if every step hurts. Is that how it feels?"

Mai Lin waved a hand as if brushing away a fly. "It is no matter about me. Mistress is feeling better today. She sees her baby coming back to her."

"Yes, yes, that's right," Grace said and let Mai Lin take the brush from her hand to continue the job. "Let's hurry now, so he doesn't leave again like that other time."

Mai Lin dressed her in a simple frock because the autumn afternoon was still warm and Grace could not be bothered with all the layers of petticoats. Her enlarged belly was visible, and she felt certain the others would understand that in her condition, she couldn't possibly be encumbered by all the usual undergarments.

She allowed Mai Lin to tie her sash, but not too tightly. Then she dashed out of the room.

"Careful on the steps, Mistress," Mai Lin called after her. "You are more light-headed than you realize."

Grace could not be bothered with such concerns, although she did find that her vision was playing tricks on her. When she went to hold the balustrade at the top of the stairs, there were two finials, not the usual one. She must remember to speak to Mai Lin about her dosage. The medicines were crucial to controlling her nervous condition, but much of the time, they left her feeling as drunk as a sailor, which was not proper of course but did add to her mood of levity. The reunion she had dreamed of was about to transpire.

She traipsed lightly down the wooden steps, flew across the wide front hallway, and opened the screen door. Grace stepped out onto the grand porch and abruptly came to a halt. Before her were swarms of people. Chinese people. She had known they had entered, but from upstairs she had not seen their distinct features, their slick black hair, their dusty lined faces, the stained or missing teeth. And the stench emanating from them almost made her gag. What on earth were they all doing here? she wondered.

Then she remembered what had taken place on this same soil about a decade before. She had learned about it on the day she had first met the Reverend in Ohio. The story of the Boxer Rebellion had been seared into her mind, and it had never been far from her thoughts since her arrival in Shansi Province.

The dear missionary families of the past had been swarmed by angry Chinese. The crazed peasants came down from the villages in the mountains. They swooped in from every desert hamlet. They bore sticks and rocks and even guns. With war cries, they rallied their own into a frenzy of violence. Grace had heard stories of it any number of times over the past four years since her arrival here.

"Foreign devils," they had shouted, "you have poisoned our wells, dried up our fields, and sent our children to heaven! Soon we shall all die unless we kill you first."

"The gods are angry that we smoked the opium of the white man's religion," others had shouted. "It is because of this Jesus person that we are slaves now and starving. We will make the rain come, but first, we begin with a rain of blood!"

Grace shivered at the thought. On an afternoon not unlike this one, the bands of barbarians had killed those who they believed were the source of their misery. Grace would forever remember the final count: 180 missionaries murdered—men, women, and innocent children. Their valiant story, and then the young Reverend Watson's contagious plan to be amongst the first brave souls returning to this land only a few years after the onslaught had taken place—well, of course, she had been propelled to join him in this frightful place. Her husband had been on the veritable front lines, and now it was her turn, too.

She raced back into the house and found a broom in a closet. As she cut back through the parlor and headed out the front door again, Ahcho appeared beside her. Grace was also dimly aware of Mai Lin making her way slowly down from the second floor.

"Mistress," Ahcho said, "how wonderful to see you up. You are feeling better?"

Grace paused for a moment and glanced at him. He looked inordinately calm. Why was no one else preparing to fight the oncoming horde? Had Ahcho not noticed them pouring into the yard?

"We must do our duty," she shouted and made for the door.

"Shall I sweep the porch for you?" he offered as he followed. "You must not exert yourself, Mistress."

Now Grace could hear Mai Lin coming along behind her. Surely dependable Ahcho and dear Mai Lin would see the situation for what it was and help. But they were moving too slowly, and she could not wait for reinforcements. Grace hurried down the porch steps and began stabbing the dusty ground at the feet of the milling Chinese. She used the straw broom to attack their bare toes. The coolies hopped back, startled, and barked in surprise at being poked by stiff bristles.

"Shoo, shoo," Grace shouted. "Away with you!"

As some staggered back, others filled in their places. She felt their bodies pressing toward her. Her heart beat faster, but she told herself she must not give up. Her husband had been brave so many times, and now was her chance to finally join him in his zealotry. She spun in circles, swinging the broom wide in the air to keep them away.

"Out," she shouted. "Out you go!"

Then she felt a warm hand on her arm and let the head of the broom drop to the ground. She felt surprisingly dizzy, but luckily, the hand held her steady. The unsettling vibrations that had overtaken her brain began to recede again, and Grace vaguely wondered what had come over her.

"Mistress," Ahcho said, "may I take this from you now?" He reached for the broom.

She looked up, more than a little confused, but trusted his kind voice. She felt as baffled as in the mornings after waking from her hallucinations. Whatever was going on in her mind? she wondered.

"This is what you want instead, yes?" he asked.

Ahcho's hand appeared before her. In his palm sat a small bar of lye soap and a white rag that she knew served as a washcloth.

"It is Friday today, Mistress. They are here for their weekly baths."

He gently touched her shoulder again and steered her in the direction of the Chinese women who stood in a line before the metal tub.

"They would be most honored to receive their soap and small cloths from the Reverend's excellent wife."

Grace ran her palms down the front of her slip and straightened it as best she could. She suddenly felt terribly underdressed. She should not be seen by these new congregants in her flimsy petticoat. Why had Mai Lin allowed her out without the proper attire? Although Grace had to question her own judgment in this instance as well.

"Am I all right?" she whispered to Ahcho.

"Absolutely." He nodded. "They are pleased to meet you."

She tried to stand taller. "As I am to meet them."

Grace pulled back her shoulders and made her way to her position beside the tub. She prepared to greet each tired and filthy new Christian with a smile, although she feared that she needed a bath as badly as they did. And if somehow her mind could be scrubbed clean as well, she would be most grateful.

Nine

Would you care for a cup of tea?" Mildred Martin inquired, her eyebrows raised.

The Martins' number-one boy poured, and Grace smiled when he held up a rare lump of sugar with silver tongs. Mildred must have saved her small store of the precious sweet for special occasions, which gave Grace a shred of optimism about this visit. She so wanted them to be friends again.

As Grace accepted the cup and saucer and placed them on the table, she hoped that her trembling hand was not too noticeable. In the four years since she had arrived in Fenchow-fu, Mildred, though only slightly older, had watched over her with a mother's keen eye. Indeed, Mildred was watching her now. There would be no hiding Grace's delicate condition.

"You do not look well," Mildred began and patted Grace's thin wrist. "But, of course, you have been through so much."

The two ladies looked down at their laps and slowly shook their heads.

"It must lead you to prayer more than ever," Mildred said.

Grace agreed, although oddly, she did not pray often anymore. She was far too occupied with keeping track of her dreams and all that business out the window. Her vigilance required a great deal of her.

"The baby will help you enormously," Mildred said, now giving Grace's hand a firm squeeze as a signal for Grace to let go, which she did reluctantly.

"My little Daisy has made my earlier loss all but disappear from my mind. Of course my earlier one never saw the light of day, unlike your dear little boy, who made it all the way to three years of age."

Grace wished her friend would refrain from mentioning her son, especially not in the past tense as if he had died, which Grace was convinced he had not. She tried to recall if she had ever told Mildred about the two she had lost to miscarriage as well. Those were terrible, but nothing compared to the open wound left by her stolen boy.

"I do hope for that, Mildred. You are most blessed with precious Daisy."

Hearing her name, the little girl rose from where she played with blocks on the Chinese carpet. She toddled over, placed a block in her mother's lap, looked up, and spat out the word "block" as if it were the most thrilling thing on earth. Grace could not help letting out a giggle. The child was just so darling. But the little girl looked up at Grace and frowned. She took a handful of her mother's fine skirt and wrinkled it in her chubby fingers.

"I believe I have upset her," Grace said.

"Nonsense," Mildred said. "Daisy, say hello to Mrs. Watson."

Daisy continued to frown at Grace as she pawed at her mother's lap. Mildred lifted her daughter and set her upon her knee. Daisy twisted her body away so as not to look at Grace.

"I won't bother you, darling girl," Grace said. She longed to reach across and touch that fine blond hair, so like her own Wesley's that it pained her heart. "But did you know that very soon you will have a new playmate?"

Daisy glanced back at Grace with a skeptical look.

"I have a baby coming soon, and he or she will be your new friend."

This seemed to finally set Daisy at ease. The girl pushed off from her mother's arms, clambered back down onto the rug, and waddled to her blocks. Grace and Mildred took up their cups and drank as Daisy commenced building a tower.

"Your Reverend," Mildred asked, "he is excited about the child?"

"Oh, yes," Grace replied with enthusiasm.

"And you believe he intends to be around more often once the baby arrives?" Mildred's voice sounded rather pinched, Grace thought.

"I assume so. We have not discussed it."

"Really? You are entering your sixth month of pregnancy, and you have not discussed it?" Mildred's eyebrows rose again. "I would think that would be a most important topic at this time." Then she leaned closer and asked, "Do you actually know where he goes when he leaves for days and weeks at a time?"

Grace set down her cup and sat up straighter in her chair, "Why, to the outlying churches, of course."

Mildred let out a stifled laugh that cut Grace to the quick.

"My dear," Mildred said, "that man is gone more often than he is here. Do you think he has any concept of the frenzy he has created with all these new supposed converts whom my husband has been left to deal with? All I am saying is that it is not always best for the mission to have your Reverend gone. And I suspect it is not terribly good for you, either, especially in your condition."

Grace shifted in her seat and wondered if she should just rise and exit at that very moment. No one should be permitted to speak of the Reverend in such disdainful and critical tones. He was head of the mission and respected far and wide. He had built the hospital in which Mildred's child had been born, and the schools where the Chinese children were taught. But, instead of leaving in protest, Grace reached up her sleeve and brought out her linen handkerchief. As she dabbed at her eyes, she glanced at Mildred and saw genuine concern on the other woman's face. Grace's hand that held the kerchief fell heavily to her lap.

"No, it is not so good for me, either," she admitted.

"My dear Grace, after all you have been through." Mildred offered a crisp rub to Grace's knee. "I am sorry to be so forward, but perhaps you can tell me: what is the precise meaning of all those belts and whatnots he has hanging about his person?" Mildred let out a thin stream of air. "What I am getting at is that I believe your Reverend has gone native on you, Mrs. Watson. Whatever are you going to do about it?"

Grace pushed her handkerchief up her sleeve again, although she feared that if she was unable to control herself, she would need it in barely a moment when she would finally burst into tears.

Luckily, Mildred continued, "The Reverend Martin and I have discussed it."

"Discussed what?" Grace asked.

"Your situation and your Reverend's changed—well, there is no other word for it—his changed *being*."

Grace nodded, although her mind raced with both the truth of this observation and the utter ignorance of it. Had the Martins' first born son been stolen from them, then they, too, would have found their *being* changed.

"When your baby comes," Mildred continued, "we wish to invite you to live here with us. No, hear me out. It is quite customary for a new mother to be cared for by a loving auntie or friend. No one will think badly of you. We cannot have you over there across the courtyard without a husband and no one but the natives to tend to you and your baby. That is not Christian of us, or of you."

Grace felt the anticipated tears rise up. She did not know what to say, so she reached out a shaking hand and held on to Mildred's own firm one. "You are most kind and good," Grace finally spluttered. "Truly you are."

Mildred smiled tightly and nodded in agreement.

"I am sure the Reverend will understand?" Grace said, half telling and half asking.

"Not to worry. I will have my Reverend Martin speak to him. This new child of yours needs to be protected at all costs. Frankly, knowing the likes of those your husband has come to associate with recently, I am not entirely confident that you should stay in your home even if he were there to be with you. I am sorry to be so blunt. But you will feel much better off here, allowing us to care for you. You may use my number-one amah and leave yours behind. Daisy is old enough to manage without her all the time."

Grace shot a startled look at Mildred, who glanced away quickly and took up her cup again.

"I do not know if I can manage that," Grace said softly. "Mai Lin relies on our employ."

"I should say it is you, rather, who relies perhaps too much upon her," Mildred said, her words slow and careful. "But there is no need for us to quibble about the details. Let's just say it is decided."

Mildred stood, and before Grace knew it, she was being helped up from her seat and escorted out of the Martins' parlor and toward the front door.

"I assume Doc Hemingway will deliver the child?" Mildred asked.

Grace nodded but did not answer.

"He did such a fine job with my Daisy. I would not possibly trust any method other than Western practices for something so important as bringing a baby into the world. Beware of the voodoo rituals of the natives, am I right, my dear?"

Grace nodded again.

"You take care of yourself, and as I said, Reverend Martin will speak with Reverend Watson. It will all be arranged."

Mildred helped Grace out onto the Martins' porch, where she promptly left her. Grace glanced around the desolate courtyard and let out an audible sigh when she finally spotted Mai Lin. The old woman was crouched under a forlorn tree, spitting betel quid into the dust.

Ten

Although it was not customary for the missionary wives to accompany their cooks, number-one boys, or amahs to market, Grace thought that a rare expedition of this sort was acceptable. She had been holed up in the compound for she couldn't recall how long, and on a cool midautumn day like this, she positively needed to walk and feel the crisp air.

She tugged her wool coat tighter around her middle, although it would no longer button shut, and held Mai Lin's arm. They wove through the sorry-looking market stalls that displayed small piles of shriveled potatoes and wilted greens. Grace began to notice that the whole setup appeared rather pathetic: the toothless vendors, hollow-chested farmers, and their gnarled-looking wives had barely any produce for sale. Grace knew that she and Mai Lin made an odd-looking couple, but somehow she also sensed that they suited this miserable place.

The old woman hobbled along, but her pace was just right for Grace at six months pregnant. To her amazement, no one bothered them with the usual incessant begging. No doubt Mai Lin was liberally threatening to douse any who approached with the Evil Eye. Dear Mai Lin, Grace thought, how could she ever get along without her?

As they left the market, Grace noticed that more people than usual were hurrying past. She was not terribly familiar with the town, but somehow the crowd seemed different to her and more frantic. Even those carrying heavy loads on poles over their shoulders or balanced precariously in straw baskets on their heads passed quickly and with great intent. Men and women practically ran as they pushed their wares on carts before them. They shouted out prices for charcoal, rice, millet, and cloth, although they seemed to have no intention of stopping for interested customers.

Just then, up ahead at the corner where two cobblestone streets met, a small troop of soldiers belonging to the local warlord appeared. They marched in the direction where Grace and Mai Lin stood, with their bayonets out and their faces stern and unchanging. Their boots scuffed in unison. Before them stumbled a Chinese coolie dressed only in a loincloth. His wrists were bound by thick rope, and his legs were in chains. Mai Lin took Grace's hand and started to pull her away as more people poured out from the small shops and alleyways to follow the prisoner.

"What are they going to do to that poor fellow?" Grace asked.

Mai Lin did not reply and only tugged at her arm again.

"Tell me, Mai Lin."

"He was caught stealing something. He is nothing. Just a common criminal. Do not be concerned."

"But what is being done to him?"

"Mistress must go back to the mission compound now."

Grace looked for a long moment into Mai Lin's lined and worried face. Then she abruptly broke free and followed along with the crowd. If an injustice was about to be committed in plain sight of all these people, she wanted to witness it, too. She would return to the mission and report on the primitive justice system in this barbaric country. The Reverend ought to know about it, and she would be his deputy by informing him. Surely, he would be proud of her.

Grace felt the filthy bodies of strangers press in around her as they filtered through the opening in the city wall. They finally stepped out into an area where farmers milled about and watered their donkeys before heading back onto the plains. As the small band of soldiers cut through the crowd, the bustle stopped. The donkeys kept chewing, but the country folk went still, their faces frozen in unchanging masks.

At the center of the wide circle made by the watching peasants, the prisoner fell to his knees and wept. He had wet himself, and his body trembled. Grace knew she should look away. It was not decent to see a man so shamed. But she could not look away and watched as the prisoner fell forward onto his elbows and bowed his head in prayer.

She stepped closer and listened as the poor fellow called out for his mother's and his father's forgiveness. He begged that his ancestors not shun him upon his arrival in heaven. Then, to Grace's great surprise, he called out to his Savior, Jesus Christ, his Lord and Master.

At that moment, Mai Lin caught up with her. Grace looked down at her maidservant and asked, "Is it possible that they are punishing this fellow because he is a Christian?"

Mai Lin shook her head in disgust. "No, they punish him because he stole what was not his. Now, we must go!"

Grace stared with wide eyes and said, "But he would not have stolen something if he is a Christian."

Mai Lin let out a surprising cackle and slapped a palm against her wrinkled cheek. Grace's cheeks flushed as she sensed the crowd turning to look at them. She must speak to Mai Lin about treating her more respectfully, especially in public.

Just then, out into the square stepped a large man in a black robe with a saber hanging from his belt. The sword had to be three feet long, with a black lacquer handle and sheath. A red braided tassel swayed from the hilt. Grace had never seen such a handsome and frightening weapon. The man wore a black cloth over his forehead and another pulled up to his nose so that only his eyes were visible in the narrow slit between. He unsheathed his sword and swung it over his head.

The silver blade caught the late-afternoon sunlight as the man performed some sort of ritual, a dance that edged him nearer and nearer to the prisoner. The soldiers stood at attention and watched while the crowd became more quiet and tense. Grace wanted to look away. She knew she would regret it if she did not, but her eyes stayed frozen on every movement of the man who swung the sword. She heard Mai Lin mumbling beside her and noticed that the old woman's eyes were shut. Yes, Mai Lin's head was bowed in prayer, although Grace could not guess to what god she whispered.

The swordsman circled the cowering figure. He bent deeply in a ritual genuflection and let out a menacing cry that echoed across the courtyard and bounced off the city walls. The crowd answered with a nearly imperceptible gasp. Two soldiers lifted the prisoner and forced his bound arms over a bamboo pole. The man ducked his head as low as he could, as if that might help him escape his end.

Grace had a most startling thought at that moment: if that were she kneeling in the dust, she would not want to give the barbarians the satisfaction of seeing her cowed. She would not bow her head in prayer. She simply wouldn't do it, devout husband or no.

The Chinese man was a better Christian than she. The prisoner and Mai Lin both prayed frantically now. Grace wanted to shout at them: what was the use of prayer when the blade was about to strike? What good could it do when evil was upon you? No such prayers could save this man, just as fervent prayer had not saved her son when he had been stolen from her.

The sword drew an extravagant arc through the air. While it twisted and curved in arabesques, Grace wondered if the terrible thing might never actually happen. Maybe the blow would never be struck. That would be the only true miracle to prove once and for all that prayers had been answered.

But as she watched, Grace knew that she would carry the memory of this moment with her for the rest of her life, and in that way, the moment would never fully come to an end. The sword would hover continuously over the kneeling man's neck. The red tassel would dance forever like a gaudy bauble against the blue sky. The prisoner's final desperate cries would echo endlessly off the city walls and across the hushed courtyard. All of it would live on in Grace's mind in an endless cycle, never bringing relief or deliverance.

The slow, steady chewing of the ignorant donkeys to her right, the wild reverberations of her own heart pounding in her ears would remain always. At least, during that unbearably long moment, Grace hoped that would be the case. For as terrible as it was to wait, it was better than the swift and irreversible end that finally came too soon.

The blade hit bone with a sickening crack.

Grace yanked a handkerchief from her sleeve and pressed it against her mouth, where it hardly muted the terrified scream that rose from her lips. Her cry was all the more deafening because of the silence around her.

A hard thud sounded as the head hit packed earth. A duller thud signaled the body falling forward onto its stump. The soldiers who had held the bamboo pole let it drop and watched without expression. Blood spurted onto the dirt and soaked into the skin of the still-twitching man. It darkened the dust in rivulets leading in the direction of the head. Lying there in the dirt, just a few feet from them, the open-eyed head stared at Grace. For far too long an instant, she stared back while Mai Lin's eyes remained shut, her lips still murmuring.

"Oh, dear," Grace said as her vision started to blacken. "I believe I have seen too much."

Mai Lin gripped her waist. "Shut your eyes!" she shouted. "Do not allow dead man's spirit inside you. Ignorant woman, you should not have watched."

With Mai Lin's arm around her, Grace did not faint. She took in gasps of air and began coughing. She bent over and convulsed, a deep cough rising up from far within her body. It was as if she needed to expel all the dust she had breathed since coming to China. The fine yellow loess carried on the wind all the way from the Gobi Desert had filled her up, clogged her mind and lungs. Grace continued to cough and felt her face flame.

Some brave person, she thought, should have stepped forward and objected or argued or pulled out his own sword, ready to fight. If only the Reverend had been here, he would have marched forward and not flinched. The Reverend would have been brave. Never had there been a white man better suited to this awful place; never one better able to change it for the good. Grace made herself stand upright as her coughing finally subsided. She would tell the Reverend about this incident, and he would see to it that no such things ever happened again. Such was her husband's influence, she believed, in this arduous land.

Mai Lin kept hold of Grace's arm as they began the slow trek back to the compound. Grace paused to fold her handkerchief and started to tuck it back into her sleeve. But Mai Lin grabbed the white linen and held it up to the sunlight. It was streaked with blood that shone with shocking brightness. Grace turned to Mai Lin. In an instant, she understood the look in the old woman's eyes.

Eleven

Ahcho held open the flap of the yurt, and the Reverend bent to enter. The circle of Mongolian men in sheepskin vests and hats looked up with pinched eyes as the fire before them billowed and smoke swirled upward and out the center hole. The desert night air had grown cold, and the Reverend had not hesitated to ask for shelter from the lookout guard. He had become bolder on his many recent journeys across the plains and western mountains. His unhealthy disregard for danger made Ahcho's task of seeing to his safety more difficult than ever.

"Good evening, gentlemen," the Reverend said in a sufficient approximation of their dialect. He bowed, and his long coat swept the richly colored rug they had set down on the hard dirt. "Thank you for your hospitality on this frigid night. We are most grateful."

The chieftain of the Mongol band nodded but did not smile. The thick fur cape he wore over his shoulders was preposterous, Ahcho thought. For one thing, it was enormous and still bore the head and claws of the wolf to whom it had belonged. Ahcho tried not to look into the dead animal's yellow eyes. Evil spirits, both alive and dead, lurked everywhere out on the plains. A person had to be careful, and the likes of these men could not be trusted. Mongol nomads had nothing to lose. They cut men's throats and left them to die by the road without compunction. Just consider the abduction of the young Wesley boy. These people stopped at nothing. Under his robe, Ahcho fingered the cool handle of a pistol he had borrowed for precisely this reason and kept secret from the Reverend. His master would not have approved of it, but then again, as a foreigner, he could not possibly be fully aware of the many hazards.

"Sit, sit," the chieftain said as he raised a hand on which flashed rings and bracelets of hammered silver. Around his neck he wore a dozen pendants, each bearing an amulet of silver.

The other men shifted on their hassocks to make a place for the Reverend and pointed to a space in the circle for Ahcho as well, but he shook his head. He would stand by the door, although after riding all day, his legs throbbed with tiredness. He was not a young man anymore, yet not for an instant would he take his eyes off his master so long as the Reverend continued to place himself in the company of such blackguards.

"You will smoke with us," the chief said.

It was not a question, and the Reverend did not seem to take it as one. He merely nodded, and the others offered a murmur of approval.

One of the men packed a pipe with a long silver stem and tamped it down with a silver tool. This was a successful band, Ahcho thought, if one could be successful as a nomad. As their guard had led them toward the chieftain's tent, they had passed through a substantial herd of sheep and goats. Ahcho had always understood that nomads traveled in small bands because they fought too often amongst themselves and were forever killing one another over minor slights. Yet he and the

Reverend had passed a good number of tents scattered about, and Ahcho wondered if they might even belong to wives and children, although he dared not ask. Nomads were notoriously private and volatile. A simple greeting could be construed as a threat. They would slice off an ear or a hand, steal your horse, and then run you off. He had heard stories.

The men silently smoked, and when the pipe came to the Reverend, he did exactly as the others had done before him. Ahcho marveled at how the American had learned to adapt so quickly to his surroundings in recent months. While he knew that the rumors about the Reverend were unfounded and outrageous, his master was indeed a changed man and not always recognizable anymore.

The chief spoke up again when the pipe returned to him. "We heard you were coming."

The Reverend smiled ever so slightly. He spoke far less often than he used to and seemed to weigh his words more carefully. Ahcho could tell that this gave him the air of a holy man, which was true as well as a good strategy.

A young buck shook his head excitedly, and his loosely twined hair thrashed about his shoulders as he spoke. "We were told you were nearby, and I said we should go out and find you before you left the region again. But our great leader was right that you would come to us. This is a most propitious day!"

The Reverend leaned toward the young man and asked, "And what did you hope for from my arrival?"

"Oh, just to see you, Ghost Man. I will tell my children, and they will tell their children. And maybe if you want to perform a miracle, that would be fine with us." He nudged his friend beside him, and the two men chuckled.

The second said, "We will shoot you and watch you not fall down, yes? That would be something!"

Ahcho clenched the pistol under his robe.

The chieftain cleared his throat, and the men quieted down. The pipe began around the circle again.

After a long moment, the Reverend spoke. "I, too, am in search of a miracle. The miracle of my firstborn son, who was stolen from me."

The chieftain bowed his head in what appeared to be genuine sympathy. "There is no greater loss than this," he said.

"Yes," the Reverend said. "And you can help my miracle come true by telling me if you have seen any signs of a small white boy with hair the color of gold."

The wolf's jaw upon the chief's brow shook slowly from side to side. "I am an old man now, and I know very little."

The men around the circle made polite sounds of disagreement.

"No, it is true," the chieftain said to his people. "I may know how to handle a horse or how to keep my people fed even in lean times such as these." Then his voice rose as he lifted his old shoulders. The wolf hide on his back rose, too. "And I enforce the law! This I must always do!" He lowered his arms, and the animal's long muzzle sagged again. "But I do not know why the Spirits act as they do. I try to keep us safe from their wrath, yet I do not always succeed."

The Reverend let out a long sigh. "That is the problem, is it not? To understand the Lord's wisdom, even when it is more painful than a person can bear."

The two men passed the pipe between only themselves, and the others watched.

"You understand that things are different out here in the borderlands?" the chieftain asked him. "Anything but petty thieving is punishable by death. Under our system, elders are held responsible for the actions of offspring. A parent may be rewarded for his son's good services, or he may be beheaded for his grandson's crime."

The other men nodded at this arrangement.

"This is best," one of them said.

The chief continued, "And it works the other way around as well. If a father harms another, his son can be held accountable and even traded for the crime. The family, and not the individual, is the unit in our law."

The Reverend shifted in his seat. Ahcho suspected that he was made uncomfortable by these remarks and not just because his long legs ached in their crossed position. He studied his master's face and searched for any sign that the same questions and speculations were arising in his mind. But the Reverend's face remained inscrutable.

"Out here," the chieftain continued, waving a finger over the abstract pattern of the brightly woven rug as if it were a map of the borderlands, "labyrinthine rules based on familial retribution keep order. It means that one can ill afford to offend. Any punishment is severe for either accident or error. You much approach every situation alert for signs of danger." He looked at the Reverend and asked, "Do you understand this?"

The Reverend's eyes became narrow and intent. "I do," he said.

"You are not an ignorant man, then?"

The Reverend did not reply but raised a single red and bushy eyebrow.

"All right. Let us assume that you are wiser than I thought," the chieftain said. "I will tell you what I know."

The Reverend whispered in English, "Thank you, sweet Jesus."

"But first," the chief said, "I will need something from you."

"Anything."

The chieftain smiled for the first time that evening, and Ahcho was not surprised to see that his teeth were all but gone. The two he had left were as black as tree stumps after a forest fire. "I am not a successful man by accident, am I?" asked the chief.

His men chuckled at this, and Ahcho could not help letting out a disgusted grunt. Even the best of these people were greedy louts. You could not turn your back on them even for a moment. Nomads, of all people, needed the Lord Jesus. Ahcho wondered when the Reverend would get around to mentioning Him.

"All right, what do you want?" the Reverend asked.

"Your boy is most precious to you. So, I think, something precious in return."

The men muttered in agreement, clearly proud of their conniving leader.

The Reverend did not hesitate. He pushed aside the swath of red cloth that crossed his chest, unbuttoned his long coat, and reached inside his vest pocket. Ahcho let out a slight puff of air as the Reverend pulled forth his handsome gold watch on its chain.

"Reverend," Ahcho said in English, "he may be lying to you."

The Reverend lifted a hand to silence him. Ahcho had seen how grief could make a person turn foolish or even temporarily insane. He had witnessed this any number of times in the past, most recently with the mistress on bathing day, but here he was saddened to see it happening with his clever master as well.

The gold of the watch shone dully as it swung in the firelight. The chieftain reached for it and clasped it in his soot-stained hands. He showed his compatriots how heavy it was by letting his hand sink under its weight. Then he brought it up to his mouth and bit down on it with his two sorry teeth. Ahcho could not bear the sight any longer and stepped forward.

"Of course it's real gold!" he shouted in their language. "It was a gift to the Reverend from his father. The Reverend John Wesley Watson is not to be trifled with, you old fool."

The two younger men hopped up from their seats and instantly pinned Ahcho's arms to his sides. Ahcho tried to pull himself free, but they held him fast.

"Please don't be offended by my man," the Reverend said quickly to the chieftain. "He is only being loyal to me. He is upset that I am willing to make this significant sacrifice to you." The Reverend pointed at the watch. "For this is certainly real, is it not? As I assume your information about my son is also completely real."

The chieftain snapped his fingers, and the men let go of Ahcho's arms. "I see this is a sacrifice," he commented, fingering the watch. "I like this sacrifice." His black eyes danced, and his despicable smile returned.

"Now you will tell me where to find my boy?" the Reverend asked.

"Yes, I will tell you what you want to know. I have seen a person low to the ground and with hair the color of this golden watch. With my own eyes I have witnessed it! You will sleep here tonight, and tomorrow I will send you in the direction of your son. He is not far from here."

The old man struggled to stand, and two of his men took him under the arms and helped him up. To Ahcho's surprise, the chieftain could not have been more than four and a half feet tall. How had he not noticed this peculiar fact sooner? The gigantic wolf hide that he wore over his shoulders had made him appear much larger. Now its claws hung down to the rug, and the old chief looked swamped beneath all that fur.

"I want you to have this," the chieftain said to the Reverend. He started to pull the thick hide off his own shoulders. "Years ago, when my son died, my people brought me offerings. That is our custom. The shaman of our tribe was ancient by then, as old as I am now, and knew he would die soon. He passed this on to me. For many years, it was the only thing that helped me carry on. I have been invincible when I wear it. Truly. You, Ghost Man, are already invincible to physical harm if the story of the two bullets is true. But I can see by looking into your eyes that you are not invincible to grief and loss. This hide will help with that."

The old chieftain held the heavy thing in his thin, trembling arms. The Reverend thanked him and bowed. The two younger men helped their leader lift the wolf skin up onto the Reverend's high shoulders. Ahcho knew he should assist with this task, but he did not. In no way did he approve of the dead thing now draped across the Reverend's back. It was a primitive, superstitious, and ridiculous garment not worthy of his fine master.

But when the Reverend lifted his head and rose to his full height with the fur hide over his shoulders, he appeared enormous and otherworldly, frightening even to his manservant. The yellow eyes of the dead animal stared out at Ahcho and caused the hairs on his neck to rise. Although the Reverend offered a proud smile, Ahcho knew that nothing good could come of it.

Twelve

The Reverend steered his trusty donkey along a precipitous path that seemed to grow narrower by the step. If he had not witnessed a camel caravan successfully approaching from the opposite way, he would never have believed it possible to traverse the path ahead. Camels, however, could be surprisingly agile, whereas an old donkey with clouded eyes and at least one sore hip was another thing altogether.

The Reverend put himself in the Lord's hands. He might survive the journey, or he might not. Since his son's kidnapping, he had steadily given up his former efforts to master his own destiny with overzealous care. It wasn't lost on him that the theistic doctrine to which he had always subscribed was being steadily eroded by a laissez-faire atheism, as dangerous as the sheer cliffs on either side of him now. But, no matter, he was on a private, nonecclesiastical mission.

In the face of great trials and tribulations, the Reverend maintained his focus and simply kept himself, his manservant, and his animal calm. Not in any higher, biblical sense but in actual practice. That seemed to be the key to survival in so many instances. The more complicated goal of maintaining goodness and virtue at all costs seemed somewhat beside the point out here in this godforsaken wasteland.

The Reverend found himself retreating to a basic principle passed on to him by his dear mother: the best a person could do in life was to maintain overall good cheer. And why not, given the dreadful way that things occurred? Although now, as he approached the obscure outpost that he felt certain harbored his stolen son, maintaining her suggested attitude felt remarkably easy.

He called back over his shoulder to Ahcho, "Nothing can surpass the evening skies of these foothills in their late-autumn glory. I find they infiltrate my whole being with serenity."

Ahcho replied with an anxious grunt.

The Reverend had noticed that his number-one boy—as loyal a man as he had ever met—lacked nerves of steel and was prone to worry. The Reverend found that if he kept up the timbre of his voice, then both his manservant and his donkey were more likely to relax. He wished he could impress upon Ahcho the benefits of his evolving come-what-may philosophy, but he did not want to bother the fellow while he was concentrating on the trail. The Reverend adjusted the animal hide on his shoulders and returned to reading.

"Sir," Ahcho called forward, his anxious voice echoing across the ravine, "shouldn't you set aside your book for the time being?"

"Heavens, no, man," the Reverend shouted back. "I need the Romantics more than ever in moments like this. A line from Wordsworth—just like the pealing of those distant bells—serves to remind me of the Lord's elegant intentions even in the face of misery elsewhere. We are blessed, are we not, to be in the midst of such beauty?"

Ahcho offered a feeble sound of agreement.

The man needed to read more, the Reverend thought. All the people here needed to read more, starting with the Good Book, then proceeding rapidly to the classics. Imagine how Shakespeare would explode their constricted lives. Personal tragedy, such as the loss of a child, would not feel so personal given the context of the Greeks and the bard. Not that Shakespeare had soothed his own soul since Wesley's kidnapping, but the idea remained that he should.

The Reverend shooed away flies from his donkey's ears and smiled to himself. The chieftain had spied his son and soon his own odyssey would be over. He could envision how this most tragic act in the play that constituted the forty years of his life was soon to come to a harmonious end.

"I feel we are on a better path now, Ahcho. Things are looking up."

"Sir, we had better not look up, but keep our eyes on the trail."

"Yes, yes," the Reverend said. "I meant it metaphorically."

No reply came, so the Reverend tried again. "Take the temple bells tolling far off in the next village. I envision them as the golden streaks of sunset grown audible. I wonder, what do those bells tell us, Ahcho?"

Ahcho did not hesitate to reply, "That people actually live up this infernal path and somehow survive its passage."

"No, not that, man. The bells are meant to remind us of the seraphim, those angels who watch over us. And what do you think of the hawks that circle below us on the updrafts between the purple hillsides?"

"I believe they are vultures, sir, circling the carrion of bodies lost to the slide."

The fellow could be a first-rate wit, but he needed to loosen up.

The Reverend shook his head, closed the book of poetry in his hand, and held it to his breast. "Ahcho," he shouted back, "I ask you to set aside your literalist interpretation. You need to be a poet at times like these. Those hawks, or vultures if you insist, are carried on the Lord's breath. They circle in sheer delight at the miracle of flight. You see, I cannot help rhyming when describing this divine setting."

"This place, divine?" Ahcho asked with a snort. "It is only divine if by divine you mean treacherous. For the Reverend, danger has become the only fascination and joy. You care more for the excitement of the hunt than anything else."

"Ah!" the Reverend replied, for Ahcho's words had pierced his heart. "Clever man," he muttered. "Terribly wise."

On they rode in silence. The Reverend forced himself to further consider his manservant's comment and determined that Ahcho was indeed correct: in the six months since his son's kidnapping, the Reverend had come to thrive more on the precipice than anywhere else. During his most recent stay at home, he had hardly been able to contain himself. The compound was far too tame for him, too constricted. What pleasure was there in huddling under a roof when his son remained out in the storm?

As a boy, the Reverend had followed his parents and two brothers down into the root cellar when tornadoes swept across the Midwestern plains. But if one member of their clan had accidentally remained outside, his father would not have hesitated to open the sloped wooden door and charge out into the winds in search of the lost. The Reverend was merely doing his fatherly duty, although, he had to admit to himself, the plains and the neighboring mountains now called to him not just of his son but of other things as well, though he could not name them precisely. Sometimes their call woke him from sleep, and he had no choice but to go.

He shook his head lightly and told himself to remain on track this morning. His goal was near at hand. He opened the leather-bound volume and slackened the reins. As the chill of the morning wore off and the late-autumn sun rose higher in the sky, the hide warmed him most pleasantly. The chieftain had been right: wearing the fur did make him feel less vulnerable to sorrow. The Reverend smiled as he recognized lines of poetry he knew by heart. He pinched shut his eyes, tilted his face into the sunlight, and recited them under his breath. He felt most blessed precisely when he made the least effort to be so.

"Master!" Ahcho called out. "Look ahead."

The Reverend's eyes snapped open. They had passed the final turn of the mountainside, and there before them stood a vast field of late-blooming poppies and, beyond it, an open expanse where deep-maroon-colored tents had been set up and people gathered.

"It is as the chieftain described," the Reverend said.

Ahcho pulled up beside him on his donkey and offered that skeptical look again. The man was a worrier, a naysayer even.

"This is where Fate has carried us," the Reverend said. "We must trust our path, Ahcho, if we are ever to achieve our ends."

Ahcho nodded, although he appeared unconvinced. "Please be cautious, sir."

The Reverend let out a laugh and spurred his donkey forward. "It will be all right, Ahcho. Everything works out in the end."

Out of the corner of his eye, the Reverend saw Ahcho shaking his head. The proof was in the pudding, the Reverend would have liked to say, but the serious fellow would never have been able to grasp that strange idiom.

Instead, the Reverend called back, "Come along!"

The poppies danced in the wind, their glorious Chinese-red skirts swaying. The Reverend knew that these flowers were the culprits that caused every opium fool to loll away his life, but for the moment he did not care. He was going to carry his son home on his lap through this field and even allow the boy to pick a few.

As they approached the crowd, the Reverend noticed the colorful glow of the tents. This primitive festival resembled a circus back home. He could recall the great excitement with which the locals ran out to the field at the edge of their town when the Barnum & Bailey train pulled to a stop. Every year, a motley-looking crew unloaded dozens of red boxcars, each inscribed with fine gold lettering and holding the most extraordinary sights: exotic animals coaxed and prodded down steep ramps and blinking in the bright sunlight. The Reverend had first seen camels in this way, and an elephant, too. Had he not witnessed them with his own eyes, he would never have believed that the Lord had such an imagination.

And, sadly, the same held true of the poor souls trapped in the sideshow. He had only spied the freaks inside that tent briefly for fear that his mother would catch him and send him home. But it had made a deep impression upon him, one that had factored into his decision to dedicate his life to the Lord and to come to China as a missionary.

Souls, the young John Wesley had realized, could be forgotten, misshapen, even mangled, and yet people were forced to live on and carry the burden of their deadened spirits for years. He had felt lucky as a boy to belong to a hardy race that lived well enough to help free others from their unfortunate lot. His soul was never in question, for he felt he had spirit in surplus—enough, indeed, to rescue others from their paltry allotment.

There on the Midwestern plains, he had pulled his small head away from the flaps of the sideshow tent and looked back across the cultivated fields of corn that rose high in late summer. The tassels swayed with such grace that he had understood, even as a boy, that something had to be done. Rows of crops were planted with care and strict order to create a satisfying harvest. So, too, it must be with human lives. People needed a way to manage the sheer chaos of their misery.

What a pure and sturdy understanding to recall at this time of rising doubt, the Reverend thought now as he approached the festival. Perhaps he would soon have ample reason to return to the timeworn theological track.

It was unbelievable to him that his dear, angelic child could be considered in that same unsightly category of lost souls by these ignorant people. Absurd but true to human nature: we don't trust that which we don't know and recognize. A blond boy was as alien as a god in their midst. Or a devil.

The Reverend felt his heart speed up as he and Ahcho halted, dismounted, and tied their donkeys to a tree. Somewhere amongst the crowd milling on the field at the edge of the mountain was his precious boy, no freak at all but his own flesh and blood.

Thirteen

A man tipped back his head and thrust a flaming stick into his open mouth. A blind charmer blew into his flute, and snakes stood upright like question marks. A giant swallowed a bucket of nails until his belly sagged under the groaning weight. Thick men clad in bright loincloths and boots circled, charged, and gripped oiled biceps, struggling to fell one another like massive, entwined oaks. Other sportsmen appeared to be flicking some sort of animal bone at a target with the goal of trying to knock yet more animal bones away while nearby an archery contest looked ready to commence. It all appeared good fun, this field day on the edge of a cliff. The Reverend felt he just might like to join in. But as he strode forward, the crowd parted and shuffled anxiously to keep out of his way.

Ahcho kept pace, and the Reverend was grateful, for he had not anticipated the shock on the faces as they looked up at him. He was a large man, he knew that. Six foot four ever since his seventeenth birthday. These country folk had no doubt never seen a white man before. And he supposed that the animal skin did nothing to make him appear more approachable. Ah, well. He would use it to his advantage. If they were intimidated by him, he could gather up his son all the quicker and make his departure posthaste. He would be the Ghost Man of their dreams if it helped him to secure his own.

He heard them whispering and assumed they spoke that very name as he brushed past. Many turned aside or shut their eyes, afraid, he supposed, of what he might do to them if they looked at him directly. Ahcho had hinted that the animal hide made even him feel ill at ease, for who knew what reason. The Reverend's number-one boy was no longer superstitious but a true Christian through and through. He glanced over at him now and nodded in appreciation of his devotion and dependability. Ahcho kept his hand under his robe and looked as tense as a rubber band ready to snap. Perhaps in this one instance, his manservant's penchant for worry was well placed.

The Reverend ducked his head deeper into the hide and balanced the wolf's jaw over his brow. When he straightened himself to his full height with the animal head now atop his own, he must have measured a full seven feet tall. The Reverend chuckled to himself, for he realized that he, too, now belonged in the sideshow tent.

He swept his arms up under the fur cloak and spun around to face the assembled crowd. The fire breather stopped tossing his fire. The giant with the nails in his belly belched quietly to himself. The flute music died abruptly, and the snakes dropped to the dirt like useless pieces of rope. Nomad mothers pulled their children into their heavy skirts and turned the babies strapped to their backs away from the great, ghostly spectacle before them.

The Reverend cleared his throat and looked about for someone in charge of this ragtag scene. He whispered to Ahcho under his breath, "Do you see any sign of a ringmaster?"

Ahcho inched closer and looked at him with uncomprehending eyes. "A ring, Master?"

"The fellow in charge," the Reverend clarified.

"No one is in charge here. That is the problem," Ahcho said, then glanced around and said, "The Reverend is aware they surround us on all sides?"

"Indeed. No need to worry, dear fellow," the Reverend said.

It was true. Around the edges of the crowd, men wearing brightly patterned jackets and matching hats sat atop diminutive, though sturdy and strong, horses. The Reverend could not help noticing the grand archery bows held in position by a clever apparatus at their sides. These horse-riding nomads had been known throughout history for their warring streak. They were nothing if not fierce. The crowd had closed ranks by now, and he was the main attraction.

The Reverend glanced over their heads and spied a sorry-looking elephant grazing amongst a herd of camels and horses. The skin on the enormous animal sagged miserably, and the Reverend wondered about the pathetic life the once magnificent creature had endured here with these barbarians. Then his face went hot as he allowed himself to consider what his boy had suffered in their midst as well.

The Reverend lifted his arms again, and the crowd stepped back a pace. His first instinct was to reassure them, but instead, he forced himself to make a fearsome face.

"Listen to me!" he began.

His powerful voice did nothing to set their worried brows at ease. If anything, hearing him speak their tongue only rattled them more. He thought he heard a fearful shriek from the back of the audience, although perhaps that was only the sound of the wind whipping up and over the cliff. The Reverend glanced at the sky and noticed a cloud bank approaching from the west. The weather on the steppes was notoriously unpredictable, and he hoped they were not in for a sudden storm. Although the quickly approaching shadows helped magnify the unsettled mood, which could work nicely in the Reverend's favor.

"Give me back my son, and I, the Ghost Man, will leave you in peace!"

Ahcho moved closer, and the Reverend could tell that even his skeptical number-one boy was impressed by his alarming tone.

"He is small." The Reverend lowered his arm toward the ground and put his hand at just the height where dear Wesley's head would have been. "And his hair," the Reverend reached for a hank of fur from the wolf's head atop his own, "his hair is the color of the sun!"

The crowd let out a gasp.

"Bring him to me, and then you may return to your festival."

The crowd stirred, and several of the burly, half-naked wrestlers marched off. The Reverend felt certain they would return in a moment's time with his son's hand in theirs. He waited and forced his expression to betray nothing of his excitement.

After a few long moments, the crowd parted, and the Reverend could not help the broad smile that overtook his countenance in anticipation. The people whispered, and several even clapped their hands, for everyone, except perhaps Ahcho, who remained as stern-looking as ever, knew that a miracle was about to take place before their eyes.

The row of grandmothers and grandfathers at the front of the crowd bowed and stepped aside. The children scurried off. Then there, before the Reverend, appeared a blond head, so blond as to be freakishly white.

The Reverend staggered back.

"Are you all right, Master?" Ahcho asked and reached under the hide to take the Reverend's arm.

The Reverend did not speak.

A stout form waddled toward him. It was not a child's face but a man's, pink and with pink eyes. He blinked wildly under no eyebrows or lashes, as if it hurt him just to see. The small creature looked painfully raw and unfinished, and the Reverend could not help but think that the Lord had left this lump of clay only half molded. He looked away in disgust. He had never before seen a more hideous human being.

"Great Ghost Man," the albino midget said, his high voice shaking. "You have come to save me!" He threw himself onto the ground and began to kiss the Reverend's boots.

The Reverend stepped out of his reach and shouted, "Stand up, man. Do not grovel like an animal!"

The midget rose and wiped tears off his cheeks with his thick arm clothed in a colorful tunic. But his tears kept coming, and the Reverend saw that the hideous fellow was unable to control himself.

"Whatever is the matter?" he asked.

"My misery will soon end," the man whimpered. "You will kill me, and I will finally meet my ancestors. I should never have been born, and now my time on this earth will be over. I am most grateful to you." The man let out a sob and raised his head and shut his eyes, as if expecting to be smote down by the Reverend in the next instant.

The Reverend swallowed. Could those be his own tears rising up behind his eyes? He had become so resistant to allowing his grief to reveal itself that he hardly recognized the sensation. There was no mistaking, though, that the man before him was wretched to his very soul. His body was a travesty and his entire being spoiled and irretrievable. The Lord had seen to that.

The midget opened his eyes again but remained cowering, still waiting for the blow. The Reverend stared into the frightened and frightening pink eyes. The man's features resembled those of other Mongols, but his skin lacked color to the point of virtual transparency. Blue veins rose up the thick neck and coursed behind fragile temples. The slick, tear-soaked cheeks resembled pulp more than flesh. He was made only of the most base of human matter and nothing divine.

Then the Reverend noticed the most hideous sight of all: red slashes cut across the backs of the fellow's hands and on his shins below the polka-dotted bloomers.

"Turn around," the Reverend shouted.

The crowd inched forward, curious what cruel thing was about to happen next to the midget. The Reverend recognized the sickening look of prurient curiosity on their faces.

"I said," the Reverend repeated, "turn around."

The midget did as he was told, his large head bowing lower on his stump of a neck. The Reverend pulled up the brightly colored tunic. Across the pale skin of the man's child-sized back appeared long scars and welts. Beside them were fresh red cuts that oozed fine beads of blood. The Reverend dropped the shirt. A fury rose up inside him that he did not recognize. A low and fearsome growl issued from his lips. The midget dropped to the ground and covered his head with his arms.

"Stand," the Reverend said through gritted teeth at the shaking creature. "Tell me who did this to you."

The midget stood and swayed before him, his eyes shut and his whole body trembling.

"Open your eyes!" the Reverend shouted.

The eyelids quivered slowly open. The Reverend looked into those unearthly portals and thought he had never before seen such fear and misery in a man. How could the Lord do this to one of His creatures? How could He so punish an innocent soul?

The Reverend reared back his head, raised up his arms, and let out a piercing cry that echoed down the cliffs and into the ravine below.

"I will smite whoever has harmed this man. He must not be hurt again!" the Reverend shouted at the crowd. Then he swung his arms around and swooped toward them. The claws of the wolf slapped the ground and stirred up the dust. The people scuffled back frantically to keep out of his reach. "If you lay a finger upon him, I will fly at you in the night and I will swallow your soul. I will suck it out of you and spit it into the valley below. If you do not treat him with respect, you and your children and your children's children will suffer a hideous punishment for all time."

The Reverend returned to the midget's side and took his pudgy, damp hand into his own and raised it up. "This is a man of consequence," the Reverend said, his voice breaking with sorrow. "This is a man."

He let the midget's hand drop. The Reverend's own head bowed as well. "The Lord Jesus," he said more softly, "and I, the great Ghost Man, will watch over him from now on, forever and ever."

The crowd remained frozen and unspeaking. The albino midget

fell to his knees, and the Reverend ran a hand over his hair. Blond to the point of whiteness, it was as fine as dear Wesley's and surprisingly soft. As he touched it, the Reverend felt tears roll down his own cheeks.

The wind kicked up at that moment in a sudden gust. Black clouds gathered overhead. The tents began to shudder, their flaps making a cracking sound in the rushing air. Rain came in an instant, hard and furious. The updraft from the ravine next caused hail to fall. Large pellets struck the crowd, and they covered their heads with their arms and fled. People screamed and shouted as they ran in all directions, seeking shelter.

Still on his knees, the midget looked up at the Reverend. His face flinched against the sudden ice that fell from the sky. "Take me with you," he begged and threw himself around the Reverend's legs. "Please, dear Ghost Man, take me!"

The Reverend kicked him off. "No, man, they won't harm you any longer. Rise up and find your place amongst them. No one here is better than you."

The man stared at the Reverend with disbelieving eyes. The Reverend would have liked to say more, to quote the Lord about the meek inheriting the earth if he could still believe it. But Ahcho had his arm and was pulling him toward the donkeys.

The Reverend looked back and saw the midget stagger off into the chaotic scene. No one bothered him, but no one helped him, either. He was a free man, with all the suffering that would entail.

The Reverend could not rush away. His heart had been broken here, and he wished to remember it always. He noticed then that no one was tending to the animals. The camels had dashed off toward the dangerous trail, and the horses had fled into the open countryside.

And the poor, panicked elephant had broken free of the chains that bound its legs and appeared altogether lost. The Reverend watched it trot off, the enormous creature's feet surprisingly dainty. The great ears flapped like sails luffing in the wind. Despite its size, the elephant, too, seemed frighteningly vulnerable as it dashed into the sheets of hail. With small eyes closed against the elements, the animal stumbled in the direction of the cliff.

The Reverend left Ahcho and ran after the creature. He ducked his head deeper into the wolf hide for protection. He wasn't sure what he was going to do, but he couldn't very well stand by as a great beast fell to its death down the precipice. Yet, as the Reverend pulled closer, he was shocked at the elephant's size. From a distance, it had appeared large, but now, standing next to it, he understood that this was one of God's grandest creations. Its scale suggested the expansiveness of the Lord's will. He could make anything He pleased, and this elephant was what pleased Him most.

The Reverend dared not go nearer, for one stomp of the animal's foot would end his life. But the animal had run precariously close to the rocky edge. The Reverend grabbed one of the chains that dragged in the dust and yanked on it hard. The animal stopped in its tracks, turned its head slowly toward the Reverend, and stared directly at him.

The small, dark eyes looked out with what could only be described as infinite sorrow. The creature conveyed a deep weariness with the world and all its follies, especially those wrought by humans who had bestowed upon it nothing but pain. The Reverend felt his heart wilt even more as he recognized and understood the animal's misery.

"Dear Lord," he whispered, dropping his chin to his chest, "why do you abandon us so?"

He set the chain back down upon the ground and stepped away. He was no match for the Lord's cruel whims. If He, in His cruelty, chose to kill one of His finest creations, whether an elephant or a precious child, then who was the Reverend to stop Him? But in one final effort, he called out to the beast, shook his fists in the air, and even stomped his foot. The animal appeared not to hear his weak voice, nor did it seem to care about footfalls that were not powerful enough to shake the ground.

Then, as if to confirm how ineffectual the Reverend truly was at saving even a single soul, a bolt of lightning struck the field of poppies only a hundred paces away, and further mayhem ensued. The crack and boom shattered the air, as if God Himself had shouted down from the heavens. The Reverend instinctively covered his head with his arms and gripped the wolf's fur with trembling fingers. The sound rang magnificently in his ears. A fire began instantly on the spot where the bolt had hit. The wind swirled with smoke and fire and falling ice as the terrifying blast continued to echo all around.

The innocent elephant took fright in this hellish moment. It dashed forward, and as the Reverend watched, the great, grand creature plunged over the cliff. Just like that. The Reverend stared unbelieving at the blank space where the animal had stood. The sleet struck hard, and fire spread, but even with disaster on all sides, there was no cause and no reason for the magnificent beast to have been sacrificed on this day. There was no possible understanding of such a pitiless world. The elephant had simply turned away from life.

And the Lord, the Reverend's good Lord, had done so, too.

Fourteen

One mild and moonless evening, as Grace sat by the closed window, she thought she heard bells—high, tinkling bells of the sort camel drivers tied to their beasts to keep them from becoming lost in dust storms. She cocked her head and listened and waited for the sounds of voices. She felt certain she would recognize her children because they would be brought home to her by a chorus of angels, or, given the bells, perhaps camels, or both.

Instead, it was her husband who returned through the open gate of the compound a little after midnight. He wore bells strung about his neck as if he were a beast of burden. She pressed her fingertips against the chilly glass. No dust swirled in the courtyard, and first he was not there and then he was. He wore his long traveling coat like a cowboy from the American West and over it the dead animal fur that he seemed to like. The worst of winter was upon them with bright, chilly days. At night, a sparkling frost covered the ground, and the moist air cut to the bone. She was glad he had the warmth of the hide, although he appeared weighed down by its heft. From her second-story window, she noticed that he walked with bowed head and downcast eyes. Two donkeys trailed behind him, and after that came Ahcho, bent lower still by their journeys.

Another trip, another return, and still no sign of the boy. In his ongoing search, Grace's admirable husband had become a haunted apparition. Had she not heard the actual tinkle of bells, the footfalls of their animals, the clapping of the pouches and bags attached to the Reverend's belt, she might have believed he was made only of sorrow and air. In the silver moonlight, he appeared to be a ghost man indeed.

"Master returns with a heavy heart," Mai Lin said.

Grace startled, not having noticed that her amah had risen from the cot in the corner. "It is he, though, isn't it?" she asked. "You see him, too?"

Mai Lin put her hand on Grace's thin shoulder and said, "Yes, he is home. Mistress can sleep now."

Grace tipped her face into the oil lamp. "Do I look all right? Pleasant enough, I mean?"

Mai Lin was too good to her, Grace thought. Her old amah's eyes did not let on about the dark shadows that Grace knew puffed under her eyes. Nor did Mai Lin mention how Grace's light brown hair had lost its sheen, or that her neck had become as thin as a chicken's and the corners of her mouth shot downward too much of the time. At seven months pregnant, her clothing bound her uncomfortably, and while her cheeks were sallow and drawn, her whole being felt bulky and unappealing. But Mai Lin chose not to dwell on these disagreeable truths.

Instead, she said, "Mistress most beautiful."

"Luckily, beauty is within. The Revered knows that. He will not be taken in by surface appearances. His mind is much on the soul." Grace stood and held Mai Lin's arm to steady herself.

"You need rest."

"I am perfectly all right. You run along now. Sometimes a wife must see her husband alone."

Mai Lin looked sternly at her mistress.

"It was not long ago that we were newlyweds," Grace said. Then, in a smaller voice, she asked, "Perhaps you have something to help us?"

Mai Lin made a clucking sound with her tongue, but Grace felt her heart quicken as she watched her amah reach into one of the many pouches that she wore. Mai Lin brought out a handful of fine powder which she sprinkled over Grace's bed. Then she touched her mistress's forehead with a finger that bore the same potion and touched her large belly with it to protect the child inside, too. Grace studied each of these magical gestures, and when Mai Lin was done, she reached for the old woman's hand and kissed the bony back.

"Thank you. You are too good to me."

Grace then heard the Reverend's heavy footfalls rising up the stairs. She was surprised that he had entered the house so quickly and had not stopped in his library on the first floor. He had taken to sleeping on a cot in there, but on this night, he must have been mad for sleep in a true bed. Still, she hoped he would pay her a visit on his way to his bedroom at the end of the hall and not wait to see her until the morning.

"Mai Lin, open my door," she said.

Mai Lin did as she was told just as the Reverend was passing.

He looked up and saw Mai Lin. "What in the devil?" he said. "Is the whole house awake at this hour?"

Grace slipped forward and hoped he would notice the way the lamplight danced on the folds of her silk robe. Surprisingly, he had on his coat and that awful animal still over his back. She could not understand how Ahcho had allowed her husband to march into the front hall and rise to the living quarters with desert dust flying off him.

"Reverend," she asked, "would you like to take off your coat?"

He stared down at his traveling attire as if noticing it for the first time. His hand touched one of the ropes of leather around his neck, and a bell sounded. "Yes," he said, "I believe I would."

"Mai Lin, don't keep the Reverend waiting."

Mai Lin shuffled forward and tried to help with the animal hide, but it was too much for her elderly arms and short stature. He yanked it off himself and tossed it onto Grace's chaise. The lace antimacassars fluttered and were instantly covered in a fine layer of dust that flew out from the fur.

"Heavens," Grace said, "that creature has seen better days."

The Reverend did not smile. He bowed his head and allowed Mai Lin to remove several leather ropes from around his neck. She started to undo the red sash that crossed his chest, but he held on to the pouch with the twin yellow dragons and would not let her. Then Mai Lin reached up to unbutton his long coat, but he brushed her aside again.

"That's enough," he said. "Leave me be."

Grace was alarmed by his gruff tone. Usually, he was the model of civility with the servants, always attempting to teach by example. Do unto others, his tone customarily seemed to suggest. Now he sounded as coarse and uncaring as the lowliest coolie.

"Reverend, perhaps I can help you remove your overcoat?" Grace asked.

He peered down at her through glasses covered in dust.

"Or shall I first clean your spectacles?"

He nodded slightly, and she took them and wiped them on her robe. When she handed the glasses back to him, his hand touched hers, and her heart swelled with the possibilities still between them.

"My darling," she said.

He sat heavily upon the chaise. A light puff of dust wafted off him and reminded her not only of the distance he had traveled but of the one between them even now, although they were finally together. It made Grace deeply weary.

"Your coat now, sir?" she asked again in as light a tone as she could muster.

"I had best keep it on," he said. "I may be leaving again soon."

Grace's shoulders drooped, and she sensed her heart literally sinking deeper into her chest. Mai Lin must have sensed it, too, for she stepped closer. Grace felt faint and wished she were lying down again, but she remained standing over the Reverend as he placed his elbows on his knees and dropped his head into his hands. If she was worn and sorrowful, then he had to be so as well. She felt it her duty to help him return to his usual optimistic state.

"Mai Lin, you may leave us now," Grace said.

Her amah looked at her with anxious eyes. Grace mustered a smile and shooed the old woman off with a pale hand.

"Close the door after you, please."

Mai Lin's expression as she did so could only be called pleading.

After Mai Lin's departure, Grace knelt down with some difficulty before her husband. The baby in her belly kicked as she shifted, but she ignored it for now. She lifted her husband's callused hand and put it upon her cheek. He flinched at her touch, but after a few moments, he settled into it, a horse newly broken. She tossed back her hair like a girl, and still he did not look into her face. She felt silly as she stroked his hand, but it was her right. He was her husband, after all, and while there was no injunction in the marriage vows for a wife to console her husband in low moments, every American woman understood this to be part of the bargain.

"You must be terribly tired," she said. "Shall we lie down together upon my bed?"

He offered a soft grunt of agreement but didn't move.

"It has been so long since we have truly *seen* one another. I miss you, my love. And I want to know where you have been and what you have experienced. Tell me all." Her own bright voice surprised her. It was true, though, that she longed to travel with him, or at least to know more about the strange journeys that took him away.

His distracted expression shifted, and he finally looked upon her. She expected a softened countenance, yet his eyes remained fierce. She was not sure she knew this man who stared at her with blazing ferocity. Where was his tenderness, his good humor, his ease?

"I have seen far too much, my dear, for your innocent ears," he said. "You would never survive out there. I should not have brought you to this land. You are too delicate a creature."

Grace let out a hearty laugh, forced frivolity taking a great effort in that late hour. "Reverend, don't you recall that I came here of my own volition? I obtained my degree in religious education, and it was my decision, not yours, to travel all the way to Shansi Province. I came for the mission, not for you. Although," here her voice rose and a blush appeared on her cheeks, "our first meeting on the green at Oberlin will be etched in my mind forever, and after my arrival here, I became more smitten with you by the day." She patted his hand and waited for his smile, which appeared faintly. "But that you came to feel as I did and we married six months later was a dream come true, even here in this land where dreams rarely survive. No, without question," she said more firmly as she made herself sit with a straight back, "China is not for the faint of heart. But remember, I am the granddaughter of farmers. I am used to rough winters and hot summers, and I know how to work. I am every bit a proper match for this country. As my grandmother used to say, 'Don't you worry about me one iota.'"

She spoke to assuage his concerns and so they could move on to what she truly hoped for—that he might simply hold her in his arms.

He gazed at her and appeared to finally take her in. He ran a rough fingertip along her cheek and said, "I recall when you first arrived how startling our love seemed. I didn't think humans could feel as passionately for one another as for the Lord. And I do recall you are a sturdy gal. But my dear, you must admit that our circumstances have been trying for even the strongest amongst us. We have endured a great loss, and I expect there will be more. That seems to be the way of this world." He looked away toward the dark window, and she feared she might lose him again.

"Let's not dwell upon it, Reverend," she pleaded and reached for his hand. "Please."

Her voice drew him back, and the Reverend looked upon her once more. As he traced her lips with a chapped finger, it took all her concentration not to swoon at his touch. He then leaned forward and placed dry lips upon her brow and kissed it. She felt tears blazing up from the back of her mind.

"I see I have overlooked you in my suffering," he said. "I have sinned most grievously by this omission. Self-absorption is the devil's work. Can you forgive me, my love?"

She nodded but had no words, only the tears that pooled in her eyes. She knew her tears would pain him and make him pull away, so she willed herself not to cry.

"I know the remedy," he said. He sat forward and squeezed her hand. "You shall go with me on the trail. It is high time you saw the outlying hamlets, the villages and the rocky roads. The churches, too, of course, and the good work we have commenced. We will journey there together."

She leaned forward, too, and looked to see if he were joking. With a child due in two months' time and in her weakened state, she was in no condition to travel. Mai Lin would have forbidden it in an instant if she had had the power to do so. But her husband wanted her at his side. That was what mattered.

"If you say so, Reverend," Grace said.

"It will help me greatly to not face the foe alone. Even with able Ahcho at my side, I find it quite lonely out there, especially when a lead goes dry and we are forced to move on without hope. For I am ashamed to admit that I succumb to sin more than I had ever thought possible."

"It isn't your fault, Reverend," she said, gripping his hand. "I recall that my father and grandfather each succumbed to the bottle from time to time. It is to be expected from real men."

"Heavens, no." His brow furrowed as he lifted his gaze. "I was referring to the sin of despair. It is the worst weakness of all, and you will help me to defeat it. I believe I have been abandoned by our Lord but not by you, my dear girl. *You* shall be my savior."

Grace swallowed with some difficulty. She wanted to argue the point, but hearing such heartfelt words, she let her head sink into his lap. She allowed herself to feel actual optimism at sitting so close beside him, until quite abruptly the stench of his traveling coat reminded her of the marketplace, of the poorest of peasants, of the sickening flesh and rotted stumps of limbs. Although she tried to will her mind not to imagine such things, Grace felt herself starting to choke and gag. Her head grew quickly feverish, and she thought she might faint. The dizziness was upon her, and the buzzing vibrations were quickly overtaking her brain.

She coughed into her husband's thigh under the filthy coat. The Reverend stroked her hair and then her shoulders with his large hand. She was grateful for the attention, although the coughing wracked her and made her ribs hurt. Her swollen belly shook, and she wondered if the baby could stand being tossed like a tiny vessel on a stormy sea.

"My dear," the Reverend said as her coughing finally subsided, "this is not like you."

"Oh, it's nothing," Grace said. "A tickle in my throat from the winter air."

"Are you sure? It sounds more serious than that. Have you seen Doc Hemingway?"

She brushed back her hair and smiled up at him. Because of the coughing, she felt certain that her face had more color than usual, and she hoped her husband would take notice. "Now, when shall we leave?" she asked.

A distracted air overtook the Reverend again, and she realized that even mentioning the road carried him away from her. But this time, she would go along. Finally, they would be together.

"Tomorrow," he said and stood. "We haven't a moment to lose."

She watched as he turned and strode from the room. Yes, she thought, not a moment.

Fifteen

The following noon, Grace, Mai Lin, the Reverend, and Ahcho, along with several donkey drivers, set out from the compound. The servants had been in a flurry all morning as they prepared for an abrupt departure, but they were most professional and uncomplaining. Grace felt she should model her own behavior on theirs in this instance. Once on the trail, however, it was immediately apparent that she did not have it in her to be as flexible as was needed. She requested frequent stops, which were terribly awkward given the exposed terrain and the fact that she and Mai Lin were the only women in the company of a half-dozen men. Mai Lin had been right: a traveling cart would have been far preferable to a lumpy donkey back, but it was too late now.

In midafternoon, their party paused under a tree by a narrow, rocky stream where only a trickle of water flowed. Grace fell asleep right away, wrapped in a warm blanket on a rug set down for her on the rough earth. She was awakened only a few moments later by the overwhelming sight of the Reverend already atop his donkey again, the fur over his shoulders, the yellow animal eyes staring down at her. No wonder the Chinese did as her husband said: he resembled some mythic god out here on the plains. The light shimmered around him, and she could almost believe as they did. He was more miracle than man.

She clambered back upon her donkey after their altogether too brief rest, and on they rode, heading across the plains in the direction of the western hills. Hunched atop the beast with her arms around her amah, who steered it, Grace insisted that they keep pace with the Reverend. She tried repeatedly to introduce topics she thought might be of interest to him, but for much of the day, he kept his head buried in a book.

Although Grace tried to concentrate on observing him and keeping herself comfortable, she soon noticed a surprising number of people out walking on the dirt roads that crisscrossed the desert plains. She wondered where on earth they were all going. On their backs they carried great bundles of what appeared to be bedding or clothing, with pots and pans dangling down. Weapons or tools of the field sagged in their weary hands. Children shuffled along, not even lifting their eyes when she passed. That was most unusual because she was normally a magnet for the young. But these families appeared too burdened to look up or speak.

"Where are they going?" she asked Mai Lin.

"The fields are no good anymore. They go to Fenchow-fu or other towns to find work."

"But there isn't any work in Fenchow-fu. There are already too many beggars on the streets."

Mai Lin offered a tsking sound.

"They should just stay put," Grace said. "They'd be better off."

"Robbers now cover the countryside. But robbers also hide in alleys in the city. They don't care where they slit your throat," Mai Lin said with a chuckle.

"How awful!" Grace said. "You must not say things like that Mai Lin. These good families will surely reach their destinations."

Mai Lin shrugged, and they carried on. Grace thought it better not to dwell upon the fates of the poor Chinese. It was terrible, but what could be done? She had first arrived in Shansi during the drought of 1907, when the Reverend had been mightily preoccupied with famine relief. He worked passionately day and night to secure financial support from expatriate Americans and congregations back home to help the starving Chinese. He quickly raised enough to build the roads that brought in the Red Cross and shipments of food from American companies to the villages. In one of their first encounters, he had described to Grace the grateful Chinese children stuffing wads of Wrigley's Juicy Fruit gum into their mouths and how he had frantically instructed them not to swallow. Of course other food was delivered as well, and then, when the rain eventually came, those same newly constructed roads then carried crops from the fields to the marketplace more swiftly than ever. It had all worked out in the end. Except that this famine of the present year seemed every bit as bad and appeared unending.

Nonetheless, Grace had admired the Reverend so during that difficult time. Her passion for him had grown tenfold in her breast. When he had finally looked up from his efforts, she had believed it an actual miracle that he professed to feel the same way about her. She hadn't allowed herself to believe he'd even noticed her in the two months since her arrival. The two were married a fortnight later on a gloriously rainy day in the small mission chapel. Falling raindrops had been far better than the usual confetti or rice tossed onto the shoulders of bride and groom. And while some in the mission had been surprised at the sudden nuptials, such was the swiftness and surety of their love for one another.

Grace had never been happier, although her subsequent explanatory letter home took some careful crafting. Her mother's agitated return telegram had brought scalding tears to Grace's eyes, but after several more exchanges, eventually a heavy box of handsome sterling place settings arrived from the best jewelry store in Cleveland, and the rift with her family was mended. Yet further evidence that everything worked out in the end.

Now she gazed at her husband, who remained absorbed in his book. It worried her that he had grown inward since those earlier, more purposeful days. But she supposed that was what personal tragedy wrought. What was the starvation and death of thousands when your own child was lost to you?

Grace tried to shake this sad thought from her mind. She forced herself to speak up in a bright tone. "I believe you must have memorized the Good Book by now, Reverend."

He looked across at her and blinked.

"Don't you think you have studied enough for one day?" she asked. "The Lord is not going to quiz you on each and every chapter and verse."

The Reverend lifted the leather-bound volume in his hand and actually smiled. "This is not the Good Book, my dear, but ancient Chinese poetry."

"Is it really?" she asked. "How absolutely astounding."

"Yes, it is. They have a knack for simplicity that the Romantics missed altogether. And they do not flinch from the hard things in life. I find their melancholia to be the perfect mirror to this desolate setting. Would you care to read some?"

Grace let out an embarrassed titter but then nodded most gratefully. Her husband was more surprising by the minute. She thought she could ride on with him for days if he was to treat her thusly, including her in his unusual passions. He passed her the book of Chinese poetry, but she did not open it.

"Go on," he said. "Read."

"I cannot," she replied.

"Why?"

"I have not learned their written language."

He stared at her with horror. "Every day in our new school we teach the illiterate Chinese children, and yet you do not know how to read the language of the land in which you now live? Why haven't you attended those classes?"

Grace bit her bottom lip.

"I do not understand why women refuse to be educated but insist instead on filling their minds with frivolous things. Ladies care more about their hemlines and hairdos than about the actual meaning of life. Here, hand me back the volume."

She passed him the book with a limp hand and thought that would be the end of it. He would punish her again with his silence. But the Reverend cleared his throat and commenced to read aloud. His voice rang out as they rode until a late-afternoon sun crept over the plains. She studied her husband in all his grandeur, although she could not help but be curious about the various specific accessories that made him quite so startling a figure now. Whatever were all those things hanging from him, especially the pouch with the twin golden dragons that sloped down from the red sash and slapped against the side of the donkey with each step? Grace bent slightly toward it and wondered at the perfect orblike shape inside the satchel. What on earth did he have in there? she wondered. But she did not dare to interrupt, although she could hardly concentrate on the meaning of the verses for all the love and admiration welling up in her for her Reverend.

She was also distracted by a continual stabbing pain that rose up from below her swollen belly. And the desert dust didn't agree one bit with her lungs. More and more often, Mai Lin had to slow their animal while Grace coughed madly into her handkerchief. Mai Lin would have to wash blood from the used ones that evening. But the Reverend read on, mesmerized and mesmerizing in the shimmering light. He remained oblivious to her various complaints, and Grace was simply grateful to be at his side.

As they reached the foothills at dusk, bells rang out from the hollows. On many of his previous trips—both those to encourage the outlying churches in his first half-dozen years in China and his more recent ones of the previous months in search of their son—the Reverend had written her long letters in his fine cursive. For pages he had carried on about the beauty of this sort of setting. She had long pictured it in her mind. His letters, she realized now, had perfectly captured the strange grace of this distant land.

The Reverend finally closed the book of poetry.

"So, what do you think, Mai Lin?" he asked. "Superior words from your ancient compatriots, yes?"

"I know these poems. There is much wisdom in them for those who care to open their clogged ears and listen."

Grace thought she sensed the older woman's stare upon her. She felt it was not her fault that she had become so distracted by life, and she promised herself she would try to do better in the realm of self-education. But for now, as the chilly day slipped into colder evening, she could not help being preoccupied with her husband's state of mind: he appeared to be blooming to life again out here. Now that he was on the trail, his dark mood had lifted. She grasped more fully that he was one man in the Christian compound and an altogether different and happier one out here in this mysterious countryside.

A camel train passed, and the Reverend had encouraging words for the drivers. He raised his hat and cheerfully flagged them on. He then instructed Ahcho to carry on ahead with Grace and Mai Lin while he circled back. Grace looked over her shoulder to see her husband's head bowed in conversation with one of the camel drivers. When the Reverend rejoined their party, he reached across and patted her hand.

"The fellow knew my mission even before I opened my mouth. The whole country is our eyes and ears now, although he insisted on calling me Great Lord Ghost Man. Imagine such foolishness."

She was grateful for her husband's determination to find their son but did not say so, for she feared she might have to choke back tears. She was grateful for so much, even in the midst of such tragedy. Pain shot up her spine again, and it took all her concentration not to have her smile collapse into a grimace.

"Do you hear those chimes?" he asked as they rose higher up the hillside. "Those used to emanate from a temple, but now they toll in the tower of our newest little chapel. Can you imagine the joy it must bring to the deprived coolie after a long day of work?"

She smiled on but still could not speak as she witnessed her husband of old returning to her. He appeared quite joyous and gay out here. Grace couldn't help wondering if she would have to become itinerant as well to enjoy his fine company.

Sixteen

At nightfall, they entered a desolate village where the Reverend intended for them to spend the night. The sole, rutted road led to an inn where a toothless innkeeper greeted them. He wiped his dirty hands upon his apron and trotted forward from his hovel. The man had his barefoot son lead their donkey drivers and animals to a stable while he called back through the open door of the inn for his wife to prepare *mein* for their supper.

"Minister John Wesley returns!" the innkeeper said with a hollow grin. He gathered the Reverend's hands into his own and shook them vigorously.

As the Reverend clutched the man's shoulder and squeezed, Grace could hardly believe the innkeeper had called her husband by his given name. Standing nearby, Ahcho had noticed it, too, and looked ready to reprimand the fellow, but the Reverend carried on with introductions as if it were most expected. John Wesley: how unheard-of. Since his arrival in China when he was placed in charge of the mission, not a soul had spoken to her husband so familiarly, not even she.

Hunched and sallow, the innkeeper nonetheless seemed the picture of contentedness as he motioned for them all to sit at a rough table outside his door. His scrawny wife appeared after a few moments and bowed, but when she saw that the Reverend had brought his pregnant wife, she lost all manners and actually clapped the Reverend on the back.

Mai Lin spit her betel-quid juice into the dust and Ahcho shook his head, but Grace frowned at them both, and they kept their comments to themselves. A pleasant smile remained across Grace's lips, although she could not understand a word the couple said in their local dialect. She was determined to be gracious under these difficult circumstances, but when the innkeeper's wife pointed at her belly and made obscene-looking gestures, Grace hopped to her feet.

"She is only expressing her excitement for us about the unborn child," the Reverend explained.

The innkeeper's wife muttered something that made Mai Lin hobble to her feet, too.

"It's all right, Mai Lin," Grace said. "The poor wretch doesn't know any better."

Apparently, however, the innkeeper's wife knew enough Mandarin to grasp Grace's comment, for when she brought out the bowls of noodles, Grace's portion was noticeably smaller than the others. She did not mind, for she had little appetite anymore.

After supper, when there was still some light left from the setting sun, the innkeeper escorted the Reverend and Grace to the barn of a recent convert. On the short stroll through the hamlet, they saw no one, although at mealtime whole families would normally have been out in the streets. The Chinese had a habit of sitting on their haunches in their doorways and scooping mush from bowls into their mouths with chopsticks. But here, Grace saw no cooking fires and no greedy mouths. No younger adults at all, just elders and children leaning listlessly against doorways, peering out with blank eyes. The innkeeper confirmed that every able-bodied worker from this hamlet had gone to the city in search of employment.

"Obviously, the fields are withered," the Reverend whispered to her. "You notice no animals in sight. No dogs or even rats. Everything has been caught and eaten."

She took his arm to keep herself from shuddering. At seven months pregnant, her steps were necessarily slow, but he did not seem to mind. The cramping in her belly had subsided, yet she did not dare move too quickly.

At a crumbling barn near the edge of the village, a man far older and even more bedraggled-looking than the innkeeper stepped forward and embraced the Reverend. Grace let out a slight gasp at the sight of the skeletal little creature clutching at the fur hide around her husband. The top of the man's bald head did not come up to the Reverend's chest, and his brown arms in their torn shirt could not reach around him, but the Reverend did not appear repulsed. Instead, he placed a large hand across the man's back and held him close.

The man pulled out a set of keys, which he rattled in the lock. He pushed open the flimsy door, and they followed him in as the innkeeper lit a lantern and held it aloft. In the flickering golden light Grace noticed the resemblance between the two Chinese men and wanted to ask the Reverend if they were father and son.

She glanced about, and although the recesses of the open room were shadowed, she could tell there was no grain for the winter stored here, no curing meat hanging from the rafters, nothing to see them through the lean months ahead. The pinched grandfather who owned the empty barn kept nodding joyfully, though, as he struck up a second lamp. He rattled his absurd set of oversized keys, which seemed quite unnecessary to Grace since surely there was nothing inside the empty barn to steal.

But then they stepped into a smaller room, and the older gentleman made a pleased sound and pointed. Before them on a table sat the most surprising antique porcelain bowls, vases, and cups that Grace had ever seen.

The Reverend bowed his head respectfully before the table and listened as the older man jabbered on about the ceramic vessels, his voice rising and falling with remarkable vigor. Grace was able to catch only a few phrases.

She touched her husband's sleeve and whispered up to him, "Do they know that these are quite old? I believe I saw pieces like them at the Metropolitan Museum of Art in New York City in the days before my ship departed for the Orient. The simplicity of design, lack of decoration, and thinness of the porcelain all suggest they date all the way back to the Han period. Does he understand what he has here?"

The Reverend smiled down at her, his face softened by the glow of lamplight. "Indeed, he does."

Grace squeezed her husband's arm more forcefully and whispered again, "We should help him sell these pieces so he can make enough to see his family through the drought. He could move away from this terrible place. Does he want us to carry them to Peking for him and find buyers? I'm sure I could do that without too much trouble."

The Reverend held his finger to his lips to silence her and said, "No, my dear, this is their inheritance. They intend to hold on to it."

Grace looked at the foolish ancient man and his foolish old son and spoke slowly to them in her best approximation of their dialect. "You will sell these and eat?" She rubbed her fingers together to suggest money and then brought them up to her lips to show eating. They had to understand.

The grandfather shook his head firmly, and the son looked quizzically at the Reverend.

The Reverend addressed the men. "Forgive my wife, she doesn't understand just yet." Then he spoke to Grace with exaggerated patience, as if to a child. "This treasure means everything to them. If they sold it, they would no longer want to live."

"Why, that's absurd," Grace sputtered in English. "They will starve next winter. Selling one or two of these vases could save their entire hamlet."

The Reverend stood erect, the fur on his back broadening his presence as his voice changed unexpectedly. "Disrespect these people at your peril," he snarled. "I have seen the errors of our arrogant ways and the punishment we rightfully deserve. Have you learned nothing since our son was stolen from us? Must we repeat our hubris again and again?"

The Reverend's enormous shadow rose up the wall in the lamplight, and Grace could not help the shiver that overtook her spine as she stared into her husband's eyes, now as yellow as those of the animal on his back. She felt shaken and betrayed. Her mind raced as she tried to grasp the meaning of his outburst, but all she wanted to ask in that frightening moment was what had become of her husband?

The Reverend had lost his senses. Mildred Martin was right that he had gone native. She had heard the other ministers whispering that he had become a charlatan, a convert to his own code, a nut. Grace could not bring herself to believe such horrors, but out here in the borderlands, she finally understood that he had become one of these—these dreadful people.

She stomped off across the straw-strewn floor. She could not locate the door in the dark until the innkeeper hurried to her side. He held the lamp aloft and escorted her out and down the rutted path back to the inn. They did not exchange a word as they walked, but the old fellow stayed beside her, all the while offering that balmy grin.

Back at the inn, Grace settled on the bench outside the door. Her back ached from the donkey ride, and the baby in her belly was restless and unhappy. The pain continued along her lower spine as the baby pressed on her nerves and muscles, but she did not dare mention it to Mai Lin. Instead, Grace coughed into her handkerchief until Mai Lin handed her a new one.

Grace felt certain she had never been so humiliated in her life as she had in that miserable barn, and yet what did it matter to be scolded in front of such silly, ignorant people? Her husband had been under much stress recently, perhaps his strange behavior was explained by that. After all, she knew that she, too, had become a different person since their loss. From her customary position by the window of her bedroom in their mission home, Grace could attest that the search alone was enough to drive a person mad. It was no wonder that he was no longer himself.

Ahcho sat quietly puffing on his pipe on a bench nearby, and although it was not proper to confide in one's servants, Grace felt she needed corroboration on her husband's changed state of mind.

"Ahcho," she began hesitantly, "would you say that the Reverend is different now and no longer the man—" She didn't know how to phrase it, so she simply let her sentence drop away.

"I believe he's not altogether of this time anymore," Ahcho said with surety. "He is more holy than ever."

Mai Lin, who squatted with her back against the wall of the inn, let out a laugh. "More lowly and lost than ever, you mean."

"That's enough," Ahcho said to Mai Lin with surprising firmness.

Grace had never quite grasped the relationship between their two house servants. Clearly Ahcho, as number-one boy, was of a higher rank than her amah, although Mai Lin hardly seemed intimidated by him. And while Ahcho's description of the Reverend confirmed his manservant's confidence and respect, his suggestion that her husband was more holy than ever only served to confuse Grace. She tried to shake Ahcho's appraisal from her mind. The Reverend did not seem more holy to her. If anything, he appeared more like the surrounding peasants all the time.

As the minutes passed, the dark and narrow street of the hamlet appeared even darker and narrower. Ahcho's admiring words about the Reverend crept slowly into her heart, and she slowly found herself willing to forgive the Reverend for his strange outburst. As a chill rose up from the frozen ground and she tucked herself deeper into her wool coat, she felt the loneliness she had come to know so well. Grace desperately missed the cheerful and forceful man she had married. But that man was no more. She had best get accustomed to it. And, as she reflected further, she had to admit that she was no longer the frivolous, carefree girl whom he had married, either.

Then she looked up and saw the Reverend approaching from the far end of the road: a giant in a fur hide, the rims of his spectacles catching the swinging lamplight. She understood that often the Chinese were still afraid of him, but she was not. They thought he could perform miracles, while she knew with all certainty that he could not. The Chinese might still hope for such things, but Grace could plainly see that the Reverend was as displaced as she. Mai Lin, as always, was right: they were both the tiniest bit lost. Grace and her dear Reverend were simply stumbling along like sleepwalkers in the Chinese desert.

The innkeeper's wife poked her head out of the inn door and barked something at her, which Mai Lin translated. Their *kang* was ready.

"Mistress will sleep on the spot closest to fire, but the *kang* grows too hot when the fire is stoked, and then, when the embers die down, it becomes too cold. Countryside is a terrible place. We wake with fleas, you will see."

"Now, now, Mai Lin," Grace said as she peered harder up the black street. "That is he, is it not?"

Mai Lin huffed, "Mistress still searches for her husband even when she is with him. Yes, that's the Reverend."

Grace glared at her but then reached out a hand, and Mai Lin took it. "You will help me to sleep tonight?" she whispered.

Mai Lin made that tsking sound, but Grace knew by the squeeze that the old woman gave to her fingers that she could count on at least one creature in this world. Grace felt the only relief she knew anymore.

The Reverend sauntered closer with one hand held behind his back, the other swinging a lantern. His long coat swished, and the amulets he wore on his belt swung freely. Grace noticed a new scabbard at his hip. Its sheath glinted in the lamplight. She wanted to ask him about it, to insist he not be armed like some barbarian, but she began to cough, and besides, she knew it would do no good. He was who he was now.

When she finally drew in a clear breath, she looked up with a feeble smile and asked in as cheerful a voice as she could muster, "Whatever took you so long?"

"I have something for you," he said.

From behind his back he brought forth one of the ancient Chinese vases, a simple porcelain one with no handle and no decoration, just a pale green glaze that caught the lamplight.

"They gave you the most beautiful one?" she asked.

"They did. That was their purpose in inviting us to see their collection. They had hoped you might accept it, too."

"I would have if they had allowed me to sell it and give them the proceeds."

"My darling, I know it is hard for you to grasp this, but they want to live and die here."

The Reverend offered the small vase to her, but she did not take it.

"You are most stubborn," he said.

"I, stubborn? It is you and these foolish people who will not help themselves. They will die out here because of their pride."

"You're right." He smiled down at her. "It is pride that will kill us all."

His voice did not sound one bit sorry. Whatever could have gotten into him?

He set the vase on the rough table. "They wish for this beautiful object to become a part of our inheritance. They want us to pass it on to our children."

Grace flinched at the suggestion of more than one child. The coughing began again, and this time she did nothing to hide it.

The Reverend sat quickly at her side on the bench and put his hand on her back. "You're not well," he said.

She brushed him away, although it pained her to do so. Yet she could not bear his pity. She would not have him thinking of her as the weaker one. It occurred to her that she was no better than the foolish peasants with their precious porcelains. Perhaps it was she who wouldn't allow herself to be saved.

"Here," the Reverend said, taking the animal cloak off his shoulders. "You will catch a chill sitting outside like this."

He draped the heavy thing over Grace's shoulders, and she flinched, smelling its wild odor. But then she settled into it and let herself lean against her husband's side as he spoke.

"Would you like to hear why it is that I brought you to this hamlet?"

Grace nodded, and although she was warming up now, she still trembled from the cold.

"The last time I was here, I sat with the ancient grandfather and listened to him into the night. He and his son, the innkeeper, had not spoken to one another for fifteen years. Can you imagine living in this miserable little village and having a relative so near and yet not speaking to one another? Shortly before midnight, the old one agreed to meet his son, but only if we did it at that hour and at that moment. When the Lord knocks, we must answer, so I returned with him to this inn, and together the three of us sat up until dawn. The grandson, who escorted our donkey to the stable today, stood in the corner watching, rubbing his eyes from tiredness but also, no doubt, trying to tell if he was dreaming at the sight of the two patriarchs finally speaking to one another.

"As the sun came up, the grandfather pronounced that their fight had been most unfortunate, and the son agreed. The ancient one said he had not felt such peace in the thirty years since his wife had died. The innkeeper repeated the Chinese proverb that says, 'One night's talk with a good man excels ten years of study.' And I reminded them then that there were two good men in their family and another growing into one before their eyes."

Grace nuzzled against his side. "Your mission thus succeeded?"

"Truly, I'm not sure anymore. I was grateful that the men found one another. Perhaps I was the catalyst. But, as you see, they're still starving. The Lord has seen to that as well." He bent and kissed her forehead, and she ached for more, but he said, "But now, to bed with you." Then the Reverend called into the dark, "Mai Lin, Mrs. Watson needs your assistance."

Mai Lin, who had been sitting nearby, grumbled as she planted herself in front of the couple. "Reverend wastes his time here," she said. "Sure a family is reunited, but who cares about these ignorant country people?" She spat over her shoulder onto the dusty road.

"Prejudice dies hard," he spoke patiently to her. "But you need to be a model, Mai Lin, to your fellow countrymen."

"And you," she pointed at him, "you need to be a model of a husband understanding his wife."

Grace's eyes popped open at her amah's disrespectful remark. "Mai Lin," she said, "behave yourself."

"Reverend does not see what is right in front of him," Mai Lin said. "Mistress is not well enough to travel. To think so is madness!"

The Reverend stood and loomed over Mai Lin, "Whatever do you mean by speaking to me this way?"

"I speak to you this way because Mistress Grace is ill."

Both the Reverend and Mai Lin looked down at Grace, seated on the bench. She attempted to stand to prove Mai Lin wrong but felt too light-headed and stumbled back upon the bench.

"Look at her, blind man," Mai Lin said. "See how pale she is? She is soon to be the ghost, not you!"

The Reverend put his hand delicately under his wife's chin and tipped her face toward the lantern light. "Yes, she is most pale."

"She carries a baby in her belly these many months, and she is all the time also very sick."

"Is this true that you are terribly ill?" the Reverend asked Grace. "Why haven't you told me?"

Grace felt her face go hot and twist into a miserable frown. A sob finally issued forth from her with decided force.

"Mai Lin," the Reverend said, "you should never have allowed her to come on this trip."

"Aeiiii!" Mai Lin let out a screeching sound, "I tell her, but she will not listen to me. And you have cotton in your ears."

The Reverend stood taller. "We shall return to the mission tomorrow. I see the error of my decision."

He knelt before Grace, and she fell weeping into his arms.

"The situation is most grave," Mai Lin said. She shrugged her shoulders and stepped away. "I can only do what I can do."

The Reverend kissed Grace's hair and held her in his arms. "My darling," he said, "can you ever forgive me?"

Grace could not answer, for the coughing had begun again.

Seventeen

After a swift return from their aborted expedition, the Reverend kept vigil at his wife's bedside on the second floor of the Watson home in the mission compound. Numerous times, she coughed up blood into a basin, but Mai Lin appeared more concerned about the several spots that stained the sheets from the baby inside. The Reverend tried not to be in the way, but on the second day Grace's nursemaid shooed him into the hall so that she might administer to her patient without distraction. He then proceeded to pace back and forth outside the bedroom door for he wasn't sure how long until Mai Lin finally stepped into the hallway and spoke to him under her breath. "We need food. The fields are dry, and there is nothing at the market anymore. Mistress must have sustenance to keep the baby inside alive. I need beans, at least, to mash into a paste. I must give her something, anything. You go and find some!"

The Reverend answered quickly, "Whatever you say, Mai Lin. I will bring food back right away."

She raised a gnarled finger and said, "Don't get lost out there. Ah-cho will go with you to see that you come back."

The Reverend felt chagrined, and he did not argue.

The donkeys had already been prepared for the outing, and the Reverend marveled at the efficiency and cleverness of his servants. In so many instances, they were more informed and wiser than he. Out on the front porch, the Reverend asked for Ahcho's assistance in placing the animal hide upon his shoulders.

"Perhaps Reverend does not need this fur any longer?" Ahcho asked. "The sun is out, and today appears to be a milder day. Your overcoat should be enough."

"You must know that I don't wear it for protection against the elements. I use it to help us achieve our goals."

The Reverend shimmied under the tattered old fur without the older man's help.

Ahcho crossed his arms over his chest and said, "The Reverend recalls his many sermons about the ineffectualness and misguided belief in superstition?"

"I do, indeed, Ahcho. You are a fine parishioner, good through and through." Then he leaned in even closer and added, "But this hide and my new weapon may help, too." He placed a hand on the hilt of a small dagger. He had been given it by the peasants in the hamlet who had also bestowed upon him the ceramic vessel.

Ahcho nodded, although the Reverend knew he would have liked to protest. The man was not a fighter, and while the Reverend had never thought of himself as a fighter, either, he needed to be prepared for all manner of treachery these days.

The two men rode out from the compound. As the Reverend looked over his shoulder, he saw Reverend Charles Martin and Reverend John Jacobs retreating back into their homes. He thought he should stop to speak to his colleagues, for it had been some time since he had last done so, but he did not want to distract himself from the important task at hand. His wife was in great need.

"How is everyone holding up?" the Reverend asked Ahcho as they passed through the open compound gates and turned onto the road that led toward the small town.

"What do you mean?" Ahcho asked.

"Are the other families of the mission faring decently? I'm afraid I've lost track of them."

"You have been gone most of the time."

"And they resent me for it?" the Reverend asked.

Ahcho did not answer, which the Reverend took to be an affirmative.

"I will make an effort when we return with the food. Perhaps we can procure enough for the others."

"We shall see, sir," Ahcho said.

"But they are all right?" the Reverend pressed.

Ahcho's eyes betrayed very little, but the Reverend thought he sensed some sort of judgment coming from his servant. Then Ahcho spoke with an evenhandedness that the Reverend admired.

"The Jenkins family lost their oldest girl," he said. "She was too hungry and ate a persimmon from the market without washing it first. She was old enough to know better, so no one understands why it happened. The illness took her in two days' time."

"Dear Lord," the Reverend muttered. "I remember her. Miranda was her name. A lovely girl, almost a woman."

"But a child still, or else she would have known better. Unless she wanted it to happen thusly?" Ahcho asked tentatively. "The servants have been discussing the possibility."

The Reverend tried not to show his alarm at such a supposition. It could not be. "I think that's most unlikely," he answered, although truly he could not say.

Only a cruel God would do such a thing, unless, he sighed, there was no God at all keeping watch over them. The two rode on in silence.

They passed through the market, where the stalls stood derelict and empty. A gathering of old hags and beggars sat on their haunches in the shade by the side of the road. When they saw the Reverend, they did not rise to their feet or even lift their open palms in hopes of a coin or two.

"Isn't this market day?" the Reverend asked. "Where are all the farmers?"

"They stay on their farms to protect them now. Bands of robbers sweep through the countryside and burn them down. Very dangerous."

"But have they no crops at all? Not even a kitchen garden to feed their families?"

Ahcho turned to the Reverend. The older man appeared baffled and apparently speechless.

"What is it, Ahcho?" the Reverend asked.

Ahcho shook his head with uncharacteristic dismay. "I cannot imagine how the great Reverend has not noticed the plight of the people on his trips?"

"Why, of course I have noticed them. I have a keen affinity for these peasant types." The Reverend looked around for coolies to corroborate this, but the streets were empty.

Ahcho's words tumbled out with surprising fury. "But your nose remains in a book, and your head is high in the clouds. You see nothing!"

The Reverend felt a flush of feeling he did not recognize as his manservant stared at him incredulously. Heat rose from his collar as shame overcame him.

"You see only what you wish to see," Ahcho added more softly. "I fear you are not the expansive man you once were."

The Reverend felt his cheeks flame fully, and his shoulders felt uncomfortably hot under the hide. He wanted to defend himself against this accusation. In the past, he had built the people fine roads and a school and a hospital. How could he ever be perceived as anything but a champion of the poor?

He swallowed the cold, dry air, and his throat constricted. He had to admit his mind was often someplace other than where it needed to be. Ahcho's accusations rang true. He did see only what he wanted to see. And yet what he saw was not one bit pleasant.

Recently, he had been preoccupied by wrestling with God. He had come to the anguished conclusion that his Lord had been steadily slipping from his grip and intended to abandon him altogether. The Reverend felt quite alone with his failed effort to clutch on to Him. But now, as he glanced at Ahcho's disappointed expression, he understood that his sorrow at losing the Lord did not matter nearly as much as the fact that he had somehow managed to lose the Chinese as well.

"I shall try harder," he finally said.

Ahcho nodded, clearly uncomfortable with the strange occurrence of his master apologizing to him.

They continued onward without speaking and the Reverend tried to take careful note of the miserable state of things around him. The empty shop windows, the frail and defeated beggars, even the few dogs that appeared mangier than ever and who no doubt would serve as some lucky person's dinner before long.

After some time, Ahcho pulled his donkey to a stop outside a forlorn-looking shop, and the Reverend pulled to a halt as well. The dusty road led to the threshold of the sunlit door, and on the doorstep sat a stick-thin boy who raised his head and rubbed his eyes.

"If you watch our animals," the Reverend said to the lad, "I will give you a coin."

The boy hurried to take the reins, although Ahcho said in English, "He may try to sell them before we come out. No one is to be trusted these days."

"This fine young fellow?" the Reverend asked as he ran a hand over the boy's hair. Instantly, the Reverend thought he felt lice on his fingers. He wiped his hand roughly on his coat and whispered to Ahcho, "Do they no longer take baths?"

"What's the point," Ahcho shrugged, "if you're starving and soon to die?"

The Reverend followed him to the doorway of the shop. He tried to peer in, but the room inside was too shadowy and the road too bright with the winter's sun. The Reverend couldn't tell what transpired within. He paused for a long moment on the threshold and knew that with the morning light at his back and his silhouette blocking the door, he would appear an impressive figure. Once again, he hoped this effect might work in his favor.

But when he stepped inside, he saw that the audience he wished to impress sat lolling on wooden barrels in what appeared to be an old-fashioned general store. The Reverend was reminded of one just like it back home and in every American village and town. This was the center of local commerce, where shelves were meant to be stacked high with every sort of goods for farm and home: tin nails and calico fabrics, thick braids of rope and sacks of flour, workmen's gloves and dainty ribbons for the piping on girls' dresses.

The Reverend could see that the intention here was the same: high shelves covered the walls, and the room was divided by a long counter. But nothing, not one thing, sat upon these dusty surfaces. A Franklin potbellied stove stood cold, although the room was chilly. A young man who appeared to be the proprietor leaned against the blank counter, and beside him sat several grandfathers, another boy, a girl, a woman with a baby in her arms, and several young men—a typical Chinese extended family, the Reverend thought, with its many appendages and hangers-on. Who could guess how the half-dozen men seated on the barrels were related to the owner of the place? But the Reverend was certain that they were.

The people did not offer the usual gasps of recognition that the Reverend had grown accustomed to upon arriving in any setting. Usually, his reputation as the Ghost Man preceded him, but here in his own town, where he had assumed he was revered, the natives eyed him with an even stare. That was all right with the Reverend. He didn't need to appear a god to all concerned, so long as he was able to obtain what he had come for.

"Good people," he began.

Ahcho shot out a hand and patted his arm. Then his manservant spoke in a quick and unrecognizable dialect that surprised the Reverend. He had thought he knew all the possible permutations of the complex language of the region, but apparently he did not.

The proprietor, who appeared to be the most robust of the men behind the counter, leaned forward to get a better look at the Reverend. He spoke quickly to his friends or cousins, who also leaned their elbows on the counter and stared.

"What are they saying?" the Reverend asked Ahcho.

"They have heard of you."

"Good, good."

"No, not so good," Ahcho mumbled.

"Why ever not?" the Reverend asked.

At that moment the proprietor came out from behind the empty counter. He planted himself before the Reverend and raised an eyebrow. The fellow was shorter than the Reverend by at least a foot, but he was sturdy and muscular. He did not look one bit affected by the famine. His eyes in the shadowed room appeared black and angry—shiny beads that sucked in the dim light. The man put his hands on his hips and lifted his chin.

"Show us, Ghost Man," he said. "Show us your miracles."

The Reverend thought he had caught the meaning of the taunt, but the others did not wait for his reply.

A bent grandfather stepped forward from where he had sat hunched on a barrel. "You are the one who turned a small white freak into a deity that no man can harm?"

Before the Reverend could answer, a different young man came from behind the counter and said, "And I hear you taught an elephant to fly."

Even a mother with a child on her hip spoke up. "I heard that you made the snakes fall asleep forever."

The Reverend pushed the wolf's head back and off his brow so they might see he was only human, like them. He bobbed his head and smiled slightly. "No," he began, "not exactly."

"You," the proprietor said as he stepped closer and poked a finger hard at the Reverend's shoulder, "you who can do so much magic, I say you will now fix the drought for us."

Another strong young fellow stepped forward and insisted, "That's right, you'll do what he says."

"The fields are cracked," one of the grandfathers added from a shadowed corner of the room. "The last time it was this bad was before the Boxer Rebellion. Foreign devils were amongst us then, too."

The Reverend understood the phrase "foreign devils" and grasped the angry sounds of agreement now coming from the other elders.

"Oh, heavens," the Reverend said, "I am not responsible for the weather, gentlemen and dear ladies. We know better than that, now, don't we?"

One of the grandmothers spat on the dusty wooden floorboards, as if to prove that she was no lady, but also that she did not believe him.

"But you made these other miracles happen, did you not?" the proprietor asked.

"Well, I—" the Reverend started.

"Because if you did not," the proprietor said as he crossed his substantial arms over his wide chest, "then you have been fooling us all along. And we are not a stupid people who deserve to be fooled."

His friends nodded in agreement.

"Of course you're not," the Reverend said. "My God, I was just thinking this morning that my servants are far cleverer than I." He looked over at Ahcho and hoped that the dear man understood that he meant this sincerely and was not just saying it to make an impression.

Ahcho blanched and stepped forward. "Ghost Man respects *all* Chinese, not just his servants."

Before the Reverend knew what was happening, one of proprietor's friends, clearly a thug, had Ahcho's long queue in his hand. "Old one," he said to Ahcho as he tightened his grip around the braid, "I see you follow the ancient ways. But we're done with all that. We're servants to no one now."

Ahcho spoke calmly to the man. "Let go of me and we'll leave."

The man pulled a knife from a sheath at his waist. "Before you go, I think I'll cut off your queue," the young thug said. "That would shock the old-timers who serve the white people. Imagine if you returned to the Christian compound with the new short hairstyle. You'd be a laughingstock. Maybe you'd even lose your easy job, old one?"

The grandfathers and grandmother who sat nearby made tsking sounds and shook their heads at this insolent behavior, but they did nothing to stop him. The Reverend waited for them to at least reprimand the young hooligan who was disrespecting an elder, but they didn't open their mouths. Such were the appalling changes of these times.

The Reverend felt he had no choice but to pull his small knife from its elaborately carved sheath. "Leave him alone," he said, stepping forward and thrusting the dagger outward.

The young man looked at the Reverend's upraised hand and began to laugh. Then the others joined him, their lips pulled back from brown teeth as they bent over in mild hysterics.

"Where did you get that souvenir, Ghost Man?" one of the young thugs asked.

The Reverend looked at the knife in his hand.

"He doesn't even know it's a letter opener," one of the others said.

The proprietor chuckled and held out his hand. "May I?" he asked.

The Reverend had no choice but to give the man his only weapon.

The proprietor inspected the knife and said, "My father sold this same model. It's a letter opener, all right, but of decent quality."

The Reverend chuckled out of nervousness, too, but Ahcho wasn't smiling. The older man's eyes burned with rage. "Unhand me," he said.

The young thug who held his queue finally let go.

"I wonder," the Reverend tried, "could I trade you this fine letter opener for some beans, perhaps?"

The proprietor let out a disgusted snort, as if he had been waiting for this question all along. "You and every other person in the province would like to make a deal with me."

"Does that mean you have beans," the Reverend pressed, "but you won't trade them?"

The man crossed his arms again and looked around at his band of thuggish friends. "I have many mouths to feed."

"I see that," the Reverend said. "But I have a pregnant wife who is terribly ill. She may not make it unless I procure some sustenance for her. She has endured far too much already. Please, take pity on her and our unborn child."

The proprietor looked at Ahcho for a translation as the Reverend, in his distraught state, seemed to have lapsed into English.

Ahcho got to the point and said, "You know what he wants. Don't make him beg."

The proprietor shrugged and stepped back. His friends turned, too, and the Reverend heard the old people beginning to chatter again amongst themselves. His chance to save his family was slipping away.

The Reverend spoke again in a clear voice. "I wish to offer you something else. Something most precious."

The proprietor did not even bother to look his way. He simply waved his hand. "I don't need anything but rain. Can you give me that, Ghost Man? Somehow I don't think so."

"I can give you something better," the Reverend said as he pulled the enormous wolf hide off his back. "This is what caused the miracles. This!"

He held the sagging fur before him in his outstretched arms. The proprietor and his friends and family turned to look at it. The proprietor sauntered back to the Reverend and ran a hand over the thick fur.

"What do I want with this mangy thing?"

"*It* is what caused the miracles. You who are from here and already a prince in this land, when you wear it upon your back, it will bring you rain, if that is what you wish. Since I started wearing it, I have been invincible. All that I have wished for has come true. It will work for you, too."

"This old thing caused the miracle of the two bullets?" the proprietor asked.

"This is what saved me," the Reverend answered.

"And what about the elephant that flew?"

The Reverend placed the heavy fur in the other man's arms. "Yes, it made that magnificent creature fly. This, and nothing else but this."

"You say your wife is starving, Reverend?" the proprietor asked, his head cocked to one side. "And you need beans?"

The Reverend nodded eagerly.

"I have beans. I have a great deal of them."

"I will trade you, then," the Reverend repeated. "I would be most grateful to trade this remarkable hide for your beans."

"For this hide that has saved you and your people, you will receive food. That seems a fair deal," the proprietor said. He looked around at his companions, and they nodded. "But first, one more thing."

"Anything," the Reverend offered.

"I had thought that your Lord Jesus made the miracles happen, Reverend."

A cloud passed over the Reverend's face.

The man continued, "Didn't Jesus make the water turn into wine and the fishes into loaves of bread?"

The Reverend took a step back. "How do you know the Gospel?"

"I went to your school as a boy. I hated it. All those nonsense tales and strict rules."

The Reverend tried to smile as he countered, "But you seem to have been a good pupil."

The proprietor inched closer. "So tell me, Reverend, did your Jesus heal the sick and feed the hungry?"

The Reverend didn't know what to say.

"Was it He or was it this fur hide that has saved you out here in no man's land? Because if it wasn't this old, mangy thing, then our deal is off. So tell me, was it your Lord Jesus or not, Ghost Man?"

The Reverend bowed his head. No words issued forth from his lips.

"Come on, which was it?" one of the thuggish friends echoed.

"Was the Lord Jesus responsible for the miracles or not?" another asked.

The Reverend finally answered. "No, He wasn't."

"I didn't think so," the proprietor said and spat on the floor. "Your Lord Jesus means nothing here, you foolish man."

The proprietor then gestured to his friends to help lift the fur up onto his shoulders. Once it was in place, he paraded around the room and said, "This was a fair trade, I believe."

The Reverend cleared his throat and finally spoke in a weak voice. "I will need five bags of beans, please."

The proprietor raised his arms, and the animal's claws rose up, too. The fierce yellow eyes glared down at the Reverend.

"Three bags," the proprietor replied.

"Four."

The proprietor motioned to one of the boys, who got up and disappeared into the back of the store.

"I can feel it working already," the proprietor announced. "I feel stronger." He turned to the Reverend and asked, "Invincible as a god, you say? I bet you enjoyed that feeling, Ghost Man. But now you are a frail human like the rest of us."

The Reverend stood with drooping shoulders and had no words left. The boy returned with four bags of beans and presented them to Ahcho.

"Bring them out a few bags of rice, too," the proprietor said. "We are friends now."

The Reverend mumbled his thanks and started toward the door.

The proprietor called out to him, "You watch it out there, Ghost

Man. Without this fur on your back and no god to protect you, you're like everybody else."

The Reverend nodded as he stepped outside into stark and painful sunlight. He could not argue. He understood as never before that he was like every other godless man in this godless land. His abandonment was complete. His heart sank deeper into his chest as he shut the door on the Lord forever. Ahcho joined him outside, and the Reverend turned his head away. He was too ashamed to look a good Christian in the eye.

Eighteen

Shortly before labor began, Mai Lin offered sacrifices to the gods and the family ancestors, although her young mistress couldn't even recall her grandmother's grandmother's name. Mistress Grace moaned with miserable, slow pains for many hours. Mai Lin gave her a special mixture of teas proven to move things along faster. She made Grace alternately bear down over a metal tub and then walk back and forth along the upstairs hall to bring forth the baby inside. The mistress had several baths, although she said that doctors in her country would warn against it. Ignorant doctors like Hemingway claimed that germs could swim up the woman's canal and infect the unborn child, something that Mai Lin plainly knew was false. The baby would come down the river to be born, so what was the harm of it getting wet beforehand?

In midmorning, the Reverend poked his head into his wife's bedroom and inquired after her health. Luckily, Mistress Grace was lying down at the time, and she quickly shut her eyes, pretending to be asleep. Mai Lin had been instructed not to mention that labor had begun, so he quickly left.

Later in the afternoon, he stopped by again, and this time the situation was more difficult to hide. Grace sat upon her chaise and paused between pacing. The pungent smell of the ointment Mai Lin had rubbed onto her belly was hard to miss, but Mai Lin's mistress merely smiled between gritted teeth.

"Mistress is better today," Mai Lin said to the Reverend, which was not a lie, for her cough had improved.

"Her complexion does appear brighter," he commented.

Mai Lin thought it remarkable that he didn't guess that the sweat on her brow and over her rosy cheeks was the first strain of the birth process. But then again, the Reverend had always been blind.

"Mai Lin, see that Doc Hemingway is called immediately if she goes into labor," he said before returning to his study on the first floor.

Mai Lin knew she should obey, but her mistress's eyes flew open, and she said, "Don't you dare. This is my baby. Lock the door."

Mai Lin did as she was told, lit the lamp, and rubbed more oils on her mistress's back and belly. There was much to be done, and having a man in the room would have disturbed the effort. She lit the sacred incense to welcome a new life into the world and handed her mistress pillows to scream into, for one loud yell would carry into the courtyard, and the Reverend would be knocking in no time with Doc Hemingway at his heels.

It was a grave responsibility, but Mai Lin had birthed more babies than she could count. She concentrated with all her being on every sign given off by her mistress's body. She sensed the pain as if it were her own. As labor progressed, her own body rose and fell with the contractions, and she told herself that this would be her last birth. She was getting too old for this. Still, she kept a hand on Grace so she could judge the intensity of the spasms. When it became too much and Mai

Lin couldn't stand it any longer, she shouted again for her mistress to push.

In the hour of the rooster, of the fourteenth day in the month December, in the second year of the Emperor Pu-Yi, in the reign of the Qing Dynasty, Grace finally let out a howl that echoed off the compound walls and cascaded into the dirt road and plains beyond. Mai Lin knew that the donkeys and horses in their stalls perked up their ears at the sound. Ahcho, smoking his pipe in the back alley, tipped his head to the side and offered a worried smile. The Reverend, seated at the teak desk in his library, set down the fountain pen with which he had been scribbling his Sunday sermon and finally allowed himself to grasp that his child had been born.

But at a moment like this, Mai Lin didn't have time for distracting thoughts. The baby was in her hands. She set its wet and squirming body on a soft pillow and cut the cord at the navel with a pair of pinking shears. Then she applied a special poultice of ash, mud, and dung to the umbilicus. In the way that she knew best, she lifted the child in her arms, pressed it against her shoulder, and slapped the tiny back ten times. A yowl issued forth. She wiped the infant perfunctorily, wrapped it, and placed it in her mistress's arms.

"Your daughter," she said.

Grace, as red-faced as the baby and wet with perspiration, held her child against her cheek and wept. "My girl, my precious, precious girl," she said.

Mai Lin knew this was only the beginning, for now she must help her young mistress to breast-feed, which the master did not approve of and so would take place only in private. Stupid Westerners, Mai Lin thought. The Reverend would change his mind when he understood that animal milk was virtually impossible to come by now.

After wiping the floor and tossing the birth cloths into the metal tub, Mai Lin returned to her mistress's bedside. The baby had begun to root, and Mai Lin took this for a good sign. This girl baby with her pinched and demanding face was not faint of heart.

Mai Lin took her mistress's wrist between her fingers and felt for her vital signs, which, unlike the child's, now appeared to be startlingly weak. She studied Grace's suddenly pale face. Only moments before the mother had seemed robust, but her skin was turning gray and chalky, her eyes glazed. Mai Lin pressed lightly again on her thin wrist but could not hear the strong current of life that she was seeking.

Mai Lin swooped up the baby and placed her in a bed of blankets on the floor. She pulled back the sheet that covered her mistress's lower half. A pool of blood glistened in the lamplight between her legs. Grace began to writhe in pain. After several moments of examining the expelled matter, Mai Lin did not feel all that she wanted to feel. Something wasn't right.

Grace tossed and moaned, clearly in as strong pain now as she had experienced during actual labor. Mai Lin had no choice but to clamber up onto the bed. Despite her thick, long skirts and awkward legs that had little strength anymore, she nonetheless made herself sit astride her mistress.

Grace's head was tipped back, her mouth gaping, her eyes open and apparently unseeing. She did not seem to notice that Mai Lin now sat atop her, but she would notice it in the next moment. For Mai Lin used all her tiny body's strength, all her years of accumulated wisdom and power, and thrust her weight steadily and forcefully into her open palms. She pressed down upon her mistress's engorged uterus.

Grace let out a scream that made her birth sounds seem like whispers. This was a cry of pain the likes of which Mai Lin had rarely heard before, and she had heard a great deal in her many years. Although Grace appeared terribly frail, the sound that came out of her had the fury and desperation of a tiger caught in a trap. Her mistress's weak arms flailed, and her bony fists struck Mai Lin repeatedly with surprising force. Mai Lin did not flinch or give up. She took in a second large breath and pressed all her weight down again. Grace's eyes opened wider, and she stared at Mai Lin in disbelief.

"You're trying to kill me!" she screamed.

Mai Lin shook her head at the foolish young woman but couldn't take the time to argue or explain. Instead, she reared up one final time and composed all her strength into a single long push. As Grace's screams and accusations slammed against the plaster walls and her hands battered the old woman's ribs, Mai Lin began to hear frantic pounding at the bedroom door.

The Reverend shouted, "Unhand my wife. Let me in, you old crone."

The final effort was done. Mai Lin had nothing left in her, and she hoped the same was true of her mistress. She lost her balance and fell forward onto Grace's sweat-soaked body in her simple white chemise. Mai Lin cared about the foolish girl in spite of herself. Then she regained her composure and carefully slid off the bed. She stood on unsteady legs as pain shot through her bent back, but she chose to ignore it.

Instead, she pulled the sheet away again and carefully inspected the bloody evidence, but still remained skeptical. She lifted the lamp and had no choice but to reach up inside her mistress. Mistress Grace writhed and arched her back, but Mai Lin was quick and sure. Her fingers finally grasped the cause. She pulled it out and did not flinch at the sight, nor was she made queasy, but instead, like a true scientist, Mai Lin carefully studied the proof in her hands until she felt certain she had found the offending remains of the birth sack.

The knocking on the bedroom door had continued all this time, and the Reverend's threats grew steadily more hysterical. Mai Lin heard several male voices now discussing in what manner to break down the door. She whipped her long braid off her shoulder, adjusted her many skirts and sashes and pouches. She cleaned the blood from her hands on the bedsheet and finally hobbled to the door. She opened it slowly and stepped aside.

The Reverend charged into the room, shouting and pointing at her. But at the sight of his wife lying exhausted in a pool of blood, he stopped his nonsense and threw himself forward to hug her and hold her weak hand. Doc Hemingway entered with less fanfare but more purpose. He held his stethoscope out and set down his black bag, the sight of which for some reason made Mai Lin laugh as she flopped down upon the chaise longue.

The Reverend turned to her and shouted, "What have you done to my wife?"

Mai Lin let out a sigh and pointed to the baby on the pillows. The blind Reverend had not even noticed his child. He finally grew quiet as he went to the baby and crouched beside her. Mai Lin let out a disgusted sound as she rose and went to the awkward father who didn't even know how to pick up his own offspring. She swooped up the baby in the swaddling clothes and placed her in her father's arms.

"A boy?" he asked.

She waved a hand at him, the dried blood on her fingers catching the light. "Be grateful that both your girls are alive."

Mai Lin could see a slight wash of disappointment flit over the Reverend's face before he determined to beam. She stepped away. The silly man had no idea of his good fortune.

At the bedside, she stood opposite Doc Hemingway.

"How did you save her?" he asked Mai Lin.

"The only way."

The Doctor leaned across Grace's sleeping body, waiting for more, but Mai Lin was too tired to talk to ignorant people.

"I will send over my maid to clean this up right away. You have done more than enough for one evening," the doctor said.

With the baby held in his stiff arms, the Reverend stepped forward and asked Hemingway, "Is my wife going to be all right?"

"It appears she hemorrhaged after the birth. Is that right, Mai Lin?"

Mai Lin nodded from her seat nearby and reached into one of her pouches for more betel quid.

"A very dangerous condition," Doc Hemingway explained. "I have lost several patients in this way. You are extremely lucky she had such good care."

The Reverend looked across at Mai Lin, and the man of so many words seemed to have forgotten them all. She held out her arms, and he came forward and gratefully handed her the baby.

"Your wife will be terribly weak," Doc Hemingway said as the

Reverend rejoined him at bedside. "She has lost a great deal of blood, and it will take her months to recover. She will require bed rest and good sustenance, which will certainly be a challenge, but I believe Mai Lin will know best how to handle her condition."

The Reverend looked across at the old amah, and from his lips finally came an outpouring of gratitude. Mai Lin didn't care about the words that tumbled from the Reverend. As he continued to thank her, she lifted the baby to her shoulder and patted it in the only proper way.

Nineteen

We shall move you over this afternoon," Mrs. Watson said. "We insist."

Then she turned and strode from the room, her skirts whisking the floor. She did not glance at Mai Lin, who sat in her customary spot on the spindle chair in the corner. Grace's amah rose and went to her mistress and placed a cool cloth upon her forehead.

"I am to live with my good friend Mildred," Grace said in a weak voice.

"Not to worry. It will be all right."

"I'm not worried," Grace said and tried to squeeze Mai Lin's hand, "so long as you're there with me."

"Mistress grows stronger by the day. But you must sleep now."

Soon her mistress returned to dozing, and Mai Lin slipped from the bedroom. Ahcho waited just outside the door, as he had come to do often in the week since the birth.

Mai Lin whispered, "That two-faced witch is stealing my Mistress."

"It is as it must be." He shrugged. "Some things are out of our hands."

She stared at him for a moment and then said, "Nothing is out of our hands. You know that. Mistress would have died had I not been here. She shouldn't be transferred so soon, and certainly not without me. We must do something."

Ahcho looked suddenly quite old as he said, "We have to accept that we can't save everyone. Some things are beyond our control."

Mai Lin put her hands on her hips. "Is something wrong with you today?" she asked. "You don't sound like yourself. Maybe you can't save your charge, but I'm stronger than that."

He shook his head and muttered, "Woman."

"Enough with the sorry face," she replied quickly. "Go now, bring me Doc Hemingway. I must talk with him."

Ahcho's brow formed a question. "And the Reverend, too?"

Mai Lin let out a slight laugh. "Have you no sense at all today?"

"I'll get the doctor. I see that the old lady is emperor of everyone now."

"That's right. And you better do as I say, old man," she said and shooed him off.

Ahcho started down the hall, but then turned back and stepped closer to her again.

She gazed into his sorrowful face and asked softly, "Are you sure you're feeling all right? Is your heart bothering you?"

"My heart is fine," he said, but then he bowed his head even lower so that his lips practically touched her ear. "I have heard word of the boy," he whispered.

Mai Lin pulled away, and he stood tall again. They looked at one another for a long moment.

"Where is he?" she asked.

"Where we expected."

"The great Gobi Desert?"

He nodded.

"And he's alive?" she asked.

Ahcho nodded again.

"But surely he lives as a slave there?" she asked.

He shook his head slowly from side to side.

"What then?"

"A prince."

Mai Lin couldn't help the harsh laugh that escaped her lips. "No, it can't be."

Once again, Ahcho nodded.

Outside the moon-shaped window at the end of the hall, dull morning light washed over the ochre saddleback roofs and the swallowtail eaves of the mission compound. Mai Lin looked past those familiar outlines to see the plains stretching on and on forever. She didn't like to think about life out there, but in this moment, the distance could not be ignored. Ahcho had traveled across it with the Reverend before the mistress had arrived in Fenchow-fu. He had returned with stories to tell and a puffed-up chest. Afterward, people had asked him questions as if he knew everything now that he had become a world traveler. Mai Lin had barely been able to stand it. But what was worse, when he returned, he had not only a swollen head but a heart condition as well, brought on by stress and the dangerous desert winds. She despised that world out there.

She looked up at him now. "You can't believe this outlandish report. It's absurd."

"The tradesman claimed he saw the boy himself."

"And you spoke to this man? When? Where was I? Why didn't you tell me?"

"Calm yourself, woman. I am telling you. I keep my ears to the ground. I know many, many things."

"Not that again," she said and waved a hand at him.

Just then she heard the baby starting to cry in her mistress's bedroom.

She reached for Ahcho's hand. "Will you tell the Reverend?" she asked. "If he insists on rescuing the boy, you'll have to go with him, and there's no way you'll come back alive. No, you mustn't tell him."

He gazed down at her with grieving eyes, and she felt certain she had never seen him so burdened.

"You'll do what's best." She squeezed his fingers before letting go. "I know you. You will."

Then she hurried back to the mother and child.

A half hour later, as Mai Lin tucked Rose Baby into her nest of blankets, she heard a tap on the door. The mistress still slept, which was a blessing. Mai Lin went into the hallway, where Ahcho stood with Doc Hemingway.

"Mai Lin, I understand you need my help?" the doctor asked, setting his black bag down on the hall table. This time, Mai Lin did not laugh at the sight of it. The doctor's silver hair and creased pink face showed his age. He had been practicing for a long time, although not as long as she.

"No help is needed with the patient," she said. "There is little sign of improvement, but we didn't expect any at this early stage."

"Quite right," Doc Hemingway agreed. "I would be surprised to hear otherwise."

Ahcho leaned in, but Mai Lin elbowed him away.

"Go on now," she said to him. "This is business between medical people."

Ahcho pulled back and spoke to the doctor. "Be careful, she wants something from you."

Mai Lin hissed at him to leave again and then wrapped her fingers around Doc Hemingway's arm in his wrinkled seersucker suit. "Mistress is to be moved to the Martins' this afternoon."

"So I heard. That is probably for the best."

"You must speak to the Reverend about this. He will trust your opinion," Mai Lin said. "He is not the problem, though. The problem is that lady over there."

"Mrs. Martin?"

"Wicked woman."

"Now, Mai Lin."

"She does not allow me to go with my mistress."

"Ah," Doc Hemingway said.

"'Ah'?" Mai Lin mimicked, her eyes flashing. "That is all you can say?"

He bit his bottom lip and looked down at her through smudged glasses.

"You must tell her that I go everywhere with Mistress Grace," she said.

"I can't do that. I can't tell a reverend how to run his household."

Mai Lin crossed her arms.

"I am sure you will be welcome to stop in anytime to see Mrs. Watson," he said.

Mai Lin narrowed her eyes at this Hemingway man and sucked harder on the betel quid in her cheek.

"What do you want me to say to them?" he asked, placing his pudgy hands on wide hips.

"Tell them the truth. Mistress Grace will die without me."

The doctor let out a slight laugh that disappeared quickly into the air.

"You do not believe this?" she asked. "I have saved her four times already. Twice with the unborn babies in the night, once when her son was stolen, and now with Rose Baby's birth." Mai Lin raised her thin arms and shook them, her many bracelets rattling. "I ask you, how many lives can a woman have?"

Doc Hemingway appeared to be studying her, but she had no patience for his slow-witted response.

"You know it's true," she barked. "Speak to the Reverend Charles Martin."

The doctor glanced helplessly over the balustrade to the front entrance hallway below and then across to the closed door of Reverend Watson's study.

"He is of no use," Mai Lin hissed, nodding down to where the Reverend had locked himself in for days. "He loves his wife, but he is unable to help her."

The doctor's shoulders sagged. "I will speak with Reverend Martin. Heaven only knows if he holds any sway over *his* wife. She is a force of nature."

"Her?" Mai Lin let out a sharp cackle. "*I* am a force of nature."

Later that afternoon as Grace continued to sleep, Mai Lin told the Martins' number-one boy and the number-two boy, his son, to rotate her mistress's bed. Mrs. Martin skittered around and objected, but Mai Lin pointed to her reclining mistress and whispered, "Quiet! Patient is sleeping."

The men carefully set the bed down precisely where Mai Lin wished.

"Astounding," Mrs. Martin muttered. "Next thing I know, you'll be rearranging my parlor."

Mai Lin did not argue but hurried to her mistress as she was opening her eyes onto the vista out the window. The corners of Grace's mouth lifted slightly. She noticed her friend on the other side of the bed and raised a hand, which Mrs. Martin then shook too vigorously.

"Thank you, dear Mildred, for so thoughtfully placing me here where I can see the courtyard and the plains beyond. I know it will help in my recovery."

Mai Lin let out a grunt of satisfaction and went to the dresser across the room, where she busied herself setting up her apothecary. She organized bottles of tinctures, a mortar and pestle, pouches of herbs, blocks of incense, cups, and needles. When she finished, she noticed that the Reverend had sneaked quietly into the room. He stood behind Mrs. Martin, who chattered at the mistress as she lay very still with shut eyes. The Martins' young daughter, Daisy, clamored around the bed, too, not helping Mai Lin's mistress to rest at all.

It was time to shoo them out, these useless people who did not understand the seriousness of her mistress's medical condition. Mai

Lin shuffled over to the Reverend, and to her surprise, he beamed down at her. The tall man knew so very little and somehow believed in all the wrong things. Now, for example, he suddenly looked convinced that it was easy for Mai Lin to keep his wife alive. She would, of course, but it would be no simple task. As always, Mai Lin thought, he had the faith and enthusiasm of an innocent child not yet schooled in the ways of the world.

"Mai Lin," he said in a fond voice, "how is our dear girl doing today?"

Mai Lin jutted out her bottom lip. "She is here now at the Martins' house."

"Yes, yes, I see that!" the Reverend said, rocking up onto his heels. "A wise decision. Doc Hemingway explained it all to me. And most excellent that you are here with her. We are terribly grateful." He awkwardly patted Mai Lin on the shoulder, and when she did not respond, he withdrew his hand.

"Reverend Watson," Mrs. Martin said, finally acknowledging him, "it is best for your wife to rest now. Out we go."

Mrs. Martin rose and gestured for her small daughter and the Reverend to leave the bedroom with her. Like an ignorant sheep, he turned and started toward the door. The grand, powerful man of previous times appeared withered in his simple black suit. Mai Lin missed his long traveling coat and the enormous hide he had worn on his adventures. She was glad, though, to see that the red sash still hung across his breast, and the pouch with the twin golden dragons swung at his side. Several silver amulets and half-a-dozen pouches remained around his neck on ropes of leather. Mai Lin assumed these talismans reminded him of the man he had once been out on the trail when his hopes had been high and foolish. She liked that man more than the meek soul he was turning into here before her eyes.

"Mistress Grace wants to see her husband," Mai Lin said abruptly to Mrs. Martin. "She told me so."

Mai Lin then pinched tight her eyes, and apparently Mildred Martin was not stupid: she recognized the Evil Eye when it was upon her. She lifted her chin, took her toddler's hand, and marched from the room.

"Really, Mai Lin?" the Reverend whispered. "Did Mrs. Watson ask for me?"

"Come," she said and gestured for him to join her at the bedside.

"Mistress," Mai Lin said, and Grace's eyes opened slowly. "The Reverend is here."

Grace let out a pleased sigh.

"My darling," he said, and Mai Lin stepped away. The Reverend bent to kiss Grace's hand. "You made the trip across the courtyard like the Queen of the Sheba on a bed of silks. The distance was as vast and treacherous as any I've traversed on donkey back, but you made it like a trooper."

Grace grimaced and asked, "Are you leaving again?"

"Oh, no, my dear, I didn't mean to frighten you. I'm staying right here with you."

A faint smile appeared, then flitted away. "Have you seen her?" she asked.

"Who?"

"Our daughter."

"Why, yes, I have."

Mistress Grace seemed to wait for more from her husband, but then she carried on. "I have decided to call her Rose."

He clapped his hands together like a schoolboy, and the cheerful sound echoed strangely in the sickroom. "Excellent. But shouldn't it be Rose Grace?"

Mai Lin's mistress now fully smiled, and the Reverend kissed her brow. "You sleep now, my dearest, and regain your strength."

Mai Lin could tell that her mistress was reluctant to release her husband's hand, but she finally did, and Mai Lin escorted him out of the room. In the hallway, the Reverend paused before leaving. He held a new hat in his hands that Mai Lin had not seen before. It was of the type worn by shepherds and tribesmen of the western borderlands—those shiftless nomads who lived on the plains, killed one another randomly, and needed fur to keep their heads warm, even in their sleep.

"Reverend has a new hat?" she asked.

His face blushed. "I seem to still have a following. News of the baby leaked outside the compound. One of the chieftains sent this gift all the way from the steppes. I gather it's supposed to bring good luck." He looked hopefully at her and asked, "Do you suppose that's true, Mai Lin?"

She scoffed and wanted to say something about the superstitious country people, but the Reverend appeared too tender now to understand.

"Check that thing for lice," she said. "It probably came off a dead man."

The Reverend inspected the hat. "It is rather terrible looking," he said, but then he went ahead and put it on his head anyway, pulled it low and patted the top. Mai Lin actually smiled at the silly, sorry man who seemed pleased with himself for a change.

Then she stepped closer and got to the point. "We need your help. Mistress's milk will dry up soon because she doesn't eat enough. Rose Baby is very hungry, but Mistress is too weak. We need animal milk to supplement her supply. Sheep or goat, whatever you can find."

"Of course," the Reverend said. "I will go at once."

He started to leave, but Mai Lin called him back. She lifted a silk cord from around her neck. On it hung an amulet: a small inlaid wooden box, and inside the box was a potion that her grandmother, the great healer, had put there herself. If anything could help the Reverend at this point, Mai Lin thought, this charm might, although she wouldn't have bet her inheritance on it.

The Reverend took the wooden box between his fingers and admired it. He let it fall to his chest, where it hung beside the other necklaces he had been given along the way.

"Thank you, Mai Lin."

He then surprised her by bringing his hands together and bowing lower than she in a sign of utmost respect.

The Reverend turned and scurried down the stairs and across the front hallway. He had made it almost to the door when the Reverend and Mrs. Martin stepped from their parlor.

"Dashing off already?" Reverend Charles Martin asked. "We never see you anymore, old boy."

The Reverend apologized and thanked them again for encouraging his wife to convalesce in their home. He said he was most grateful. But then, without further explanation, he pushed open the screen door and hurried off the veranda into the gray late-winter afternoon. Mai

Lin watched from the second floor as the Martins followed him with their eyes.

"Where on earth did he get that hat?" Mildred Watson asked.

Her bald husband with a hawk's nose shook his head. "When he finally shed the animal hide, I thought he might be regaining his senses."

"You're too patient, Reverend Martin. That man is head of the mission in name only."

"Let's not forget that he lost his son not yet a year ago."

"Others have lost children as well. You need to bring it up with the mission board back home. We must have strong leadership here, not some half native in disreputable garb."

Mai Lin had to restrain herself from spitting betel quid onto Mrs. Martin's prematurely silver bun. The Reverend Martin put his arm around his wife and tried to kiss her temple, but she brushed him away and went to her young daughter, who was howling like a wild animal from the parlor. Mrs. Martin's daughter was a lousy specimen, too, Mai Lin thought, nothing like the good girl, Rose Baby.

Twenty

Grace's children came to her in a swirl of dust and sunlight. Motes of light floated behind her closed eyelids, and when she opened them the sun danced low over the sill before her, bringing with it the children. She thought she heard them crying. She dozed and dreamed and woke again and heard them crying again, this time from quite close. She squinted down at the soft bundle beside her. Rose. Her Rose. Grace's heart welled up, but her arms were too tired to lift the baby to her breast.

"Mai Lin," she whispered.

The old woman was there, just where she was needed. Grace had never known anyone so reliable. Something cool wetted her lips, and another cool cloth covered her brow. The heat that flamed up at the touch of Mai Lin's fingers startled Grace. She realized she must be terribly ill. That wouldn't do. She pushed herself up in her bed and said, "I shall feed my daughter now."

"Rose Baby drinks goat milk and tea I combine for her. Reverend brought it to your daughter three days ago."

"I've been sleeping all that time?"

"Off and on," Mai Lin said as she withdrew the cloth from Grace's forehead and replaced it with another one.

"But I want to nurse her, Mai Lin. I must."

"If Mistress insists, but you must eat, too."

Mai Lin lifted the baby, pulled back Grace's gown, and helped put the child's mouth to her mother's nipple. The baby rooted and mewed. Grace tipped back her head against the pillow and let out a surprising laugh. The pull of the infant's mouth on her tender skin sent a shooting pain through her, but she didn't mind. Her daughter was alive. And she was alive.

Mai Lin spooned tea into Grace's mouth and then a mash of beans and something else she didn't recognize. She no longer cared for food except that she knew she must eat it to keep up her strength for the sake of the baby. After another sip, she felt woozy again and wanted to sleep but made herself swallow more.

The baby pulled back her tiny head covered in thin, pale hair and let out a high-pitched howl. Grace fumbled with her breast and offered it again, but the infant's body stiffened as she cried, her face turning scarlet.

"What have I done wrong?" Grace asked. "Why won't she take it?"

"Mother's milk is not enough for her," Mai Lin said. "You hold Rose Baby in your arms. That is better."

Mai Lin covered Grace's chest and spooned her another mouthful. She then lifted Rose into her mistress's arms and showed her how to feed her daughter from a strange-looking contraption that resembled an urn with a hard spout. As unappealing as the setup seemed, Rose drank the milky liquid.

"Have we nothing with a softer teat?" Grace asked. "The poor girl has to suck on hard ceramic. This is terrible. I can't even feed my own child properly."

Grace began to weep so suddenly, she shocked herself. As she cried, her chest grew tighter and she began to cough. She had grown accustomed to the endless paroxysms, but now she could hardly bear the pain they caused to her tender female parts and to her aching ribs. Her entire body was wracked by the coughing, and she realized she hadn't recovered much at all from the birth. She remembered that entire episode only vaguely, as if it were a story of great adversity that had happened to someone else. That is, until she felt the pain again when the coughing cut through her. Then she understood it was she who had endured almost too much to bear.

When the coughing finally subsided, Grace said to Mai Lin, "I almost took my leave of this world after Rose was born, didn't I?"

Mai Lin nodded.

"I remember it now," Grace said. Her dreams and memories of the past weeks flitted past, and she searched them for what had actually happened. It was a haze, but one sensation persisted throughout. "I felt certain it was my time to leave."

Mai Lin stood over her with a worried expression. "Mistress was in great pain after the baby came, greater even than in birth labor. Something got caught inside. Your body needed to get rid of it and couldn't stop bleeding until you did. But, you are much better now. You will be well again soon."

Grace looked beyond her amah and out the window into the shadowed courtyard below. Chinese children stood in straight lines before their classroom doors as the ministers and ladies of the mission drifted about in their dark robes.

Grace let the baby bottle sag in her hand. "But truly, I was ready to leave this life," she repeated, more to herself than her amah. "I wanted to join my other children, the ones out there."

Mai Lin lifted Rose away from her mother and placed her on her shoulder. Grace did not object. The old woman patted the infant's back and said, "But you would have left this very real small one behind. That would not do. She needs you."

Grace did not answer but looked out the window again, this time beyond the courtyard to the flat plains streaked by the red fingers of sunset. She could tell she was making her maid uneasy with such talk, but it was true. She had wanted to go. Her time had come. But her daughter was here, and Mai Lin was right to say that Grace must now stay. For Rose's sake, she must hold on a little while longer. She lifted her frail arms, and Mai Lin placed Rose back into them. The baby leaned against her chest, and Grace felt a weight upon her heart. Mai Lin looked down at her with those same worried eyes, and Grace hated to pain her old amah so.

She attempted to lighten her voice as she asked, "Wherever did the Reverend find the precious milk for our girl?"

"He wouldn't say. But Mistress knows he is a most resourceful man, yes?" Mai Lin shifted her heavy skirts and sat on the edge of the bed. She appeared to almost be smiling. Clearly her amah was trying to rescue Grace from the dark cul-de-sac of feeling that she had wandered down.

Mai Lin continued, "He performs many miracles. Everyone knows this."

"Tell me, what do they say about him these days?" Grace asked.

"This morning," Mai Lin began, "Mrs. Martin's number-one boy told everyone the story of the two bullets. The latest version is that the Reverend caught the bullets in his giant hands."

"Oh, my!" Grace said. "What else?"

"Elephants tried to stampede a crowd, but the Reverend stopped them with a clap of thunder and a bolt of lightning that he threw down himself."

Grace giggled. "I believe it's true."

"Some even say he charmed the snakes to sleep for one hundred years. And others say he turned dead crops into most satisfying grains."

Grace lifted her sleepy daughter up before her and rubbed their noses softly together. "Your father is a great man, little one," she whispered. "Never forget it."

Mai Lin chuckled and said, "I don't believe anyone will ever forget the great Ghost Man who once lived here."

Grace glanced at her. "What do you mean they won't ever forget him, Mai Lin? He is still with us and well?"

"He is well," Mai Lin said as she stood abruptly and tucked in the covers at the foot of the bed.

"And he is with us? He no longer travels the way he once did?" Grace asked.

Mai Lin stopped fussing and stepped toward the window.

"Tell me," Grace cleared her throat, "where is my husband now?"

Mai Lin bowed her head. "He brought us the milk, and then he went away again."

Grace let out a sharp sigh. She looked beyond the wall that surrounded the mission compound. The yellow dust of the desert reflected the late-afternoon light. All that golden brightness hid the roughness of the roads and the dryness of the lone river. It was a terrible terrain, inhospitable and cruel. And yet her husband was out there somewhere in the vast expanse of desolate land once again. Grace, who normally studied the horizon for hours, couldn't bear to look at it for another moment. She shut her eyes and tried to feel the beating of her baby's heart against her own. It was the one solid thing she knew anymore.

Twenty-one

Grace half woke again to the sound of a child crying and fell back asleep. When she heard it for a second time quite a bit later, she lifted her head from the pillow. The wooden shutters were drawn, so she assumed it was nighttime. She heard soft footsteps in the hall and then weeping, this time not a child's, but a woman's weak sobs. For once, Grace could tell that the sounds were real and not in her dreams. She was grateful to notice the difference.

She pulled the covers away and swung her legs over the side of the bed. She had walked only twice in the six weeks since Rose had been born and both times with Ahcho holding her up to keep her from falling. She put her bare feet onto the cool floorboards now and felt grateful that her body didn't crumple under her weight. In the corner, Mai Lin snored in her cot with Baby Rose asleep on a low mattress beside her.

Grace didn't bother with her silk robe, which lay on the chaise longue. She inched forward, trying not to concentrate too hard on each step for fear of jinxing herself. She thought only of the crying that continued from beyond her door.

She made her way across the room without stumbling and held

tightly to the handle as she tried to regain her strength. Her legs felt as heavy as bags of desert sand. She could feel her blood coursing slowly through her veins. It was a strange sensation to notice something that normally went unnoticed. A steady pumping and whirring sound had replaced the nervous humming vibrations that she had grown accustomed to for so long.

Grace had overheard Doc Hemingway explaining her condition to the Reverend. After the birth, she remained in grave danger still of dying from blood loss. It would take months for her body to fully recover. Slowly, and with the help of iron-rich foods, she would make enough new red blood to be strong again, although finding decent food was nearly impossible now.

Without the proper amount of blood in her body, Grace was prone to coldness and to an annoying swishing sound in her ears that threatened to take over her entire self. She felt surrounded by the sensation of blood as it propelled itself through her. She thought it odd that she now noticed the coursing of blood precisely because of a lack of it. There wasn't enough life in her veins, so she throbbed all over with what little was left.

She opened the door and waited for her light-headedness to subside. Then she commenced to inch forward again, holding on to the banister at the top of the stairs. The crying seemed to be coming from Daisy's bedroom at the end of the hall. Grace stopped before the slightly opened door and paused before entering.

As she stood, she looked down at her pale bare feet and flimsy gown. A shaft of light coursing through the moon window at the end of the hallway shone on her full figure under the thin, white cotton.

She should have put on her robe, she realized, but it was too late now that she had come this far. Her body looked foreign to her—plump and bent and sagging under the weight of all she had been through. Her breasts hung like overripe fruit, and she could not imagine anyone seeing her and feeling anything but sorry. Like a much older woman, she had nothing to hide anymore. Decorum or custom or female vanity was lost on a body that had endured too much. She was no longer the girl whose primary concern had been to appear appropriate and bright in the face of the future. The Martins would have to forgive her. The crying was what mattered. Grace understood that now. Everything else was immaterial.

She pushed open the door and slipped into the room. Mildred Martin sat in a straight-backed chair beside her daughter's bed, her head of prematurely silver hair bowed. Normally, Mildred wore it up in a tight bun, but now it cascaded down her back in a shimmering river. She wept softly into a handkerchief.

Grace went to Mildred and put a hand ever so lightly on her shoulder. The seated woman didn't flinch or in any way acknowledge in words that another body had entered the room. She merely reached up her own pale hand and placed it over Grace's. They both kept their eyes on the now sleeping child. Grace didn't see anything wrong with dear Daisy, who normally filled the house with her rather demanding voice and busy antics. She was a handful—robust and not sickly, so Grace wasn't sure why her mother sat and seemed to worry over her now.

Then Mildred, as if guessing Grace's thoughts, reached forward and lifted Daisy's sleeping wrist into the air. The child's arm, thinner than Grace had remembered it, sagged like a catenary. It swung slightly as if a breeze had caused it to sway. The bowed bones appeared made of rubber. They curved unnaturally, and Grace felt a pain rise up in her chest. Her ears filled suddenly with the sound of her own throbbing blood, as if she might drown in it.

"Dear God," she whispered.

"Rickets," Mildred said as she delicately set her daughter's arm back on the covers. "The poor child isn't getting enough milk or green vegetables or meat. Her body is leaching away calcium and vitamin D until the bones can no longer remain solid. She is starving, Grace."

Mildred turned suddenly in her seat and flung her arms around Grace's waist. She pressed her head against her friend's loose stomach, and quickly her tears soaked through the thin material of her nightgown. "I can't stand it any longer," Mildred said. "We must get out of here."

Grace's fingers gently stroked Mildred's long hair from the top all the way down her waist. Then her hand softly settled upon her back.

"It may already be too late," Mildred added, her shoulders shaking with tears. "The trip back home could kill her."

"Don't think that way. But you're right. You must go."

Mildred pulled away from Grace and wiped her eyes with the sleeve of her robe. She studied her friend with deep fondness and curiosity. "But what about you? I didn't think you'd make it, dear Grace, but you are stronger than anyone I know. How have you managed with such loss and with a husband who is forever gone from your side?"

Grace pulled herself free from her friend. "Don't think about me now. It's Daisy and you that we must consider."

Mildred leaned forward and asked, "But what about your precious girl, your baby?"

Grace stepped close again and placed a palm on Mildred's cheek. "My baby," she echoed.

Her friend flinched at Grace's touch. "My heavens, your hands are icy cold. We must get you back into bed. That Mai Lin should watch over you better. You're not well."

Grace realized she was trembling all over, her teeth chattering silently. It was true, she wasn't well. She let Mildred take her arm.

"You must leave for America with us," Mildred whispered. "You and the baby can't possibly stay here a moment longer. My Reverend is trying to book us passage on a boat out of Shanghai. We'll get you a berth, and you will join us." She turned Grace toward her and spoke sternly. "Even if that husband of yours refuses to go, you must not stay. For the baby's sake, please, Grace, say you'll consider it?"

Grace nodded, but now she needed to concentrate on every step. The whooshing of blood in her veins was growing unbearably loud again, and she feared she might collapse. It was time for Mai Lin to administer to her. She longed to drift into sleep again and imagined the relief of her soft bed. Another chill passed through her body, and she shook violently. She shut her eyes and willed herself to be transported to rest. But with her body so cold, she understood she would have to cross a vast and snowy tundra to find peace again. Grace allowed herself to be carried back to the fields at home on a wintry morning. She tried to remember the fun she'd had as a girl in newly fallen snow.

Twenty-two

The steady bang of a hammer, the wail of a saw on wood, and the intermittent whispers that drifted up from down below: Grace had listened all day, and although no one had told her what was taking place around her in the Martins' household, she sensed it. Earlier in the afternoon, she had left her bed briefly to glance over the banister. She had seen planks of wood being carried in by Chinese carpenters. And now Mai Lin was here and brushing her hair as the last streaks of day crossed the pink desert and sliced her in two. Grace's image in the mirror showed her half in deathly shadow, half in radiant light. She knew that both sides were accurate reflections.

Mai Lin had not returned from the Watson home across the courtyard with the black dress that Grace had requested. Instead, in the Chinese custom, she had brought Grace's white wedding dress and now had put her into it and tied the bow at the back. The simple lace dress that fell to her ankles belonged on a girl, Grace could see now, a carefree ingenue. But within it now stooped the body of a woman, her chest ravaged by consumption—another thing she had had to figure out for herself—and a belly that would never again carry a child. Her body had made that latter point clear, although Doc Hemingway was too much of a coward to share with her the diagnosis.

Mai Lin would have kept fighting on her behalf forever, keeping her alive and as strong as she could, but Grace hated to think how the effort had aged her dear amah. When Grace had first married and moved into the finest house in the compound, Mai Lin had stood by the front door to welcome her, her chin high, her arms crossed over her chest, her sturdy back divided in two by thick braids over each shoulder. Now she was shriveled to an impossibly small size. Her face had lost its broad strength and was hatched by a thousand lines. Grace worried that she alone had inflicted great trials upon her maid. In the mirror, she looked into her own gray eyes and then at Mai Lin's ancient face and felt ashamed of the false optimism the old one attempted on her behalf.

"Mistress is ready?" Mai Lin asked.

Grace rose from the dressing table and went to the door of the room without help, although Mai Lin hobbled along beside her, nervously touching her elbow. "I believe I am stronger today," Grace said. "Please don't worry about me so."

Mai Lin bowed a little and stepped aside. As Grace proceeded cautiously down the stairs, she was aware of the ladies gathered below: Mrs. Jenkins, Mrs. Parker, Mrs. Carson, and even some of the unmarried women—Lucy, Gertrude, and Priscilla—with whom Grace had enjoyed sweet and simple good times. They were all in black, of course. Grace should have worn her black dress as well, but she hadn't wished to offend Mai Lin, who believed white was the proper color of mourning. In any case, Grace knew that the precious child wouldn't mind either way. What was in one's heart was all that mattered.

She dared not look at the ladies too closely, for she needed to concentrate on each careful step until she reached the first floor. And then, when she could have gone to them, she did not. She had nothing to say, and they must have sensed it, for they didn't step forward to greet her, either. It had been a long time, she realized, since she had enjoyed convivial company. Her Wesley boy had been stolen almost a full year before, and ever since, she had been on such a strange journey. In the past many months, she had become lost in a netherworld as she sought her children. She now fully inhabited a place of waiting, a purgatory, a desert all her own that suited her more than the society of these good people. She knew that they meant her well, but she suspected that the sight of her ghostly pallor frightened them and made them wary.

She allowed Mai Lin to steady her as she stepped into the parlor. There before the empty hearth stood the men. Reverend Charles Martin's fine bald head was bowed, and the others, in respect, stood in a circle with him, their faces long and expressionless. Their black suits created severe silhouettes, and Grace admired their stern, handsome profiles. She remembered when the Reverend had looked as upright and sure as these gentlemen.

She leaned toward Mai Lin and whispered, "Has anyone informed the Reverend?"

Mai Lin shook her head and made that sorry tsking sound. The poor woman was worn out. She took Mai Lin's hand in her own and held on tight.

"Not to worry," Grace said. "We will manage without him."

She went toward the one person in the place who mattered at this time: the child's mother. Mildred sat by herself beside the small coffin, her hand up to her mouth, a handkerchief gripped in white knuckles. The coffin had been made here in the parlor, and fresh sawdust dotted her black lace-up shoes.

Grace did not pause but knelt down before her friend, although it made her dizzy to do so. "Dear one," Grace began, and she studied Mildred's sorrowful countenance and saw that it was a mirror of her own after losing her son, "the untimely departure of a child is the greatest trial God sets before us. We are so sorry for your loss."

Mildred's gaze drifted away from the coffin and landed on Grace's face. Her brow tightened and became furrowed, and a look of confused amazement passed over her, as if perhaps she didn't recognize her friend. In her own grief, Grace remembered, she had mistaken people for apparitions. It was understandable that Mildred might do so now.

But Mildred didn't speak with a dazed or confused voice. Instead, she asked quite firmly, "Whom do you mean by 'we'?"

Grace squeezed Mai Lin's hand. "Why, Mai Lin and I."

Mildred looked at Grace with a cold stare and asked, "Where is your husband, Mrs. Watson?"

Grace stood unsteadily, and heat rose up from her collar. She looked about the room and noticed the others watching and waiting for a reply. And yet she had none. "I'm afraid," she said after a long moment, "I don't know."

"Of course you don't know," Mildred said with no kindness in her voice. "For many months now, you haven't known a thing, have you? You have no idea what we have gone through without anyone steering us or leading us forward. Those of us who have survived have done so with no help from your errant husband."

Grace could feel herself beginning to sway and was grateful when Mai Lin steadied her. She wished to be back in bed. Mai Lin's potion had worn off, and the swishing of her blood in her ears was like a rising tide that might soon drown her.

Mildred continued, "But that is behind us now. We are leaving, my husband and I. The other families are departing as well. As soon as we bury our daughter in this wretched soil, we shall abandon this land, and, God willing, we'll never see it again."

Grace did not appreciate her friend's harsh tone one bit. It made her feel feverish and more alone than ever. But when she looked down into Mildred's distraught eyes, Grace understood her hardened heart. Her friend was doing all that she could to remain strong precisely because she was not. Grace wanted to pat her friend's hand, which was damp with tears, and tell her to let the sorrow take her. There was no point in railing against it. Her grief, the grief of any mother whose child has been stolen away, was far too much to bear.

Strangely, Grace wanted to welcome Mildred into the painful society she had come to know and now champion. Mildred didn't yet understand that the ghosts win out in the end. It would be so much easier if she simply let them do so. It didn't matter if Mildred left this land on the next boat out of Shanghai, or if she stayed here for the rest of her days. She, like Grace, would never leave behind the plains of North China. There was no escaping this vast and desolate land. Grace understood that now. Once entered into, this desert of loss surrounded even the sturdiest of souls forever.

Then, as if to prove Grace's assumptions correct, a miserable wail escaped from the lips of her friend. In an instant, her husband was beside her. The other gentlemen stepped nearer, too. They bent forward and offered concerned faces. Grace looked around and saw that the ladies had slipped in closer as well and glared not at Mildred but at Grace. She wondered if they thought she had done something to produce her friend's outcry. Yet how could they imagine such a thing when the true culprit was death itself?

"I am deeply sorry, Mildred," Grace said. "I loved dear Daisy. You know that I did. I love all the children."

Reverend Martin held his sobbing wife against his side and said, "Yes, of course you do. We all know that about you." He tried to smile, but his eyes were clouded with tears as well.

Grace looked more closely now at the stony faces around her. She suddenly recognized what she had not noticed in the year since Wesley's kidnapping. Her fellow missionaries were no longer the large-hearted and determined people they had been when they had first arrived in Fenchow-fu. Grief lined their brows, and constant worry made their lips pinched and stern. She could sense the heartache that filled their breasts. They had seen too much, experienced too much, and it had left them in a state of constant grief.

There was Mrs. Jenkins whose oldest daughter, Miranda, had died suddenly earlier that spring. The lady's body appeared hollow now, her once proud chest caved in and her shoulders curved as if she were a coolie bearing a heavy load across her back. And Reverend Powers, once a robust and striking gentleman, had lost so much weight that his clothing hung on him like a scarecrow. And yet it was his eyes that bothered Grace even more: they had grown dull, the sparkle of light that had once shone in them with curiosity and even delight all but extinguished.

These people, her good and noble American compatriots, appeared to her not only worn down but lost. Grace recalled how their mission had once required that they stand tall and sure. They were to be models to the godless here. They were to rise to their better selves and overcome any personal faults in an effort to bring unadulterated good to a poor, deprived race. Now their fervent purpose had grown as faint and forgotten as the soil that blew away on the wind across the plains outside the compound.

Grace looked back at Mildred, whose tears rolled down her husband's dark lapel. Reverend Martin held his wife tightly. Grace tried to ignore the frantic pumping of her heart that caused her vision to blur. She kept her eyes focused on the spot where Mildred's cheek met her husband's chest. The question that buzzed in Grace's mind was as loud as the sound of her feeble, determined blood doing its work. Where *was* her husband? Grace wondered with surprising ferocity.

She made herself look away and out the window of the Martins' parlor to the view of the dirt yard at the rear of the compound. In the tradition of Chinese walls, a large and handsome moon gate had been strategically placed so that the Martins might look beyond their property and onto the windswept plains. Out there, the dead grasses of the previous season swayed and yellow dust stirred. Grace could sense the spring sun starting to warm the land. A mild though persistent heat had begun to burn the dry, useless weeds. Her husband was out there in that rising fire.

He continued on and on in his endless search, though Grace feared he had forgotten what exactly it was that he looked for. Of course each day he hoped to stumble upon evidence of their son. And yet she had come to realize that the Reverend was now upon a quest for something else as well. He had not found it, and yet he continued, not nearly as defeated as the lesser ministers here with her now. No, her Reverend carried on in spite of it all. He was an extraordinary man. She wished he would be satisfied with only her company and love, but he wouldn't be the man he was if he would. He was out in that wilderness looking for something. Something large and significant. Grace feared he was on a mission to discover nothing less than the Lord Himself.

She shook her head ever so slightly and let out a little puff of air. It was dawning on her that by conducting his fruitless odyssey, the Reverend had been steadily losing not only his faith but his dear extended family here in the compound as well. These people, his people, had had no choice but to turn their backs on him. Her husband had lost not only the Lord but these decent souls. He, of all people, was utterly alone.

She understood with sudden and striking clarity that she was the last one on earth still able to reach him. Wherever he had gotten himself to, she must go there now. It fell to Grace alone to fetch him back, even if it killed her to do so. Death was not nearly as troubling as she had once assumed, except for the thought of her baby. There was Rose to consider. And yet her husband was somehow calling out to her, too.

Mildred drew her head away from Reverend Martin's shoulder and spoke more calmly. "Grace, you can't care for your baby here," she said. "She won't survive it. You'd be killing her. Don't you see that?"

And, in an instant, Grace understood her situation and grasped what was required of her.

"Yes, Mildred," she said, "I do."

"Then say you'll leave China with us?"

"I will come along soon thereafter."

Mildred shook her head and looked toward the other ladies for confirmation of Grace's foolishness. But Grace stepped nearer and spoke with as much conviction as she could muster.

"Dearest Mildred and Reverend Martin, I don't know of two more generous and worthy people than you. You are upright and pure of heart. You are good, good Christians. You have saved me these past months by sharing your home and your care. And yet, now, I find that I must ask you for even more."

Through their swollen and exhausted eyes, the Martins looked at Grace most willingly, for they recognized their better selves in the description she had painted of them, and like all true Christians, they wished it to be true.

"Will you take my precious Rose with you when you leave this place?" Grace asked.

For some time, no one spoke, and so Grace continued, "The Reverend and I will follow as soon as our business here is finished. I cannot leave him now. You are loving parents, and I wouldn't dare to presume that my Rose could ever replace your dear Daisy in your hearts. But if you should take her with you and allow her even a fraction of your love, I would be most grateful. And soon, I will join you. Surely, I will, by and by."

The Reverend Martin looked ready to speak but then seemed to think better of it. Grace thought she recognized a brief glint of light in his eyes behind the veil of sorrow. Mildred's expression was simpler. She nodded slowly and seemed to grasp the request as only a mother could: above all else, she would see to the child.

"Good, then," Grace said. "It's settled. I can never thank you enough. May God bless you both."

She turned and let Mai Lin steady her as she walked out of the parlor without glancing at the others. In the hallway, although it was past the time for her to return to bed, Grace chose instead to step out through the screen door and onto the veranda. She couldn't bear to hold her baby one more time, knowing she might never see her again. So she let Rose sleep on upstairs under the care of Mildred's amah and her new family. Grace told herself not to remember the warmth of Rose's tiny body pressed against her side, her hands clenched over Grace's heart. Just the image of the precious child in her mind's eye was enough to start the unpleasant whirring sensation in her feeble body again. Her blood beat wildly as she looked out at the deserted courtyard. Her arms felt heavy at her sides, as if weary from carrying the weight of her daughter. And yet they were painfully empty.

As she stepped down from the porch, Grace told herself not to notice how her body ached with loss in every possible way. All around her appeared abandoned. The yellow-brick school building stood shuttered. The chapel at the far end was also closed. Several of the houses, too, were already boarded up. Crates of packed possessions stood stacked on carts, waiting for donkeys to pull them away. And yet none of it seemed nearly as desolate to Grace as the single glance backward that she allowed herself. She looked one more time at the Martins' house, still full of people, including her Rose.

Then she turned again and crossed the cracked earth toward the Watson home. As Mai Lin walked beside her, Grace shaded her eyes and squinted up at the front porch. She was surprised and most glad to see Ahcho standing just inside the open door, a broom in his hand. The dear fellow had been keeping after the infernal dust even though no one lived there anymore.

Twenty-three

Mistress Grace came slowly with Mai Lin to guide her. Ahcho held open the door to the house that had not been a home for months. His heart lifted at the thought of the baby arriving at its proper residence, but when he did not see the small bundle, he hoped that everything was all right. He had seven children of his own, and they each had seven children. He was a happy man because of it, even in these lean times when they had been scattered to the winds. It was known in his family that a baby placed in his arms would soon be charmed to sleep. He hoped he would have the opportunity to show this to the Reverend and his wife with their daughter.

Mistress Grace paused at the threshold and said, "Thank you, Ahcho, for all you have done to maintain things while I was away. You are most good to us."

Ahcho bowed solemnly and hoped that his face didn't betray his concern, for he couldn't help noticing that she didn't look at all well. Her sallow complexion matched her dingy white gown. All of her seemed covered by a yellowish tint: her fair skin, her lace dress, the white stockings, and her light brown hair all dusted by a thin layer of loess, the loamy deposit that he spent far too many hours each day sweeping ineffectually from the floorboards and rugs.

At night, he would shut and lock the front door, and in the morning, he'd still find small piles of the dusty sand pushed up against the walls and crammed into every crevice of this, the finest home in the Christian compound. Try as he might, Ahcho was unable to keep it clean. He had an impulse to use the broom to whisk the loess off his mistress now, or to at least employ a washcloth and lye soap, but of course he would never do such a disrespectful thing. It fell to Mai Lin, if she did her job properly, to help free their mistress of the dirty cloud that surrounded her.

"Mistress is hungry?" he asked. "I will prepare your dinner."

"No, thank you, Ahcho. Very kind of you, though."

She walked with gentle steps into the parlor, where he was pleased to have dusted only an hour before.

"I'll eat something," Mai Lin said.

Ahcho ignored her and stood instead behind his mistress as she looked at the lone photograph on the mantel. Inside a dark wooden frame, intricately carved with vines and blossoms, was a daguerreotype of the Watson family. With eyes pinned on the photographer, the Reverend stood in a light linen suit, his collar buttoned high, his gold-rimmed glasses glinting in the sun, and a clear expression on his face. Beside the young Reverend stood Mistress Grace. She wore a simple smock with black boots hidden under the shadow of the hem and held a rumpled linen hat in one hand. She, too, stared directly into the camera and did not smile. They didn't hold hands but stood shoulder to shoulder, a matched set, although he was so much taller. Ahcho was proud of the handsome and serious young couple at the start of their important work here in Fenchow-fu, where they would do so much good for others.

Standing in front of them was their small boy, Wesley. He wore knickers and a sailor top. In his arms he held a heavy-looking glass jar filled with American pennies, his greatest treasure. Ahcho remembered picking up the annoying coins from the floor and scolding the little boy to fetch them himself from then on. Ahcho regretted ever speaking harshly to the lad, who in the photo squinted with ferocious curiosity out at the world.

Ahcho wondered if Wesley's mother was noticing now that neither parent touched the child. No hand rested protectively on his shoulder, no fingers reached for his small hand. He was not tucked into his mother's side. Instead, little Wesley seemed all alone as he glared into the years ahead, poised to conquer, full of great seriousness and strength for someone so small. He had the countenance of a future leader, someone like his father who would bring people together to accomplish great things. Could the boy have been a prince all along? Ahcho wondered now.

Grace turned abruptly from the fireplace and cleared her throat, attempting to hide what Ahcho suspected were tears. "You must bring me to the Reverend at once," she announced.

Ahcho clasped his hands behind his back and bent forward as if he had not heard her correctly. "Madam?"

She turned to Mai Lin. "I shall see my husband now. I have important family business to discuss with him."

Mai Lin reached for Mistress Grace's arm, but she pulled away.

"I don't want to hear either of you telling me that I can't go. After I see my husband, I shall sleep for days and will be a most agreeable patient. But if you make me stay here, I swear I will not rest for a single moment and will make us all miserable."

She crossed her arms over her chest and waited for a reply. Ahcho didn't dare shoot a confirming glance at Mai Lin, but he could tell by the clucking sounds emanating from her that she agreed with him that the mistress's plan was most absurd.

"Why, I don't know where the Reverend is," he said.

Grace stamped a delicate foot on the carpet, and a cloud of yellow dust wafted around her. "Of course you do," she said. "You've known all along. You know far more than you let on. I don't hold it against you, but this is most urgent. You must take me to him."

Now Ahcho did look at Mai Lin, but she could only offer a mystified expression. What had come over their feeble mistress, Ahcho wanted to ask, to make her suddenly so strong a soul?

"I really ought to change out of my wedding dress, but we haven't the time," Mistress Grace continued. "I saw the Master's traveling coat hanging on the hook in the hall. Fetch it for me, please, Mai Lin."

Ahcho used his calmest voice as he said, "I don't mean to offend, Mistress, but you don't look well enough to make an expedition. You appear to be quite ill. Wouldn't you rather be in your bed with your baby at your side?"

Mistress Grace appeared to blanch for a moment at this commonsense suggestion, but she answered, "It is precisely because of my condition that I can't hesitate. I shall ride on donkey back. I have done it before. I am quite able."

Mai Lin returned with the Reverend's ragged traveling coat and held it up. The mistress slipped her arms into it. When she took an awkward spin in the long coat, it swished and more loess hovered in the air before settling on the rug.

"It's good you don't mind donkey back," Ahcho said to humor her, "because we no longer have a wagon."

"Is that so?" Grace asked with little concern in her voice, no sign that she grasped her situation. "How about a horse?"

"Long gone, I'm afraid."

"Ah," she said brightly. "Well, as I said, I'll be fine on a donkey. Thank you, Ahcho. I will wait outside on the porch for you. It is a lovely spring afternoon. The fresh air will be good for my lungs. But do come along and don't dawdle, please. I must see my husband today, and nightfall will soon be upon us."

Ahcho bowed, but he was not pleased. When the screen door wheezed shut and they heard the mistress's footsteps recede, Ahcho and Mai Lin stared at one another with wide eyes.

"Aieee!" she said in a harsh whisper. "They are cuckoo, the two of them."

"Don't be disrespectful," he said. "The Reverend is a great man. He built the roads and the hospital and—"

"Yes, yes," Mai Lin said, "I know about his accomplishments, but that was some time ago. He's no longer a great man."

"I disagree. The Reverend has faced terrible trials recently, but he will always be a great man, and his wife a fine lady."

Mai Lin waved her hand at him.

"They just need rest and peace," Ahcho said. "That's all."

"True," Mai Lin had to concede, but then she sidled up to him and poked at his chest with a bent finger. "Which, I do not need to tell you, they won't find on a dangerous journey to the Gobi Desert. And have you considered that their new baby might be kidnapped out there like the other one?"

She looked up at him with searching eyes, but Ahcho was not a man to discuss grave things lightly. It worried him terribly that a family's fate rested in his hands. He was no god, nor had he ever been meant to be one. For weeks now, he had tossed and turned sleeplessly. He wasn't any closer to understanding what to do than the evening he had shared a bottle with the traveling trader who had told him of the golden-haired prince who was surely better off wherever he was than this sorry lot here.

Ahcho pinched shut his lips and looked away.

"Sometimes," Mai Lin said with a coy singsong in her voice, "the Fates decide things for us. Our role is simply to sit back and watch."

Ahcho gazed into her sparkling dark eyes. For once, she appeared to intend nothing but good. As annoying as Mai Lin could be, she was loyal and sometimes even wise. For a rare moment, he allowed himself to relax. Perhaps, just this once, she was right. The Good Lord was watching over them all. Ahcho, as a simple servant of God, had only to steer the donkey on its path.

Twenty-four

As the other families attended the burial of the Martins' daughter, Mistress Grace and Ahcho plodded out from the compound and into dusk. She fussed for many miles, but he didn't listen. She was flabbergasted that they had only one donkey now. Had she known that the old gentleman would have to walk the whole way, she would have insisted on some other mode of transport. He didn't wish to be disrespectful, but this was a ridiculous notion. Nor did he mention that he had borrowed the donkey from the Martins by bribing their number-two boy with a precious cigarette. This sorry animal was one of the very last beasts of burden in the compound and had to be returned to them without fail this same night so that it could cart that family away the next morning.

On they walked, Ahcho holding the reins of the tired animal. As he tromped along before it, Grace sat perched upon its back in her long white dress, both legs dangling over one side against a thick blanket. It was not lost on him that they resembled that blessed man and woman on their way to Bethlehem. Although he did not mean to suggest, even in his mind, that they were that sort of couple. He wished only that he could promise his mistress as warm a greeting as the shepherds had given the Virgin Mary on that deep winter night so long ago. If only he could bring her to as pure and simple a setting as the stable where the straw had been warm and the animals had stood guard. He longed, most of all, for her to hear angels singing all around. He liked to think of the cherubim, those chubby babies whose cheeks were always pink and whose voices no doubt rang out like high and happy church bells. He longed for his mistress to hear such sweet music and not the frightening cries of the banshees that cascaded down from the craggy mountains in the near distance.

But he knew too well the sort of place where he was taking her, and that by doing so, he had become an altogether different character from one inspired by the Good Book. He was now like Judas, a man who loved his master so, but through some will not entirely his own was forced to betray him. This part of the story Ahcho had never fully understood. He needed the Reverend to instruct him again on this most disturbing section of the Bible. For he had grasped that the betrayal was wrong, and a sign of human weakness, and yet it was somehow also blessed, for only through this betrayal had Jesus been brought back to humankind as a true God.

Ahcho shook his head at this paradox of faith and fate, evil and goodness. It reminded him of the old superstitions, which he refused to believe any longer but which crept into his thinking just the same. Somehow Judas's story made sense, and yet it did not in any rational way. Ahcho fancied himself a man of science, as he had been taught by his master, and so preferred for things to be explicable. And yet sometimes they clearly were not. If only the Reverend were here.

Ahcho knew that his master would not want Mistress Grace to find him at his current location, and yet, for some reason that only

God, and perhaps the great Reverend, could understand, it had fallen to Ahcho to bring her to him. As they traipsed over the dry, rocky ground and each footfall ached, he kept repeating the story in his mind. Judas had been deeply loved by the Lord. And Judas had loved the Lord every bit as much, if not more, than the other disciples. Yet somehow that love had turned and twisted and turned again, in the manner of the desert wind that lifted the sand into the air at sunset now, swirling around Ahcho's boots and around the poorly shod hoofs of this last, forlorn donkey. Ahcho's mouth filled with the sorrowful grit that Judas must have tasted, too.

The rocky trail had passed through the plains, and the foothills grew nearer. Ahcho tried to think of the words that the Reverend would have used to admire the dark purple shadows, but he couldn't recall even a single poetic phrase. He chastised himself for not better absorbing the great man's wisdom. It was as if all the profound lessons he had learned were slipping away in his master's absence.

In the last light of day, Ahcho turned toward the abandoned hamlet. Having lived in Fenchow-fu all his sixty years, he knew every trail through the plains. He could have shut his eyes and still known the way. And yet the landscape around them was too mysterious to ever be truly grasped. The sun hung low in the sky, and the moon had also risen. Orange sunset bathed the mistress's face in a golden glow, but when Ahcho turned to see a dead tree by a dry riverbed, or the stark boulder that marked the last turn in the road, these things stood silhouetted and silver against a darkening backdrop. The brightness of day ebbed before his eyes, and all was sketched in charcoal. The edges became smudged as each thing grew softer and more forgiving. The cool night air caressed his cheeks and dried the sweat from his brow.

Ahcho wished with all his heart that this hallowed peacefulness could last, but he knew better. The night was only the night and the desert as menacing as ever.

"Not much farther, Mistress," he said. Then he bowed his head and added too softly for her to hear, "May God and the Reverend forgive me."

Twenty-five

Ahcho placed his aged fingers upon the rope handle of the door that hung now on only one hinge. The wind, suddenly up, rushed across the desert miles and shook it slightly, as if insisting they enter. He looked down upon Mistress Grace and wanted to brush aside her strands of hair covered in golden loess, but he did not. Ahcho did, however, think it appropriate to brush the yellow loess from the shoulders of the Reverend's traveling coat that she wore. He wished he had his whisk broom to do the job properly. His fingers left marks on the oilcloth as if the mistress had been pawed by a bear. The front of her gown where the dust had crept under the coat was clearly ruined. A mustard-yellow tint had seeped into the fine lace so completely that Mai Lin would never get it close to white again. Their mistress appeared as bedraggled as a street urchin, which suited this setting more than she could know.

"Perhaps you would prefer to wait out here, and I will bring the Reverend to you? You will have a moment to compose yourself, and I can help the Reverend do the same."

"Dear Ahcho," she said with that same unreal, happy lilt in her voice, "you are such a good fellow, but you mustn't try so hard to save us from ourselves."

She chuckled faintly, and then the coughing began. Ahcho knew his mistress was not well in several crucial ways. Her body was still weak from childbirth and also wracked with illness, but he worried just as much about her mind. He let her lean into him as her narrow shoulders heaved with the paroxysms, and he could feel her delicate body shudder under the massive coat.

Ahcho looked about to find a seat for her, but there was not a bench nor a log nor even a rock in the deserted courtyard.

"I believe we should retreat," he said more emphatically. "I will put you back on the donkey, and I can trot us home to safety. You will be asleep in your bed in no time."

When her coughing finally subsided, she looked up with a scarlet face lined by yellow dust. Yellow loam glistened on her chapped lips, and more mixed with spittle on her chin. Her eyelashes stuck together to form stars encrusted by it. Poor girl, he thought, for in that moment, she resembled a child more than a woman. A frightened child made dimly aware of her mortality by the onslaught of a fever and a cough more than by ever having seen life played out in others. She was still so innocent—ignorant, really—and more desperate than she would acknowledge.

"Please, Mistress Grace," he said with unusual familiarity, "we must leave before it is too late."

She reached for his hand, and he hoped she was finally about to heed his words. But instead, she lifted it to the rope handle, turned, and pushed open the door.

The dark room before them swirled as motes of dust were caught in the last streaks of day. Sunset skidded over the threshold, exposing emptiness—a chamber that had once held buckwheat grain or sacks of hemp waiting to be taken to market. Dried game may once have hung from the low rafters. Now a swag of herbs swayed in the afternoon breeze with a lonely rustling.

"I see I'm wrong. No one's here," Ahcho said. "I brought you all this way for nothing. So sorry! We will go now."

Grace stepped down onto the dirt floor and held up her hand. "Sh-sh-sh," she whispered as she walked deeper into the room.

Ahcho, practically stumbling over her heels, repeated, "Please, Madam, we go."

But now she had reached the door that led into the second chamber and smiled at him over her shoulder.

"I must warn you," he began, but it was too late.

Grace had turned the handle and pushed open the second wooden plank. Smoke curled out from the darkness of the back chamber, and Ahcho followed his mistress as she continued toward the lamplight. More than the stinging smoke, he hated the stench. Ahcho pulled out his handkerchief, one of the master's own, and offered it to the mistress, but she shook her head. He lifted the thin fabric to his nose and tried not to gag. Mistress Grace did not stop but proceeded into the room, which slowly came into focus as Ahcho's eyes adjusted to the dim light.

The sight was the same as it had been when he'd come here before: all around them on dingy mats lay mere stick figures with sallow eyes and sunken cheeks. Some sucked on opium pipes as the oil lamps were fired up and smoking. Ahcho tried not to look too closely for the source of the constant moaning. In a corner, the same young girls huddled, their heads upon one another's bare breasts, their legs and arms riddled with sores. They looked like tattered dolls, flung about unclothed and uncared-for. Their eyes stared fiercely in search of something—food, no doubt. They didn't even have the strength to rise and curl themselves around the visitors and beg. Ahcho almost missed their pathetic attentions, but he could see that they had lost all life.

The smell was unbearable, and Ahcho tried again to hand his mistress the Reverend's handkerchief. This time she took it, but she didn't press it to her nose, where it might have done some good.

"We've seen enough," he whispered. "I will ask if they know the Reverend's whereabouts, but then we must leave. They have the sickness."

Grace studied the prone figures. "These people?" she asked, finally taking in the drugged and ill bodies.

"The cholera, Mistress. That explains the smell."

As he said it, she finally pressed the cloth to her nose and began to gag. And yet she still did not turn back. Instead, Ahcho followed his mistress as her dusty, cracked boots shuffled toward the niche where the gamblers had once tossed their dice and raised their voices in drunken boasts. Only one or two men sat on the hard ground now, their legs splayed and their backs slumped against the damp mud walls.

An oil lamp flickered from where it had been placed upon a barrel beside a straw mattress. Upon that primitive bed lay the shriveled figure of the old proprietress of the brothel.

Ahcho stepped around the corner and now saw what had stopped his mistress in her tracks. There, in the darkest shadow, seated on a small stool placed against the wall, was the Reverend. His head remained bowed, and his hands lay folded in his lap, the fingers nervously fingering the sack that held the orb. Ahcho noticed immediately how sallow and ill shaven his cheeks had become. The man needed his proper ablutions. Ahcho stepped closer and would have given anything to attend to his master, or at least fling away that terrible hat given to him by the nomads. It pained Ahcho to see it still cocked crookedly upon the Reverend's head.

Mistress Grace, however, did not appear nearly as upset by the sight of her husband as Ahcho had anticipated. She heaved a deep sigh, and her shoulders drooped with relief. Her entire being appeared to grow calm in his presence. Ahcho couldn't imagine such a reaction: for him, the sight of the Reverend brought forth an almost violent urge to do something.

The mistress inched closer, and Ahcho sensed that she wished to reach out to the Reverend, who remained sunk deep in his own thoughts. No doubt he was praying. Clearly, she wanted to rouse him and make him know that she had come for him. But she did not. She remained quiet and waited to be noticed by the man who was a shrunken version of his former self.

The Reverend's back sat curled and bent. His long legs were crossed like a scholar's, and his tattered trousers and worn boots trembled. Upon a closer look, Ahcho could see that all of the Reverend's thin limbs were shaking. The great man had been reduced to nerves and sinews with very little meat or muscle on him any longer. Ahcho could tell he was exhausted and needed food. He was wasting away.

Ahcho became aware of the raspy, irregular breathing that emanated from the proprietress under a coarse blanket on the bed. The smell of decay and human stench in this corner was so severe, it made

Ahcho's eyes burn. He longed to remove both his master and mistress from this wretched place.

But Mistress Grace seemed undaunted by sight and smell. She moved closer and reached out a delicate, tentative hand toward her husband's shoulder. Her pale fingers hovered, unsure and yet brave, until she finally bestowed a firm grip upon him. The Reverend flinched at being touched, his gaze whipping upward and all about like the eyes of a cornered animal. He staggered off the stool and fumbled with the red sash across his chest until his hand took hold of the pouch that hung at his hip. Once he had it in a tight grip, he grew calm again and seemed to finally see his wife standing before him. To Ahcho's surprise, once the initial shock of being interrupted at his prayers subsided, the Reverend did not appear one bit surprised to see Mistress Grace.

"My dear," the Reverend said, his hand fiddling with the pouch and his eyes darting uneasily about the room.

Ahcho cringed to see the great man so weakened. What had happened to him here? This place had changed him in ways that Ahcho feared might be unalterable. At that very moment, poisonous opium, or something worse, must be coursing through the Reverend's veins, otherwise why would he behave so strangely? He needed to be carried home immediately, fed, and straightened out. A good bath would surely help.

For the first time since the mistress had suggested this nightmarish visit, Ahcho was able to imagine that something good might come of it. He and Mistress Grace would bring the Reverend back to his senses. Although night had descended outside by now, they would, metaphorically speaking, lead him out of the darkness of this vile hovel and into the pure light of the mission again. The Reverend needed merely to be carried forth, and soon they would all live together in the finest house in the compound. Ahcho waited for her to tell her husband this plan so that their journey home might begin.

"My darling," she replied in a voice as thin and weak as her husband's.

They didn't step closer, although clearly they had missed one another's company. They were proper people who did not show private emotions in public. Ahcho approved of this.

"You are attending to the sick?" Grace asked.

The Reverend's gaze drifted down to the proprietress's shriveled face, which poked out from beneath the covers. He nodded somberly, and Ahcho felt reassured that the Reverend was maintaining his good practices. Perhaps he really had been praying.

"Master offers last rites to the old, evil one?" Ahcho asked hopefully.

The Reverend squeezed the pouch on his hip with white knuckles and said, "No, I was merely wiping the liquid away. I can hardly keep up with it. She is seeping something terrible. I remember a goat that once ate nettles and managed to swallow a segment of barbed wire. Her insides oozed out of her for days. This illness is not unlike that."

"Oh, how awful," Mistress Grace said.

Ahcho hoped the Reverend might agree that the condition here was equally terrible, but he did not. Instead, he bent over the dying creature and whisked away flies. Then he bent closer—far too close, Ahcho felt—and pinched his fingers against the greasy scalp and pulled out a bug.

He held his hand up to the lamplight and exclaimed, "Aha! I have rescued another soul."

"Dear God," the mistress said.

Her knees buckled, and Ahcho caught her arm and steadied her.

"Yes, dear God," the Reverend said and shook his head as if remembering someone fondly from his childhood.

"We must go home now," she said, regaining her composure. "Our compatriots are all setting out tomorrow morning on their long journey back to America. The compound is soon to be empty, and we must not abandon ship like the others."

"A ship?" the Reverend asked, distracted again by the gasping breaths of the body below them on the mat.

"You are the captain of our ship," she reminded him, finding now a firmness in her voice that Ahcho admired. "You must return to it before it sinks."

"Our ship is sinking?" he asked.

"Not literally, my darling," she said.

"Ah." He raised himself up. "You mean figuratively. This is a crucial distinction. Listen closely, Ahcho," the Reverend said, pointing at him. "Your mistress has something to teach you. She is a clever girl. And brave. My goodness, she is brave to have come all this way and to have left behind a life of ease."

"Don't concern yourself with that now, my love," she said as she took her husband's arm and began to walk him away from the sickbed. "None of it can be helped. We are what we are."

The Reverend patted her arm and agreed, "We are."

"What's done is done," she said as she steered him across the room.

"Done, all done," he murmured.

They were making real progress and had almost made it to the exit of the interior chamber when the Reverend looked down at her and shouted, "Unhand me!" He wrenched his arm free as if she had held it in an iron grip, which clearly she had not. Ahcho couldn't help wondering whatever was the matter with the Reverend's mind.

Grace stumbled back.

The Reverend began scratching his shins under his pant legs. He brushed aside his jacket, lifted his shirt, and scratched his inflamed belly. Ahcho knew he would have to work hard to rescue him from the maddening insects, but luckily he had many methods and would not hesitate to try them all until the battle was won. Perhaps his master's unstable mental condition could be corrected by proper fumigation.

The Reverend stopped and fixed his eyes on his wife. "Woman," he said both sternly and loudly, "have you ever seen a louse living in a pair of trousers?"

The men and women asleep or lost in a haze of opium on their beds turned to stare with vague interest in their eyes.

Grace replied, "No, dear Reverend. I have not."

"Well, then, you cannot possibly understand."

The Reverend began to pace as he spoke. He lifted his long arms, and Ahcho could not help recalling the sermons that had made his master famous in this land. His stature, his wisdom, the truth that fell from his lips had rung out over the little chapel, echoing as far away as the hills and the desert beyond. Ahcho's Reverend had preached of man's sin and God's forgiveness and the hope, the pure and absolute hope, of eternal rest and salvation. Ahcho had felt it—he had known it—in the Reverend's words. There was a better world beyond. Heaven awaited us, all who believed and repented. Ahcho knew this because the Reverend had spoken of it.

"The louse," the Reverend continued in his grandest oratorical manner. Several in their deathbeds stirred. "The louse regards the trousers as a fine and prosperous home. He feels he has attained a well-regulated and honorable life. A decent life. A godly life. But soon, flames will come over the hills. Fire, the like of which has never been seen before, will spread. Villages will burn. Cities will fall. And then the lice will perish!"

The Reverend bowed his head in what appeared to be abject sorrow, and Ahcho waited for uplifting words to rise from his master's throat. Hope was waiting in the next sentence, Ahcho was certain. They would escape this wretched place.

But the Reverend looked around the room, taking in the miserable creatures whose lives leaked out of them in smoke and blood and bodily fluids. He growled, "And the man you wish to be, how does he differ from the louse?" He waved his arms at the evil on all sides and asked, "Is this not trousers?"

The mistress and Ahcho waited for more, but the Reverend's expression shifted again, and he appeared suddenly lost and confused. He pulled his spectacles away from his eyes and wiped them on the tails of the filthy shirt that hung below his threadbare jacket. He did not speak again to his sorry parishioners but only muttered to himself, "Heaven and earth are my dwelling, and my house is my trousers. I am no better than the Confucian lice and no wiser than the Daoists who invented this parable to illustrate Confucian profligacy. I am Liu Ling, a gentleman corrupted by my narrow, spoiled vision of the world. I am, without question, a louse."

The Reverend placed his glasses back upon his nose, and Ahcho noticed that one of the lenses was cracked. The Chinese gentleman's name the Reverend had spoken sounded familiar, but Ahcho could not place it at first. Then it came to him. He recalled that Liu Ling had been a drunken, hedonistic poet of the Han Dynasty, many hundreds of years before. In his incoherent and impromptu sermon, the Reverend had been citing a foolish ancient argument, a common Daoist story invented to illustrate Confucian corruption. The Daoists hated Confucian immoderation, but the Daoists themselves were heathens of the first order, too, believing as they did in the dangerous old superstitions. Mai Lin's frequent mutterings about Fate and Destiny were an example of their wrongheadedness. All those old religions were like haggling crones at the market, Ahcho thought. They had nothing of use to say anymore.

"Reverend," Ahcho said, "you shouldn't be bothered by such stupid, outdated arguments. Your way is far better and more modern. Don't fill your mind with such absurdity."

The Reverend looked up. "You believe that's so?" he asked.

"Of course I do! And you do, too!" Ahcho answered with what he hoped was a strong enough jolt of enthusiasm and reality to dislodge the Reverend from the shoals of religious relativism where he had momentarily been beached. "Come now, the Mistress is right, we must go home. The little chapel is waiting for you. Tomorrow is Sunday!"

"Ah," the Reverend said, his voice far off again. "Sunday is the holiest of days. But you know, some religions say that Saturday is the chosen day."

Why was the Reverend bothering to concern his great mind with other religions? Ahcho had the urge to knock some sense into the bedraggled man. But at just that moment, Mistress Grace beat him to it. She pulled back her tiny fist and socked the Reverend in the arm.

That finally got his attention, and he stared at her with remarkably fond eyes and a charming smile. "I have been ignoring you again, my love," he said. "You must learn to speak up, but that love pat you just bestowed upon me also works quite well, too. I gather that today's women employ that method quite often. Gone are the meek feminine souls of yesteryear."

She let out an irritated growl and said, "You must listen to me."

"I shall do my best to concentrate on your every word," the Reverend said, "although parasites, hunger, and overall misery and fatigue can drive a mind to distraction."

He raised his bushy eyebrows and actually smiled. This was the Reverend that Ahcho knew: clever and bright and true. And yet Ahcho felt he should not be encouraging his wife so. Modern did not mean undisciplined.

Mistress Grace planted herself before her husband, her hands on her hips, and spoke with surprising authority. "While you have been occupied elsewhere, I was forced to make the most difficult decision of my life. Our precious daughter, whom I love with all my heart, needs a safer and healthier setting to grow up in. America, not here. But I'm not well, Reverend. Not well at all, and I fear I wouldn't survive the long journey home. Also, I couldn't possibly leave without you, my love."

He smiled at her in genuine, fond reciprocation.

"So," she continued, "I have asked the Reverend and Mrs. Martin to take her with them when they leave Fenchow-fu tomorrow morning. They will raise her until we are able to be reunited. I can't bear that I might not see dear Rose again, but at least she won't die of some disease or starvation or be kidnapped in this frightful land. I came to fetch you back to the compound tonight so we may bid them farewell in the morning."

The Reverend's calm expression shifted. Ahcho waited for his master's former sternness to erupt. The baby was leaving the mother and father. That could not be right. Such a decision about a family should never be made by the wife. This was unfathomable. The balance of things was all askew. The Reverend needed to set her straight. It was not too late to do so. There was still time to be reunited with their child this very night. If Ahcho had known that this was his mistress's reckless plan, he would not have hesitated to find the Reverend right away.

But, much to Ahcho's dismay, the Reverend merely put one hand into his pants pocket while the other remained gripped over the round shape in the pouch with the twin golden dragons at his hip. He fiddled with the strings that closed the bag and with the red cloth from which it hung.

"Did you hear me?" she repeated.

The Reverend nodded but still did not speak.

"What on earth is in that infernal pouch that swings at your side?" she asked. "You clutch it as if it were the Holy Grail itself. Let me see it!"

The Reverend yanked the pouch upward and tucked it inside his coat. He buttoned the few sagging buttons as quickly as he could with trembling fingers. "It is something," he said.

"I know it is something," Mistress Grace said. "You have carried it with you ever since our son was stolen from us. What is in that sack embroidered with the twin golden dragons, Reverend?"

He patted at the thing behind the worn fabric of his suit jacket and bit his bottom lip. "Ahcho, help me," he stuttered and lifted a finger to his lips to suggest that he wished their secret to be kept. "I'm not thinking clearly enough to explain."

It pained Ahcho to see his master's plaintive expression, and he wanted to help the hungry and confused man. Also, Ahcho didn't like the mistress's insolent tone, but he supposed that was how things were with young women these days. So he sucked in his breath between clenched teeth, looked at his feet, and began.

"Mrs. Watson, on that tragic day, which I wish barely to mention, we found something left behind by the kidnappers. The Reverend, of course, is not a man of primitive superstition, but he does somehow believe that carrying this object with him at all times will help him in his search to find his son."

The Reverend nodded his approval at this explanation, and Ahcho felt he had done his duty to his master as best as he could under these trying circumstances.

Mistress Grace frowned. "But what is it, exactly? I must know."

The Reverend's whole body vibrated, and he swung his head wildly from side to side. Then he began to scratch his legs again, next his arms, and Ahcho thought he could feel his master's misery. The man needed a bath, a good meal, and sleep to restore his nerves and mind.

"I'm afraid it would not be wise for you to know, Mistress. It is better if the object stays quietly with the Reverend. We don't need to concern ourselves with such silly superstitions, am I right?" Ahcho tried. "We Christians don't believe in old wives' tales. We are people of Jesus, not country types who see witches flying about after dark and spit over our shoulders when we pass wells and spin around three times before planting. We believe nothing of the sort."

The Reverend and Mrs. Watson bobbed their heads, as if weighing the validity of each custom.

"Come," Ahcho said with more force than he had ever used in speaking to either of them before. "I insist. We go now!"

"Such a good man, Ahcho," the Reverend said. "Good to the core."

The mistress nodded in agreement, and the couple seemed warmly united in this one thing. But still the Reverend did not budge from the center of the dimly lit room.

Mistress Grace turned to her husband and quietly asked, "Have you anything to say about my plan? It's hard for me to imagine that you feel nothing for our daughter."

"My darling," the Reverend said and moved closer to her. He pushed a lock of dusty hair from her brow. "It is *because* I love our child dearly that I trust you to know what is best. I don't know much anymore about anything. I'm in a miserable state. Really, I know so very little and never did." These last words were spoken with great sincerity.

Ahcho let out a tsking sound of the type that usually issued forth from Mai Lin. The Reverend's self-assessment was all wrong. And honestly, how could he turn over such an important decision to a member of the weaker sex, especially one who herself was clearly so weak? Had the Reverend not noticed how ill his wife had become in his absence? Did he not see that she, too, was a withered and unhealthy soul, or did the Reverend's feebleness of body and mind make him blind to her condition?

The Reverend took his wife's hands into his own and continued, "I have been a sorry husband and an even sorrier father. I leave this next chapter to you because you are the wiser one. I see that now with great clarity. When God made woman of man's rib, I can only think that inside that bone was stored the very best of humanity. Why else do we suck on the marrow for so long if it were not the most precious part? You are by far the better half."

Grace nodded, a slight smile on her face, but Ahcho did not see any such thing clearly. The Reverend had always spoken in this colorful way with examples that were meant to illuminate, but now the man's words were merely pretty pictures and nothing more. Ahcho felt he had to rid his master of the terrible lice and whatever poisons went through his veins so that he could regain his senses and become a precise thinker again. He was the man of the household, and he needed to behave as such.

Mistress Grace wavered happily before her husband, her body swaying. She shifted, and dust rose and clouded her boots and the hem of her dress and the ragged bottom of the traveling coat. The Reverend did not seem to notice her strange attire, the sickly pallor of her skin, and the brume of dust that surrounded her. Instead, he appeared as smitten as a boy first in love.

The Reverend gripped his wife's hand more tightly, but he did not offer her the shoulder that she needed to lean against, nor did he put his arm around her as a husband should to hold her upright. The Reverend only gazed with hopeless love in his eyes. He was quite useless.

"You will return home with me, then, if I am the better one," Mistress Grace said. She gazed up into her husband's blue eyes and added, "And you will do as I say from now on."

She did not ask him but instead told him. Then she extracted her hand from his, turned, and proceeded toward the door. After several paces, she looked back over her shoulder and beckoned.

This was not at all how Ahcho would have liked the discussion to go, but he could see that his mistress was crafty. She was using the Reverend's erroneous perspective to trick him into returning to safety. Ahcho did not approve of this notion of the modern woman, but if it worked to bring the Reverend to safety again, he could not disagree.

"I shall come along soon, dear Grace," the Reverend said. "Quite soon."

Mistress Grace looked back toward her husband across the smoky room, and a strange look of recognition appeared over her face. "You say you will follow me soon, Reverend?"

"Precisely," the Reverend said. "I still have business to attend to here."

"You must attend to the dying?" she asked with great feeling.

"Yes, the dying. I feel it is my task now."

She nodded and gazed at him sympathetically, unwilling, though, to challenge the enormous mistake that seemed about to occur.

"Tell me, do they still believe you are a Ghost Man?" she asked.

The Reverend's head swayed as he replied, "I think not. I may, however, be a man inhabited by ghosts."

"Ah," Mistress Grace said as she chuckled lightly to herself, "I understand."

The Reverend smiled similarly, and the two of them appeared amused at some bizarre notion that they alone shared. Ahcho did not condone this perturbing union between them, but he felt helpless to correct it.

Then Mistress Grace turned and departed from the room without another word, neglecting to protest or insist but instead leaving her husband surrounded by pariahs and jackals of the first order. Ahcho could tell that something had transpired between them, some comprehension that he sensed was neither prudent nor good.

The Reverend and Mrs. Watson needed fervent prayer and careful instruction. But who would minister to them, he wondered, now that the Reverend Charles Martin and the others were leaving? It fell to reason that the task would be his. Ahcho, the first and most sincere of the Reverend's converts, as the great man had always said, would have to carry on the mission.

He straightened up taller and hurried after his mistress, who had already escorted herself outside. He neglected to say good-bye to the Reverend but made the decision that he would return the following day to bring him home as only a man could. He had always been dependable, but now he saw that it was his turn to fully take the reins.

When Ahcho stepped up and over the threshold, the desert night air struck him with its coolness and clarity. The moon and stars blazed in a pure black sky. Yes, he could do it. He could run the mission and carry on until the Reverend was well again. He even pictured himself behind the simple podium in the chapel. A small sea of Chinese faces would look up at him hopefully. Perhaps, in time, and using the best of the Reverend's practices, their numbers would rise again. Ahcho would pray that it was not sacrilege to envision a good future arising from his master's tragedy. But since he did so in the name of the Father and the Son and the Holy Ghost, he suspected it was acceptable.

Twenty-six

Later that same night, Mai Lin helped her mistress back into bed on the second floor of the Watson house in the mission compound. The fever was upon her again, and Mai Lin wished she had been firmer and not allowed the young woman to go out on the foolish expedition to find her husband. Ahcho had explained that they had actually seen and spoken to the Reverend, but he'd chosen not to return with them. The willful girl had risked her life for naught.

When morning came, and the other families of the compound met in the courtyard below to bid farewell to their servants, Mistress Grace remained delirious and unable to rise from her bed. Mai Lin kept cool cloths on her forehead and spooned water over her parched and dusty lips. As the donkey carts finally started to lumber away under the weight of the Americans' many possessions, Mai Lin leaned out the bedroom window for one last glimpse of Rose Baby.

Mildred Martin sat beside her husband upon their buckboard, a bundle held lovingly to her chest. As the American caravan pulled out of the mission gates, Mai Lin allowed herself to wonder if the wicked Mrs. Martin was not quite so evil after all.

Mistress Grace continued to sleep fitfully all that afternoon, calling out often for her baby girl. Mai Lin had to admit that she might improve more quickly with her husband at her side. When Ahcho announced he intended to try again to retrieve the Reverend that very day, Mai Lin entreated him to do so posthaste. The parents would find solace together at this difficult time with their daughter now gone from their lives. Ahcho set out before midday, and the afternoon passed slowly in the desolate compound. Mai Lin liked the quiet and even managed to nap some, but mostly, she attended to her mistress, who appeared to be feeling better as night fell again. The moon came up, and still Ahcho had not come home. For a brief while, Mistress Grace sat against her pillows and sipped broth. She asked for Rose Baby once again, but when Mai Lin started to answer, the grieving mother interrupted.

"I remember now," she said. "I can feel it in my heart that she's gone. My whole body knows she's no longer at my side."

Then, finally and for the first time all day, Mistress Grace slept soundly, and Mai Lin did so, too.

Later, much later, deep in the dark hours, Mai Lin awoke in her cot to hear camel bells approaching. She went to the window and opened the shutters and saw only darkness, but still she kept watch. The mistress must have sensed her vigilance because she shifted in the bed and let out a soft, indistinguishable sound—a question that hung on the quiet air. Mai Lin went to her and placed a wrist on her forehead. The fever had broken, but the young woman still breathed restlessly, her chest heaving as the fluid thickened. Mai Lin returned to the window and was about to close the shutters against the chill when she heard it again. This time the bells sounded quite nearby, followed by a soft thud on the ground directly below the window.

Mai Lin leaned out and saw the shape of a tall figure whom she hoped was the Reverend. The man stood, and the long queue down his back glistened in the moonlight. There on the ground at Ahcho's feet was a bag of sand, or maybe, if they were lucky, a bag of rice. Mai Lin could already imagine the taste of it.

But she sensed that her old eyes were deceiving her as they often did, and so she squinted harder. Something wasn't right. A few paces from the porch steps, Ahcho fell to his knees. Mai Lin then made out the shape of what lay on the ground. She quickly closed the shutters with a clatter, and the mistress awoke.

"Is something out there?" her mistress asked.

"You sleep," Mai Lin said. "The fever is finally better, but you still need rest."

"They have returned. I know it. Ahcho has brought my husband back to me."

Mistress Grace pushed herself higher in the bed, pulled off the covers, and reached for her robe. Mai Lin wanted to yank the covers over her legs again, but her mistress was already putting on her slippers and sliding down from the bed. Such a foolish girl to imagine she was well. But sometimes, Mai Lin thought, you had to let the river run its course.

"Help me, Mai Lin. I must see my husband right away."

Mistress Grace's voice fluttered forth both feeble and determined. For once, Mai Lin did not argue or explain. She lit a lamp and carried it in one hand as with the other she held her mistress's arm. In this way, the frail young woman made her way into the hall, down the steps, and across the front entrance.

Mai Lin held open the screen door, and Mistress Grace flew past and down the porch steps. The cool night air struck Mai Lin as most dangerous. It would reach down into her mistress's lungs with wet fingers and cause the cough to return. Mai Lin knew the damage it could do. Not to mention how her husband's death would affect her patient. She had taken care of her mistress after childbirth and after the loss of her unborn children, but this final blow she felt she could do very little to counteract.

Mai Lin hobbled to the edge of the porch and looked to the ground where her mistress had thrown herself over the Reverend's prostrate body. Ahcho knelt beside the sobbing woman and patted her back ineffectually. He looked up at Mai Lin and snapped his fingers, and she knew that he was right.

She belonged there beside her mistress. She was needed to wrap an arm around her, to steady her shaking shoulders and silence her cries. Mai Lin let out a hard grunt, but she couldn't seem to make herself take another step. Instead, she crossed her arms over her chest and let out sounds of the variety that she knew Ahcho hated.

The Reverend was dead. What was the news in that? she wondered. He had been dead to the household for months.

Ahcho snapped his fingers again, and this time Mai Lin expelled an exasperated sigh and moved forward. She spat a satisfying wad of betel quid over the side of the porch and began her slow descent to join them.

"Quick, Mai Lin, bring the lamp," Grace cried. "I must see my beloved."

Mai Lin held the lamp over the Reverend's bloodied and dust-covered body. With her other arm, she held the shivering woman.

The lamplight showed the Reverend's face in a most unfortunate expression. His eyes were open and wild. The Spirits had no doubt entered him already. They had flown in and by now fully inhabited him. Mai Lin reached quickly to correct the situation and tsked at Ahcho for having overlooked such an important task. He was no good at anything if he couldn't be trusted to remember this simplest of precautions. Such an old fool, Ahcho, to believe the Jesus business and forget all else.

Mistress Grace ran her hands over the Reverend's chest, where blood was dried and matted. Her fingers swept over his head and untied the string around his neck that held in place the foul nomad's hat. Mai Lin's mistress pressed her palms against the Reverend's skull as if she hoped to squeeze the life back into him. Even in the low lamplight, Mai Lin could see the vermin on his scalp. She tugged on her mistress's nightgown sleeve, but it was too late. The critters were quick, and Mai Lin knew she would have her work cut out for her tomorrow.

She shook her head, and the mistress must have noticed and misunderstood, for she gripped Mai Lin's hand and said, "Don't despair, Mai Lin. He has gone to where he is needed most."

Mai Lin patted her mistress's hand, for it was she who needed comforting. But then Grace pulled away and asked Ahcho, "How did it happen?"

"An idiot with a pistol wanted to see if the Ghost Man could survive another bullet."

"Ah," the mistress said. "They believed in him until the end."

Mai Lin wondered how her mistress could twist the circumstances around so. As far as she could tell, no one believed in the Reverend any longer except for the two who grieved over him now.

Ahcho sat hunched, his head bowed. His cheeks looked more sallow than ever, and his chest had become concave, as if the life had been pulled from him this night as well. Mai Lin wondered if she would have another patient to care for the following day. His heart, she worried, his good and weakened heart.

"But where are my husband's glasses?" the mistress asked.

Ahcho answered softly, "They must have fallen off."

Grace reached over and patted his wrist and said most reassuringly, "Don't worry, he'll see just fine without them where he's going."

"In heaven," Ahcho said.

The two devoted ones nodded in unison.

Mistress Grace then busied herself by investigating the Reverend's jacket pockets, and Mai Lin fretted about whatever other pests she might encounter. Her mistress's hand paused over the red cloth that lay across the Reverend's bloody chest. Her fingers reached for the pouch that lay on the dusty ground beside him. The twin embroidered yellow dragons were filthy now and had lost their sheen. This was the pouch that the Reverend had worn at his hip since their boy's departure. He had kept a hand upon it much of the time, as if it were his own personal rosary.

Ahcho's head snapped upward as he watched her untie the small sack. He looked too beleaguered to object, but then he managed to say, "No, Grace, leave it alone."

Mai Lin wanted to chuckle because she had never heard the proper number-one boy of the finest house in the compound call his mistress by her first name. Ahcho might very well be a changed man tonight, too, she thought. Perhaps he would be less strict and not so much of a scold. For her sake, she hoped so.

Grace opened the pouch all the way and lifted out something round and white. It sat on her palm in the lamplight. The globe glowed as if it emanated a soft, low flicker. Mai Lin leaned toward it to get a better look.

"Hmph!" she said, for she recognized what it was right away.

Grace looked at her, waiting for an explanation, but the answer was so obvious that Mai Lin didn't want to be bothered.

"It's quite lightweight," Grace said.

"Of course," Mai Lin scoffed. "It belonged to a child."

Grace recoiled at the word and dropped the thing onto the dusty ground. "This is a child's skull?" she asked. "Ahcho, explain this object to me."

Ahcho bowed his head and repeated the obvious. "Yes, it belonged to a child."

Mistress Grace began to cough, and Mai Lin knew the night air was the culprit. "No more talking," she barked. "Mistress needs to be in bed. I must take you there now."

Grace continued to hack, the sound rising from deep inside her, but as Mai Lin began to lift her up by the arms, she pawed at her husband and wouldn't let go of his lifeless body. Finally, Grace's fingers reached into his breast pocket and pulled out one of his handkerchiefs. She waved it in the air, and Mai Lin noticed that some of the Reverend's blood from the bullet wound had stained the filthy fabric.

Grace did not seem to notice. She let Mai Lin lift her to standing, calmed by holding the little stained square of linen close to her lips.

Ahcho remained hunched over the Reverend. Mai Lin did not need his help. She could haul her patient back to bed herself. Ahcho was the one with the more difficult task. Tomorrow he would have to dig a hole in soil as hard as stone. Mai Lin laughed to herself and waited for the mistress's cough to subside so they could begin the slow climb up the porch steps.

Twenty-seven

In the shadowy territory between wakefulness and dreaming, Grace's body brimmed with loss. The ache, which grew more intense as she slowly entered consciousness, was not merely physical. She was now a hollow vessel filled to the brim with nothing but grief and illness. Her eyelids flickered open, and she called for Mai Lin to push open the shutters. Outside, day appeared again, casting its stark light on her sorrow.

Grace felt she deserved her unhappiness. She had left her husband behind in that horrible place, and there was no undoing that fact. She rolled over and buried her head in her pillow and longed for sleep to take her again. She wanted Mai Lin to administer to her, even in the morning. She wanted to sleep forever.

But, as she turned in her sheets again, Grace allowed herself to consider her final moments with the Reverend two days before. While it pained her to do so, she also sensed another feeling starting to creep over her. Was it possible that she and her husband had achieved an understanding before they had stepped away from one another forever? She considered this possibility and tried to take solace in it. And, if so, what was it that they had finally shared?

She pictured him again in the wretched opium den. His feeble and withered self brought forth her quiet tears. She recalled what he had said before turning to go: he wished to attend to the dead. Grace sat up in bed and realized that her husband had been signaling to her something both grave and important. And, although she had not understood it fully at the time, she had signaled back, as if they were ships acknowledging one another across a vast and dark sea.

She couldn't go back to sleep now, for the thought in her mind was too potent. With his kind and gentle beacon, he had wished for her to see something on the flat horizon ahead. He had shone forth a light across an inky ocean, lighting her way to a distant shore. She would meet him there. That was what he intended. She would meet him there again someday quite soon.

Grace rose quickly from her bed, slipped on her robe, and shuffled to the window, where she leaned against the sill. Dizziness darkened the edges of her vision until the courtyard came into focus. It was bare. It had always been bare, but now there was nothing but the blankness of cracked ground, a lone tree on which the light green leaves of spring had appeared again, and footprints in the dust. Beside those marks in the earth lay the path where her husband's body had been dragged.

She placed a hand upon her congested chest and understood that while the world outside her window was empty of people, her lungs, her whole body, were filled to overflowing with grief and illness. She sensed a strange paradox: she was most fraught with life when all around her appeared serenely barren. Her mind wanted the quiet of the courtyard to inhabit her, too, but her rattling chest and pain-wracked body left her agitated and full.

She returned to her bedside and lifted the small white skull from the table. Mai Lin stood at her elbow and made that tsking sound that Grace had come to understand meant she had things she would not say.

"You knew what was in the pouch all along?" Grace asked her.

Mai Lin shook her head, and her black braid slapped her hunched back. "I did not."

"But you have suspicions now about why the Reverend formed such a strong attachment to this gruesome object?"

Mai Lin shrugged, no doubt another sign that she knew more than she was letting on.

"Maddening," Grace said. "The lot of you are maddening." She climbed upon the bed again and sat. Her head spun from the minor exertion.

"Mistress must rest," Mai Lin said. "The damp air was very bad last night."

"What was very bad last night was having my husband finally return home to me—dead." Grace flopped against the pillows.

She waited for the tears to commence where they had left off the night before, but they did not. Her hand squeezed the skull, and somehow it made her not weak and sorrowful but angry and strong.

"Please have Ahcho come to me straightaway."

Mai Lin ignored the request as she fussed with the potions on her mixing table.

"Now, Mai Lin!" Grace said. She knew she sounded like a petulant child. "I would like to see him now," she repeated more calmly.

Mai Lin let out an exasperated sigh, one of her many heaving sounds that needed no translation. "He is very busy this morning."

"Whatever he is doing can wait."

Mai Lin offered a beady stare, but Grace did not flinch.

"He is digging a grave, Mistress."

A surprising heat rose up Grace's neck as sudden tears pooled behind her eyes. The Reverend was truly gone. Her Reverend was to be buried this very day. She thought she might collapse if she allowed herself to consider that she would never see him again. She cleared her throat and carried on in a firm voice.

"I shall not keep Ahcho for long. He can return to his task straightaway. The Reverend's soul has already flown, and his body—well."

The truth was that her husband's body had become a filthy, foul-smelling thing some time ago. She shivered at the memory of his dusty and blood-covered flesh. The meticulous man she had married and admired was a distant memory. His body, like her own, was of no consequence any longer. It was their spirits that mattered. That was what the Reverend had said all along.

"Please," Grace tried more softly, "ask Ahcho to come?"

Mai Lin turned and left.

Grace tipped back her head and shut her eyes. The child's skull felt cool against her belly through the thin robe and nightgown. It was cradled where once she had carried her children. Her body had borne so much, and now it was empty. Her hip bones protruded, and the flesh of her stomach was pulled taut. She had not eaten since—she couldn't recall exactly when. Behind her eyelids darted small suns, and the buzzing in her head carried on as it always did. Her ears filled with the whoosh and pulse of thin blood.

Strange, she thought, to have less and less attachment to the body just when it was trying its utmost to demand her attention. Her head throbbed, and the coughing began again, though she refused to notice it. She hacked for many minutes until she leaned over the side of the bed and spat blood into the spittoon Mai Lin had placed there for that purpose. Grace felt her insides weighing her down just when her spirit wanted most to lift up. That was all right. She would inhabit this weak frame a little while longer until, like the Reverend, her soul was ready to fully take flight.

Then she heard the children, always eager to welcome her. Accompanying their high, angelic voices came the clatter of camel bells, approaching ever nearer. Grace smiled and tried to listen more attentively. Yes, bells and singing voices—that was what came to her now that she no longer concerned herself with her illness.

"Mistress," Mai Lin said and shook her arm most rudely.

"Don't interrupt, Mai Lin," Grace said, her eyes pinched shut. "The children are about to arrive."

"No, Madam," her amah clarified, "it's only Ahcho."

Grace opened her eyes. The vision had seemed so real, every bit as real as the man before her. The poor old fellow stood with bowed head before the bedside. Yellow dust covered him. His cheeks were bisected by still-damp streaks where tears and sweat had fallen. Grace wondered if she should feel ashamed for not having wept more this morning. Ahcho appeared a more dedicated mourner than even the Reverend's wife.

In Ahcho's arms were the many leather cords and amulets the Reverend had worn. There hung the camel bell that she had heard moments before. And the bloodstained strip of red cloth, which swung lifelessly, no longer strung across the Reverend's proud chest. The pouch that had held the skull drooped like a flayed body. Each of these languishing objects appeared to have had the life sucked out of them on this day.

Grace pointed to the red sash, and Ahcho handed it to her. She undid the silk string on the pouch and touched the twin embroidered dragons with her fingers. Then she placed the skull back inside, pulled shut the ties, and made a bow. Mai Lin and Ahcho both nodded in approval, and Grace realized that they thought she was tucking away the skull so that she might forget it, when, in fact, her intention was quite the opposite.

"Where did this thing come from?" she asked, holding up the pouch that now bulged with the orb inside.

Ahcho cleared his throat, and Grace sensed that he fought to hold back more tears. "I came upon it the night your small boy was taken." Ahcho's head began to shake from side to side. "I should never have given it to the Reverend. The sight of this awful thing tortured him from that moment on." Tears popped forth and began to cascade down his wrinkled cheeks.

"No, you did right, Ahcho," Grace said, hoping that her clarity might help him to regain his composure.

It was very unlike the old gentleman to show emotion of any sort, much less to fall to pieces in her presence. She knew that he, more than she, would regret it later, and she wished to spare him the humiliation.

Ahcho pulled one of the Reverend's handkerchiefs from his pocket and blew his nose with a harsh sound. "It tormented him and kept him searching when he should have been home with you and the mission."

"Nonsense, he was a responsible father and had to keep up the search for as long as he was alive."

Ahcho dipped his head lower, and Grace sensed something else in his silence, something unspoken.

"Ahcho, have you more to tell me?"

He did not lift his gaze, and his dirt-stained fingers fiddled with the amulets. Her voice remained calm, but her mind was humming from her jangled nerves, and she could feel her desperate pulse ringing louder in her ears. He knew something. He had known something all along.

"Where did this skull really come from, Ahcho?" she asked.

His head bent even lower. Grace looked at Mai Lin, but her face betrayed nothing as she sucked on her unpleasant betel quid.

Grace pushed back against the pillows as her lungs ached. She took in short breaths and tried to ignore her frantic pulse. If she could only ignore her body's painful symptoms, she might be able to think properly.

"Why would the robbers leave this skull behind?" she pressed. "And the question remains: where did it come from?"

Ahcho finally lifted his head and stared at her with swollen eyes. "From the village of Yao dao ho not far from here," he said softly.

Grace let out a ragged sigh. "You have known this all along? So may I assume that the Reverend knew this as well and searched that village for our son?"

"Yes, many times."

"But no clues arose from those visits?"

"No."

Grace tried to breathe evenly. After a long moment, she said, "Well, we must search there again. That is what the Reverend would have wished for us to do. I will do it in his name."

She pulled back the covers and slipped her legs over the side of the bed for the second time that morning.

"I will wear the Reverend's traveling coat," she said to Mai Lin as she stood and her shaky legs held her. She reached for the necklaces in Ahcho's arms and continued, "I never understood these strange talismans in his lifetime, but I believe I will wear them now. Perhaps they will protect me in some unexpected way."

She lifted the leather ropes out of Ahcho's hands and placed them over her head. He did not help her, for clearly he did not approve. Grace no longer cared. She tried to focus on the camel bell's sweet sound as it landed against her frail chest. Even though the amulets around her neck were quite heavy, Grace thought she felt herself growing lighter, freer, just by wearing them.

"You will take me there today," she said.

"Oh, no, Mistress." Ahcho spoke up and took a proprietary step closer. "That is not wise."

He was old enough to be her grandfather, and Grace suddenly sensed that he was of another time than she. Of course he would say no. That was what old people always said. But she was a young American woman, and modern times required that she take command of her situation. She began to cough again, but that reaffirming thought imbued her with confidence. "I will be perfectly all right," she said. "We will go this morning."

She turned to Mai Lin for confirmation, but the old woman was shaking her head, too, and making those awful tsking sounds again.

"Mai Lin, I ask you: am I not a grown woman, completely capable of making my own decisions?"

Mai Lin offered a baffled shrug but had to agree. "Yes, Mistress is a grown woman."

"And I have a right to live my life as I see fit?"

Mai Lin's head bobbed from side to side as she considered this and finally pronounced, "Mistress must do what she must do."

Grace thought she saw a trace of a smile on Mai Lin's face, and it warmed her to think that she and her amah still had an understanding.

"Fate takes you where it will, and you must let it," Mai Lin continued. "This is the way of the river, even when it is dry and dusty. We must bend and flow, or we will be swept aside by dangerous desert winds."

"All wrong, foolish woman!" Ahcho suddenly shouted, unable to contain his high-and-mighty opinions any longer. "We are Christian soldiers now. We fight against silly old ways. We are not overcome like a camel in a dust storm that lowers its head into the sand and waits to be suffocated. We must exert our will and not allow Fate to carry us willy-nilly. This is what the Reverend taught us!"

"Quite right," Grace said, mostly to calm him. It was touching how precisely Ahcho quoted her husband. "Though," she could not help adding although her mind remained dizzy and somewhat confused, "in a way, isn't that what I am suggesting for myself? I *am* taking my life into my own hands."

"But you are a girl!" Ahcho said.

"Right again," she agreed with no intention of belaboring the argument. He was an old fellow, and she needed to preserve her strength for the journey ahead. "Now, let's carry on."

Her words only inflamed the suffering man more. Ahcho turned to Mai Lin and began to speak in a rapid dialect that Grace had never heard issuing forth from his lips before. Mai Lin returned his fire with equal fury. Grace was shocked at the sounds. She had grown accustomed to the ever-changing dialects in this land, the inconvenient way language shifted from village to village. But apparently, the servants had had their own tongue all along, which they had somehow kept hidden from her. They argued rapidly back and forth now in words she could only vaguely understand. All these years when they had been speaking Mandarin to her and the Reverend, they had been perpetuating a ruse, as they also used another, more local dialect as well. What else had they been hiding about their true selves? Grace wondered. She was astounded and could not help chuckling, although the two continued to disagree quite vehemently.

"What is he saying?" she asked Mai Lin when the argument had slowed.

"He says he forbids you to go. He is the big honcho around here now. Mr. Big Man."

Mai Lin spat a long shot of tobacco juice into the spittoon. Grace had expressly asked her not to do that, but at this moment, it seemed precisely the right thing to do.

"Explain to him that I will go with or without him. This journey must be carried out no matter what."

Mai Lin rattled on, and Ahcho raised his voice and then his hands in another show of emotion Grace had never seen from him before. The ancient man was irate as well as heartbroken.

"Tell him that I know the Reverend would approve of this mission," Grace said.

Ahcho ran his fingers over his slicked-back hair and pressed his palm against his receding brow. Mai Lin let out a triumphant laugh.

"He has agreed?" Grace asked.

"He is an old fool," Mai Lin said and waved her hand in Ahcho's direction as she turned away.

"That's not nice, Mai Lin," Grace said.

Then she spoke to Ahcho directly in the formal tongue they had used for years. "I am terribly sorry to have upset you, Ahcho, but you see, I have nothing else to live for. I must go forward. There has to be something I can do, otherwise I am lost, utterly lost. Do you understand?"

She reached a hand across and squeezed his bony arm under his tattered, dust-covered black robe. The poor fellow was trying so hard to maintain a semblance of what had been. But Grace could see plainly that it was no more. None of it was anymore.

Ahcho appeared to have returned to his senses. His crisp posture made him tall again.

"Yes, I understand," he replied and closed his hands together. "But Madam will find nothing in Yao dao ho. It is an empty village, all the people gone, and it is dangerous to travel anywhere now, even to the market in Fenchow-fu. Why risk a destination that has no purpose? Instead of pursuing this mad investigation, you must pray, Mistress Grace, and grow strong again. You are not well, and you must ask the Lord to help you. Jesus heals the sick who are patient and good. Not those who gallivant about like wild women."

He shot a harsh glance at Mai Lin, who let out a hiss of disapproval. Grace herself was taken aback by the sternness of his little speech. She had never heard Ahcho say so many words at once, and certainly none that carried such stern judgment.

"You have always worried far too much, Ahcho," Grace said. "I appreciate your concern, but, as I have explained, if you are unwilling to join me, then I shall go alone with Mai Lin."

Grace turned to her amah, and although she sensed the older woman's uneasiness to allow her patient to embark on this expedition, she also knew that Mai Lin was stubborn and would not allow Ahcho to win an argument.

"I will go with you," Mai Lin said with her customary nod.

"Thank you, Mai Lin," Grace said.

Ahcho turned and marched from the room.

Twenty-eight

Mai Lin lugged a bundle after her over the cracked ground of the marketplace and up the road to the shop that in better times had been the heart of Fenchow-fu. She yanked it across the threshold and was aware of the old ones crouched on barrels and the young ones who lounged against the counter and lay splayed on the floor. She could not be bothered with such lazy bums and wanted only to do her business and get back to the compound. The mistress was waiting for her and most urgently wanted to leave for the unfortunate village of Yao dao ho. It was a foolish plan, but Mai Lin took it as her duty to help the young woman fulfill her destiny. The river was flowing fast now, no longer with water but with dust. Who were they to try to stop it?

With some effort, she lifted the heavy bundle onto the countertop and untied a lace corner of the white linen tablecloth. American forks, spoons, and knives tumbled out. Ridiculous utensils, she thought, far too complicated and fussy. But the sterling silver was of the highest quality and had to be worth something, even in these bare times.

A young fellow with a big swagger and a white scar under one eye stepped forward. He lifted a spoon and then let it drop again onto the pile with a clatter. The cocky man did not bother even to look closely or confer with one of the grandfathers who stood nearby. He simply turned away.

"I know, senseless things," Mai Lin tried, "but you can melt them down. Real silver!" She lifted a spoon with a florid *W* engraved upon the handle and bit it with hard gums.

One of the grandfathers shuffled closer and inspected a spoon. "Very fine," he said, and Mai Lin thought that at least the old man had not lost his sense.

The younger man glanced again at the gleaming treasure—all of the Watsons' place settings sent to them after their wedding, mailed in a wooden crate all the way from the town of Cleveland in a province called Ohio. Mistress Grace had cried the first time she had shown Mai Lin how to polish it. Such a sentimental and homesick girl, her mistress had been back then.

"What do you want for this junk, old woman?" the young swaggerer finally asked.

Mai Lin bristled at his rudeness and sucked harder on her betel quid to keep from mouthing back. "A camel."

The fellow let out a deep laugh that echoed against the empty shelves. His friends in the back of the store paused over the gambling table, but when they saw that their leader was only dealing with an old woman, they returned to their mah-jongg.

Mai Lin placed her eye upon the young man, and although it took a few moments, he stopped his foolish laugh and grew quiet. He placed a finger to the white scar under one eye. It glistened, and Mai Lin knew that it now burned. She stared harder, and Swagger blinked several times.

"I have a camel," he said. "But it's not for sale."

"I will borrow it, then," Mai Lin said.

He started to chuckle again, then caught himself. As he considered her proposal, she reached into one of the deep pockets of her skirts and pulled out the child-sized skull. She placed it on the counter and turned it to face him.

"What is that thing, you witch?" he asked as he shifted so the hollow eyes would not find him. "Get it away from me."

The grandfathers moved closer. They nodded and muttered to one another, but none reached out to touch it.

"Fine," she said. "I will put it away."

And she did. The grandfathers watched her carefully now, and Mai Lin wondered why none of them spoke up and told the young man who she was. They knew, the elders knew, but they were cowards, every one of them.

She had seen the pistol tucked into the young man's belt. That thing wasn't worth her concern. Her time had not come yet, she knew this. But these grandfathers had lost all of the old understanding. They were too intimidated by the new generation to teach them as they needed to be taught. No wonder the young thought they could rule, when really all they could do was swagger.

"I will borrow your camel for one day in exchange for all this silver," she announced.

The young man, finally coming to his senses, looked at the elders. Although still mongrels and rogues, they nodded their approval.

"Good," Mai Lin said.

Then she turned and started toward the door, avoiding the indolent women sleeping on the floor. She had barely noticed them on her way in and now could see that they were not worth seeing. Pathetic creatures who sold themselves for men's pleasure, they deserved to be spat upon, but Mai Lin refrained. Several lay sprawled on a thick carpet of fur. Mai Lin paused and knelt down to touch the flea-bitten hide. Her ancient eyes did not deceive her this time.

"Get away from us, you old hag," cried a girl who showed too much flesh.

Another said, "Don't let her touch you with those disgusting hands!"

Mai Lin chewed on her lips to keep from spewing forth at the nasty girls. She sensed young Swagger standing over her now, his hand on the pistol. Mai Lin pushed herself to stand, and of course the rude fellow did not help her up.

"I want this wolf hide, too," she said.

"You want this, you want that," Swagger said, pointing the gun at her. "You better leave before you get something you don't want."

The girls tittered at this, but Mai Lin studied the young man with calm eyes. She could see that his time was soon to come, maybe not this day, but soon. She shuffled over to one of the other empty counters and yanked a satchel off her shoulder. She reached inside with both hands and poured out onto the dusty wood many bars of lye soap. On top of the heap, Mai Lin tossed wads of toweling material torn into small squares. Washcloths, the Americans called them.

"What useless things are those, old one?" young Swagger asked. He laughed, and the girls laughed, too.

"You smell worse than cattle," Mai Lin said.

Swagger stepped toward her and puffed out his chest. "You are one to talk, foul woman."

"That's right, I am an foul, old woman. Not a handsome young buck like you, who should not be covered by filth and lice."

He glanced down at his pistol and spun the cylinder, but Mai Lin could tell he was listening.

"And these lovely ladies," Mai Lin could not help spitting that incorrect word in their direction, "they should not be disgusting like me. They are not rancid old women. Not yet, anyway."

"All right, all right," he said. "I will keep the bars of soap. Now, get out of here before I decide you have lived too long."

Mai Lin glanced at the grandfathers and grandmothers who slouched on the barrels and benches around the edge of the room. None of them even looked up, that was how far things had gone in this land. Mai Lin turned back to Swagger.

"I will take the dead animal hide for the soap and rags. That is a fair trade."

He raised the pistol and pointed it directly at her forehead. Mai Lin did not flinch or turn away or say a word. His hand trembled ever so slightly, not enough for the others to notice. After a long moment, she reached out and gently pushed the gun aside.

The young man waved it toward the girls reclining on the rug and shouted at them, "Get up, lazy bitches. Bath time outside, now. Move!"

Their robes fluttered after them as they scurried out the door.

With his pistol, he pointed at the hide. "You can see by the bullet holes that it didn't do what it was supposed to do. My idiot brother thought this mangy thing would protect him. He was a romantic fool and got what he deserved. Go ahead, take it, old witch."

"And you will get what you deserve, too," she could not help saying.

Then she sucked on her quid and made herself stop speaking. Instead, she hobbled to the hide, grabbed a tattered corner, and dragged it over the dusty floorboards.

Outside, she gave the last bar of soap to a boy who helped her up onto the camel. His thin arms strained as he heaved the wolf hide over the emaciated animal's back. As she set off for the compound, she glanced back and saw that the boy was biting into the lye. There was no end to human ignorance, she thought. It was rampant all around and surely meant to drive her mad.

Twenty-nine

Later that afternoon, they struck out, Mai Lin seated at the front of the sorry camel and Grace holding on to her. She had taken a chill, and the heavy hide felt good over her back. She even pulled the animal's jaw to cover her fallen bun and wore it like a hood. With each step of the camel's stiff legs, the bells and amulets slapped against her chest. She didn't mind being burdened so and even allowed herself to sway back and forth with the animal's stride.

As they passed through the open iron gate of the compound, Grace glanced back. The yellow brick buildings caught the light, and the yellow dust of the courtyard reflected it. All was golden and solitary. The swallowtail eaves of the nicest home in the compound rose as handsomely as ever. It was a beautiful, though melancholy, sight. How long would these buildings last, she wondered, with no one here to tend to them? No movement stirred, and with their departure this day, the mission was now empty.

It was hard to imagine that such a blank and monochromatic setting had once bustled with life. The children, Grace wondered, as she had so many times, where were the dear children? She turned frontward again and looked up the road to the desert, where she suspected they had lived all along.

Mai Lin hummed one of her toneless tunes and mumbled to the camel in some tongue that only they understood. Grace had given up trying to grasp what took place around her. Her mission was no longer to grapple with this barren world. She needed simply to find her son. She felt certain that some clue on the dry road and dusty plains ahead would lead her to him.

They had not gone far, with Grace dozing and Mai Lin muttering peacefully, when she heard a man's voice calling after them. Mai Lin's hearing was no longer reliable, so it fell to Grace to look back.

Behind them came Ahcho. He limped quite noticeably but pressed forward as best he could in their direction. He was a righteous man. Grace understood that now. He was her husband's most ardent follower, and she felt chagrined for having quarreled with him that morning when she had realized that she must make this trip to Yao dao ho. In her grief, she had behaved childishly.

"Mai Lin, stop!" she shouted.

The old woman pulled the reins and glanced over her shoulder. "We wait for him?" she asked.

"Of course we wait for him."

Mai Lin spat into the dust.

Ahcho was slow to reach them, but when he did, Grace reached down and took his aged hands into her own. "Bless you, Ahcho," she said.

He bowed, and she could see that he was much fatigued.

"Are you all right?" she asked.

"I'm fine, now that I've reached you," he said.

"If you're not too tired," she asked, "would you be willing to escort us the rest of the way?"

Ahcho bowed and replied in his proper manner, "If you will permit it so."

"I would be most honored," Grace said.

Then Mai Lin reluctantly turned the reins over to Ahcho, and he began their slow trek onward. After a short while, the heaving of the camel's stride lulled Grace back to near sleep.

"Mistress," Ahcho said as his step slowed and he strode alongside the camel.

"Hmmm?" Grace asked from a dreamy place.

"I have prayed all night, and my prayers have led me here to join you."

Grace nodded. Such a good man. Such a good and honest man.

"I believe," Ahcho continued, "that it has fallen to me to tell you about the origin of the child's skull. I must be honest, even if it hurts me to bring you pain. This is what the Lord Jesus tells us we must do to achieve the gates of heaven."

Grace's eyes opened only slightly. Ahcho's gaze was upon the cracked earth, and his shoulders sloped.

"Don't worry so," she said. "Of course you may tell me, my dear man. There's no doubt that you shall see heaven when your time comes."

"But this is about the Reverend," Ahcho began, "and something he never told you."

Grace suddenly felt fully awake, although she did not show it so that he might continue. "Yes?" she asked, as if with vague interest.

"Years ago," Ahcho said, "when your belly was ripe with little Wesley, I accompanied the Reverend into the plains and hills on a visit to the outlying churches. He was intent on rebuilding them since their abandonment after the Boxer Rebellion."

So far he was telling her nothing she didn't already know, but Grace offered an interested sound to help him carry on. Ahcho seemed so uneasy, and yet what could he possibly have to say to warrant such nervousness?

"The Reverend Watson was most brave and determined as he tried to help the heathens know the great Jesus."

"Yes, he was quite zealous at his task," Grace said. "Go on, then, tell me what you recall."

And although her eyes remained shut, she listened most attentively. She let her head loll to one side and occasionally muttered an encouraging word so that he would continue. With each step, Ahcho revealed the tale of what had happened many years before in the insignificant hamlet of Yao dao ho.

Thirty

All those years ago, the door to a hovel had swung open and the whitest man ever to enter a miserable hamlet west of Shansi had ducked his head below the lintel and stepped inside. After him came an almost equally tall and thin Chinese man. Ahcho shut the door behind them, and the Reverend removed his Western-style bowler hat and held it in his large hands. Inside the room, the peasants who lived there did not appear awed or even surprised. Instead, they carried on as if unaware of the remarkable strangers in their midst. Ahcho had rarely seen such lack of interest before but supposed it was because they were preoccupied with the dying boy.

A Chinese medicine man let out a low, mournful cry as he swung a smoking lantern slowly back and forth over the child who lay on a straw mat on the floor. The pungent smell of incense drifted across the room. The medicine man wore a matted sheepskin vest, tattered robes, and several belts across his chest, each bearing animal-skin flasks and silk pouches. Two elders stood nearby, one with his eyes crusted over from blindness, the other frowning down at the scene.

The boy's mother knelt at her child's side and held his fingers, which resembled brittle twigs.

Ahcho spoke to the elders in their dialect. "We are on a great journey, Grandfathers, and have stopped for the night. Your neighbors told us about the dying boy. The Reverend here would like to help the child to be saved," he said.

Torches appeared at the window just then, and a row of faces pressed against the soot-covered panes. The elders conferred with one another. Finally, the one with blind eyes shook his head. "We want no help."

They turned back to the sick boy, and the medicine man rubbed packed herbs and oils onto his chest.

The Reverend whispered in English to Ahcho, "They seem to be performing some sort of primitive last rites. That can't be doing any medical good."

"It is the custom," Ahcho replied.

"I left my Bible in my bedroll on the donkey's back. I shall go for it."

Ahcho caught his arm. "Better for the Reverend not to go out there alone."

"You're right. And the poor child might not make it until I got back."

"Your own words will do just fine," Ahcho encouraged the young minister.

The Reverend stepped forward and was about to speak when the mother threw herself over the boy as if to protect him.

"Has the child finally passed to the other side?" the Reverend asked Ahcho. "Sometimes it's so difficult to discern even the simplest of things with these people."

Ahcho shook his head, and they watched the mother cradle her still living son. She began a song, her words unrecognizable but the meaning of her lament clear. The Reverend appeared moved by the sorrowful sounds. His young wife was expecting a child soon. Ahcho knew that she had lost two others already. Out on the trail in those months, the Reverend bent his knees each night and prayed beside his *kang,* or straw mat. Ahcho had overheard him asking that their child be born alive and healthy. He also prayed that the native children survive, and even thrive, as well.

"How is it, oh Lord," the Reverend had asked in his nightly prayers, "that one child is spared when others are dying?"

Ahcho thought of those words now as he and the Reverend listened to the mother's lament. "Spare my son, dear God," the woman sang. "Spare none other than this child, my own."

The Reverend cleared his throat and interrupted. "In Jesus's name," he began, "we ask thee, O Heavenly Father, to take this boy here before us into your loving arms."

The mother turned suddenly and seemed to fully see the Reverend. Her eyes grew small and sharp and glinted in the lamplight. She rose from the boy and shouted. Her hands flailed and pointed at the white man. The crowd outside banged on the mud walls of the hut, which rattled the windowpanes. Ahcho pulled the Reverend by the jacket sleeve toward the door, but the woman was too quick. She stumbled forward on bowed legs and planted herself before him.

The Reverend raised himself up to his full six foot four inches and stood perfectly erect and ready, his fingers on his gold watch chain. He was a young man and terribly thin, but he knew how to appear as solid and unyielding as an elder statesman.

"Calm, now," he said. "Calm."

The mother looked all the way up into his blue eyes behind the gold-rimmed glasses. "Ghost Man!" she shouted. "You may not take away my son!"

The mother lifted her thin arms and struck her fists against the Reverend's chest, pounding the buttons of his vest and the white handkerchief folded in his pocket. Although she was trying to injure him, her blows appeared to be as mild as those of a small child. Ahcho stepped forward to insist that the woman stop pestering the Reverend, but the Reverend waved him off.

"Madam," he said as he reluctantly took her by her narrow wrists, "my heart goes out to you. Your son is in my prayers."

The crowd tapped at the glass. Ahcho could sense men moving around outside, positioning themselves before the door.

"Sir," he whispered, "we must go."

The Reverend spoke only to the mother. "I have come to help you and your boy to find peace in his final moments."

The mother's arms appeared to grow tired, and her angry movements ceased. She dropped to her knees on the packed dirt floor, and the Reverend helped ease her down.

"Go away, Ghost Man!" she said, more softly. "Go out of my house." She pointed toward the door, and the Reverend looked that way.

At just that moment, the crowd flung it open on its leather hinges and stood blocking the threshold. They stared with frightful expressions, their voices hushed at first, then steadily rising.

Ahcho helped the Reverend take the mother by the arms. When she was standing, they looked about and saw that there was no chair for her to settle into. Ahcho knew that any furniture had been used for fuel that winter. The mother swayed between the two men until she threw herself onto the dirt again beside her son's mat.

The medicine man picked up the lamp and continued his ritual, apparently unperturbed. But the crowd at the door was restless as the people jockeyed to see inside.

Ahcho tugged the Reverend toward the door. The young minister paused one more time to speak to the incense-filled room. "May the Lord Jesus Christ accept your son into his great care and grant this boy heavenly grace for all of eternity. Amen."

Neither the elders nor the mother nor the medicine man offered any acknowledgment of the Reverend's words.

"Come," Ahcho said, "that's all you can do."

The Reverend turned and made his way into the onrushing crowd in the courtyard. Flames from the peasants' torches danced dangerously close to his head.

"Ghost Man!" the people shouted, having heard the mother christen him inside. "Go away, Ghost Man! Go away and leave us alone!"

They pawed at the Reverend's topcoat, pulled at his sleeves, and tried to reach up to his hair. In all their travels, even the long trip to the Gobi, Ahcho had seen country people fawning over the Reverend many times. Villagers frequently picked at him with meddling fingers. They stroked his clothing as if it were made of heavenly material and reached for his magical glasses that transformed his blue eyes into startling gems. And although Ahcho and the Reverend tried to dissuade these strangers from their primitive notion that white men were gods, they had benefited from such ignorance more than once when offered a home-cooked meal or a comfortable place to sleep.

But this crowd showed none of that awed curiosity. They pressed closer and shouted into the Reverend's face. Ahcho was pulled away from his master and tried to return to him, but many struggling bodies intervened. He saw that there were hands on the Reverend's back and more hands on his arms. Odors of sweat and soil and excrement surrounded them, and the pressure of damp flesh felt far too intimate. All of this was extremely unpleasant for Ahcho, but it was the Reverend he worried about. The people clawed at him, not to be saved but to overpower and crush the life out of him.

Ahcho hit at their backs with his fists but could not push back through the crowd. Over their heads, he tried to shout and signaled to the Reverend to press on in the direction of the village gate, where their donkey driver had their animals prepared and waiting. Ahcho had no choice but to watch helplessly as the Reverend made little progress.

The big man appeared to be trying with all his strength to stride forward, but the crowd had his legs in a tight grip. As the Reverend strained, his legs stayed anchored, and suddenly his upper body fell. He came crashing down like a toppled ancient pine.

Years later, in the hours after Wesley was kidnapped, the Reverend had wept as he had revealed to Ahcho all that had happened next in the miserable hamlet of Yao dao ho. He spared nothing when he described the circumstances. As the crowd began to suffocate and stomp over him, the young minister prayed that he be allowed to live long enough to see his child born. Then, as his efforts to get loose from the crowd became more impossible, he prayed to the Lord the same prayer he said at every deathbed he had ever visited: let this sweet and singular life be cradled in Jesus's welcoming arms. Let this life be saved in death. Only now it was his own life he wished to be held peacefully for all eternity.

The villagers pressed down upon him, pinning him to the hard ground. The Reverend felt a blow to his head, another to his ribs and back. The peasants kicked and punched him, and the pain made his great body writhe and convulse. He said his prayers louder, more insistently, and at the same time he tried with great concentration to crawl forward. But someone still had him by the legs, and the blows to his body were coming faster. The Reverend took in the pain and let out a scream of both anguish and fury.

"Save me, dear Jesus!" he cried. "Save me, oh Lord!"

The sound of his own voice helped him muster his strength. The Reverend pulled his knee close to his chest and released his leg in a mighty kick behind him. There came a crack: the furious blow had landed on something solid but yielding, and it broke. Yes, the Reverend later explained, it was sickeningly satisfying—the same sensation he had felt as a boy when crushing rotten pumpkins in the fields with his boot.

He kicked again and again, each time with greater success. And as he did so, the Reverend felt himself being lifted up. He was certain in that moment that the Lord had him under the arms and was raising him higher, back onto his feet and toward salvation. He pushed with his arms and threw the bodies off his back. A great strength coursed through his long limbs, and then, in a final surge of spirit, he stood and ran forward. His legs were free. No one clung to him any longer. They had let him go. And, to his amazement, the crowd did not follow.

It was a miracle: the Reverend was saved. He had called out to the Lord, and the Lord had answered.

He reached his donkey and threw himself upon it. Ahcho met him there, and even in his cumbersome robe, he quickly clambered onto his animal, too. The donkey driver beat the beasts to get them moving, but they were already edgy and eager to escape the torches and needed no encouragement to bolt through the village gate. The frightened visitors made it into the desert, the hamlet of Yao dao ho a quickly receding nightmare.

Although the Reverend was rife with pain, the miracle of having been saved coursed through his veins with a fiery lightness that gave him renewed energy. In those first moments of freedom, he felt certain that he had seen the Lord on this very night and been chosen by Him. He was alive with hope.

Then, like Lot's wife, he was tempted to look back over his shoulder. The Reverend wished to merely stamp in his mind the place where God had allowed him to escape doom. But in one quick glance, he saw what he would never forget. For what he spied caused a great fissure in his faith that the Reverend, and even Ahcho as well, had tried to repair ever since.

Back through the dilapidated village gate, the Reverend saw that the coolies of Yao dao ho had formed a half circle around a man who knelt on the ground. It was a father, holding a limp child in his arms. He rocked the small body as the people around him fell to the ground and wailed. They threw back their heads and cried. In an instant, the Reverend understood.

He understood and yet he turned away again. And for that, he could never forgive himself. He did not stay and offer his condolences, for he knew it would mean his life. As he moved out into the desert, the Reverend stared up at the night sky. He reached for his handkerchief and found it gone. His glasses were missing, too, trampled under the villagers' feet, and so, for him, the stars blurred and burned like a low fire overhead. Then a cloud crossed the trail and blocked out the moon. The Reverend bowed his head in that shadow and understood that he would remain under it forever onward.

He could not erase the image from his mind of the limp child in his father's arms. Pain shot through his ribs with each step of the donkey. Blood trickled from his mouth and over his jaw and onto the backs of his hands that held the reins. But his true pain was in remembering.

The Reverend had shouted for his Lord, and his Lord had answered. John Wesley Watson had received divine mercy. The Lord had decided that he should survive. But in that instant of looking back, he had seen the reason he had been spared. Under the light of the torches and a million stars overhead, a child lay dead, his life stolen from him by a ghost man.

Thirty-one

Grace sat bolt upright on the camel's back and could no longer pretend to be lulled or sleepy. She didn't care any longer about Ahcho's delicate feelings for his beloved master. She wanted to know the truth.

"Are you suggesting there's a connection between this accidental murder in the village of Yao dao ho and the kidnapping of our son?" she asked.

Ahcho's pace slowed, and he mumbled a reply at the rocky trail.

"Speak up, Ahcho. You must finish the explanation, much as it may pain you to do so."

"The Reverend became suspicious when he spied a torn scrap of his handkerchief in one of the kidnappers' pockets. Later, when I gave him the child's skull they had left behind, he became more concerned. Then, on our travels, we heard that amongst the people of the borderlands, the family, not the individual, is responsible for any crime. It seemed quite likely that your boy was taken out of retribution. But to what end, we did not know. So the Reverend did not give up the search. He wanted desperately to find his son."

"Or perhaps, what motivated him most was a desire to not face his own guilt," Grace said. "We'll never know."

"You do know, Mistress," Ahcho said. "You know he was a good man."

"Oh, for heaven's sake, I know he was. But the point is, he was a man—a flawed and miserable human like the rest of us."

"Don't blame him, Mistress. I should never have told you."

"Ahcho, it's good you told me. I'm actually glad to know my husband as he truly was—a far weaker and more imperfect person than I ever allowed myself to realize in his lifetime. But," she added softly, "who am I, a failed mother, to cast such aspersions?"

Grace wanted to think carefully about such matters so very much, and yet her mind was spinning. Blood whooshed in her veins, filling her ears with a desolate wind. The coughing began again, and Ahcho stepped closer and helped her remain balanced atop the camel as the paroxysms took her.

"Mistress should rest now," Mai Lin said. "We will stop, and I will give you something to help with the pain."

The coughing subsided, and Grace whispered, "No, we will press on until we reach our cottage. We can stay there for the night and then set out for Yao dao ho again in the morning."

Mai Lin sucked on her teeth and offered Ahcho an urgent, worried glance.

"I must tell you, Mistress," Ahcho said with sudden enthusiasm, "I have great news. Your boy lives west of here. I've heard word of him."

"Yes, yes, how wonderful," Grace said, but the dizziness and whirring circled her like the vultures overhead. She could no longer think clearly and badly needed rest. "You will tell me all about it later, Ahcho. I must sleep now. Really, I must. I'm dead tired."

So, as Grace dozed, they trudged along the sandy trail that cut through high grasses, climbing ever so slightly toward the foothills in the near distance. She loosely gripped Mai Lin's waist and shut her burning eyelids. When she opened them again, the Watson family cottage had come into view. She had not seen it since the morning after her son had been stolen from them. The path narrowed and became as rocky as a dry riverbed. She could not imagine how their buckboard had ever made the journey that first and only time one year before.

Grace's head bobbed as her illness lulled her back to sleep even on the lumbering beast. The fever was upon her. Her limbs felt impossibly heavy, and her neck could barely hold up her head. She dimly understood that she was far more ill than she had realized.

Then, in her cloudy, chimerical mind, she saw herself drift into the Reverend's study. Her white nightgown caught the moonlight that cascaded through the open window shutters. Her husband sat bent over his desk, as he had often done in the evenings. She tried to tell what year this was. The hunger in her gut gnawed away as much from fear as a lack of food. The famine had gone on for so many months. Yet when she looked down at her belly, she noticed that it was large. In her dream, she was pregnant with Rose. Yes, she could tell by the expression on her husband's face that little Wesley had been taken from them not long before.

Grace slipped closer to the Reverend's elbow and bent to see the sermon he was working on. To her surprise, he had left only blots of ink on the page and no words. He muttered something, apparently unaware of her. He took off his spectacles, rubbed his eyes, and looked across to the high bookshelves as if he might find his next phrase on the spines of the leather-clad volumes.

The small skull sat on the desk before him, liberated from its hiding place inside the silk pouch with the twin golden dragons. On this cloudless, moonlit night, Grace saw it there and sensed that he used it to remind himself of his duty, his weakness, his sinful life, as stern a warning as Jesus's cross. Grace shivered at the sight of it. She wished he had just buried it long before in the desert where it belonged.

She followed the Reverend's gaze across the room and was startled to see little Wesley seated on the floor in the corner. He played with one of his Chinese cloth dolls. Over his pajamas he wore a padded and colorful Mongolian robe and hat that she didn't recognize. On his small feet were those darling silk shoes Mai Lin had brought him from the market. Grace thought it must be long past her son's bedtime, but he appeared busy and contented as he marched his doll back and forth across the blue carpet, using the branches of the woven cherry trees as a bridge to safety. He looked every bit the little prince that he was.

"That's a good boy," she whispered. "Let your father concentrate on his work. He has much business to attend to."

Grace rested her hand on her husband's shoulder. The Reverend started slightly, although, like Wesley, he did not seem to see her.

"Oh, love," he sighed.

It made Grace's knees weak to hear his trembling voice. "Yes?" she answered.

Although he couldn't hear her, he must have sensed a certain attentiveness surrounding him there in the shadowy study.

The Reverend spoke to the empty room. "There is so much yet to be done. But these people," he pointed with his spectacles toward the dark window that overlooked the courtyard, "they don't want us here. We try to bring our faith, but the desert will swallow our efforts in no time." He put his glasses back on. "It's all for naught. Such changes are coming, my love. I fear we had best heed the future and step aside."

Grace had never seen him in such despair, but of course he would feel that now with his beloved son so recently taken from them. Grace gently stroked her husband's arm and touched his fine red hair. She knew that nothing she could do would help erase the concern that clouded his brow or the weary look in his eyes.

"Grace," he whispered. "Dearest Grace."

At the sound of her name, her heart lightened. The Reverend was always so much alone with his mission. For him to remember her in a time of need was a victory of sorts.

"Why, Lord, in your infinite wisdom, did you take our treasure from us?" the Reverend asked, his voice suddenly rising and crashing against the bookshelves. "How can I carry on in your name when you're a wrathful God and not the tender, wise one whom I once believed in?"

His shoulders began to shake. Tears appeared in his strained eyes and fell onto ink-stained hands. He took out his handkerchief and blew his nose. Grace could feel herself shaking, too, although she wasn't sure if it was from sorrow or joy. In the Reverend's sudden questioning of his faith, he became for her more beautiful and human than ever.

But now she saw that little Wesley was upset by his father's worried tone. The boy rose from the blue floral carpet, his handsome robe fluttering.

"Come, darling, everything's all right," Grace said and reached out her arms toward him.

The boy stood in place and began to wail.

"Come to Mother."

Grace slipped nearer to her son and put her arms around him but felt nothing in her grasp. It was air, all air, though still warm where his body had been. She tried to breathe into her congested lungs and hoped to capture his pure, sweet smell, but it was gone.

Grace awoke as the camel shifted unsteadily over the rough terrain. The body she wrapped her arms around was that of an old woman. Ahead, the Watson cottage rose nearer. It stood silhouetted against the endless blue sky as she had seen it on their first day here. From this distance, the surrounding scene appeared quite lovely, with the nearby river and the willow tree.

But as they came nearer, Grace could discern that the cabin was but a shell now. On the rough earth around it lay wooden boards, useless bricks, and scraps of metal. It had been looted, and the terrible desert weather had done serious damage to the structure as well. The walls of the house remained, but in places the roof had already caved in, and the glass of the windows had all been broken and gaped open to the winds.

"Let's go first to the river with the willow beside it," Grace said and pointed. "We can settle in at the cottage afterward."

The camel lumbered on until they stopped at the edge of the dry river. Ahcho helped her down from the beast. The wolf's hide was most cumbersome, but she wrapped herself in it to control the shivers. Ahcho took her arm, and together they stepped down into the riverbed where the willow dragged its tendrils against cracked ground. She had remembered the branches as fuller and more protective but knew that she should be grateful the tree was still alive at all given the terrible drought.

"Please bring the trowel, Mai Lin," she said.

As her amah unpacked the satchel slung over the camel's side, Grace looked again at the plains. She and the Reverend had watched their futures rushing toward them across that expanse filled now with dried stubble and dust. She searched for smoke on the horizon but saw none on this clear, early-summer day.

Why had it happened? she asked herself again as she had so many times before. Only now, when she finally knew the answer, she sensed somehow that she had been asking the wrong question all along. Perhaps there was no question, just an acceptance of what was.

Grace untied the embroidered pouch with the twin golden dragons that hung from the dirty red sash. Mai Lin hobbled down into the riverbed and handed her the tool.

"Ahcho, do you mind?" Grace asked. "I believe the Reverend would be most grateful."

Ahcho took the trowel, bent down onto his knees, raised his hand, and struck the hard dirt. For some time, Grace and Mai Lin stood over him as he scratched and dug.

Standing in the river of dust, Grace held the pouch close to her chest under the great fur. She had learned from Mai Lin that each thing carried with it a life and a destiny that could not be ignored. She had learned to listen for portents sent on the wind and offered by the smallest of signs. Sometimes the future spoke to us with smoke on the horizon. Or with the dance of a handkerchief fluttering on the wind or a skull tossed down on firm soil. Each person and thing had its say and was of consequence. There was no way to undo the past or to correct the way things had gone, but attention must be given to the secrets whispered along the way. Ghosts spoke to us all the time, if we were only willing to listen. Not to do so was hubris. She could see that now and suspected that the Reverend had understood it in the end as well.

The shovel in Ahcho's hand chipped away at the hard-packed land, sending puffs of dust into the breeze. He paused to wipe his forehead with one of the Reverend's handkerchiefs. Grace could feel her husband here with them in each gesture of his devoted manservant. Her Reverend had not abandoned her but was with her still and would be always. The poor man had been so busy arguing with God, hashing out the ever-narrowing parameters of his faith, that he had quite forgotten to ask for her simple forgiveness. She wished he had understood that her love for him could have offered shade in the manner of the willow tree in all seasons and years. Ah, well, she would show him soon enough, when they met in the sweet by-and-by.

Ahcho finished the shallow, makeshift grave, and Grace wondered if she should say a few words. Bow her head. Offer a prayer. Something. But she decided that the time for last rites was long past. If anything, Mai Lin should mumble incantations as she had so many times over Grace's ill body before administering her potions. No, this skull needed no ceremony. It simply had to be gotten rid of expediently, returned to the soil where it belonged. It had cast its spell long enough.

She untied the embroidered sack, lifted out the child's skull, and placed it in the hole. Then, with her pale hands, she brushed the desert dirt back over it. The loess felt painfully soft in her fingers, like the silkiness of good, rich baking flour back home. Every week she had helped her mother prepare pies for Sunday supper. Today was a Sunday, was it not? Grace had lost track of so much—the days blending together and gone in a haze. And the loved ones, so many loved ones, gone, too, she knew now for good.

As the sun began to slice the horizon, she thought she could hear the voices of her family echoing down from the cottage nearby. Yes, it was the hour of Sunday supper, and she could hear the familiar rattle of silverware set down upon the table and the clink of glasses being filled by her mother's fine silver water pitcher. If Grace had been a good girl that week, she was allowed to light the candles. She glanced up at the house and expected to see it softly lit from within, but there was no light coming from that bleak cabin. She was far, terribly far, from home.

Shivers took her again, and her chest ached as the cough began. When it subsided, her body was soaked with sweat. Her skin was burning up, and yet she liked the heft of the hide on her shoulders. She finished the burial task and used the side of her hand to make the rough surface smooth.

She rose from the dusty riverbed and turned toward the cottage. Mai Lin helped her on one side and Ahcho on the other. She wished they wouldn't fuss so, but they continued to jabber their concerns as she shuffled forward.

"Mistress, truly I must explain to you," Ahcho said with great urgency. "The boy is out there. I heard about your son. He lives. And he is a prince."

Grace smiled. The old man worried far too much. Of course her son was alive out there. Of course he was a prince. "Yes, Ahcho, I know," she said, patting his feeble hand. "Thank you for telling me. I have known all along."

Then she stopped to cough and felt a swoon come over her. She may even have fainted. For in the next moment, she was at the base of the porch steps and Ahcho had her in his arms. The old man carried her up onto the porch, and she looked out at the horizon.

The blood-red sun hovered there, and the fields appeared bruised and painfully beautiful. This surprising beauty was why the Reverend had brought her here. She recalled his fierce and upright silhouette as he had stood against the setting sun. She had imagined him as fiery and pure as that red ball, his body bursting into a holy conflagration. It had not come to pass, although his bones would become one with this sandy soil soon. His ashes would turn to yellow dust. She looked down at her hands and saw that they, too, were already yellow from the loess.

The harsh land had won out in the end. Harsh but striking and filled with a strange history and life that could not always be understood but simply had to be accepted. The hills where he had traveled in search of their son rose in the distance, shadowed and purple. Ghosts were everywhere out there. They spread a lonely blanket over the landscape, as thick and impenetrable as the fur over her shoulders. They nestled deep into their ghostly sorrows, as she did into the heavy hide.

"You may set me down, Ahcho," she said softly.

"Madam does not wish to be carried inside?"

"I am perfectly all right," she said, and the coughing began again.

She stood and held on to Mai Lin. Her vision blurred momentarily but then returned. Even as she gripped the ancient flesh of her most trusted amah, Grace sensed she was alone. She had become as barren and as hollow as the house before her. There would be no more filling up of the heart.

The screen door hung before them on one hinge. The tired mesh flapped gently in the breeze. With all of her, she ached to have the Reverend beside her at that moment, although she was also glad that he had been spared this forlorn sight. She wondered, in the end, if he had come to believe in ghosts, as she had. That seemed possible, given the other changes that had come over him. And, if so, might he have allowed himself the comfort of imagining that their sorry cottage was inhabited by spirits now? Crowded with them, the setting might not seem so miserable after all. Perhaps she had been right to hear voices cascading down from the porch. She thought she heard little Wesley's happy cry now just inside the door.

As Ahcho held it open and Grace was about to step inside, she looked down and saw something tucked beneath the threshold. She knelt and found a copper coin half hidden where it must have fallen: an American penny, a young boy's treasure, now a gift to her.

Grace turned the dark coin over in her hand, examining it, squeezing tightly, hoping to feel something. Yes, her dear boy. He was here with her. Then, with trembling fingers, she placed it inside the pouch that had held the skull.

She stepped cautiously into the large, open room that had been stripped of the charming furniture that her husband and Ahcho had made prior to her first visit. Grace found herself drawn to the few items still left behind by scavengers. She touched the surface of things. She shifted a pot on the iron stove, traced the crack in a simple ceramic vase, and dragged a finger in a spiral over the dusty wooden mantel.

She could hear Mai Lin and Ahcho whispering to one another. They were far too worried about her. Mai Lin appeared at her elbow as she stood before the stone fireplace.

"Ahcho has prepared a mat for you. You must sleep, dear Grace."

Grace looked down at Mai Lin and was not surprised to hear the old woman's voice caress her name so sweetly. She had never been spoken to this familiarly by her servant, but now that seemed most right and appropriate.

"Yes," Grace said. "Sleep will be good. But first, help me with this, please?"

She opened the pouch again and gestured for Mai Lin to keep it open as she used her hand to swipe dust from the mantel inside. A yellow cloud rose from the embroidered dragon's mouth, and Grace tied shut the silk strings.

"Thank you, Mai Lin."

Grace felt satisfied. She had brought something to this distant corner of this distant land, and she would leave with something: an exchange of dust for dust.

Ahcho called them over to the corner where the children's cribs had once stood. The clever man had constructed a makeshift mattress from heaps of dirty straw there behind the tattered calico curtain. He patted it down, sending a cloud of dust into the air.

"Thank you, Ahcho. You have been most kind."

"It is not much," he said, his voice full of sorrow.

"It will do," Grace replied and let him help her down.

Grace lay still under the warm hide and listened to the gentle rocking of an overturned tin bucket on the floor. Weeds that grew between the floorboards rustled their dried pods. A breeze passed through the house with little resistance, issuing a hollow sound like someone's faint breath.

Grace took it all in: the wind and dust, the rising storm out there, the unsettled air inside. It was as the Reverend had once described it. A gentle, eerie peace settled over the place.

In the dimming light, she looked up at the sky through a hole in the roof. Earlier they had ridden under an achingly blue sky with pristine wisps of summer clouds. Now she could see denser clouds forming, low and tan and ominous.

"Is a storm coming?" she asked.

"A sandstorm, perhaps," Ahcho said. "We will be protected well enough in here."

"Good," Grace said. "Very good."

She did not sleep but remained alert and waiting for something. She could see out one of the open windows. The air had begun to swirl with crimson clouds. A storm was coming, no question about it, quite quickly from across the plains.

Grace shut her eyes, and in no time the first drops of rain fell. Water from the sky landed with a soft patter on the tile roof. She felt certain that this portent was auspicious. The future was most welcome, if seen in the right light.

Mai Lin lifted her head and made her drink from a small vial, Grace assumed to help her sleep.

"It's finally raining, is it not?" Grace asked.

Mai Lin nodded, or at least Grace thought she did. The storm had darkened everything, and night appeared to be descending fast. Grace glanced around the cottage and could no longer make out even the outline of the door. The screen flapped, and loose boards creaked. The air moved, and she swore she heard rain dripping from the eaves and spilling onto the packed ground. Out the window, she thought she saw great sheets of rain crossing the land. Soon the soil would yield to it.

But why weren't Mai Lin and Ahcho celebrating? The old pair had sat down with their backs against one of the cabin walls. They slumped against one another, and Grace blinked several times but could have sworn that she saw their hands intertwined on the gritty floorboard between them. My Lord, she thought, perhaps they were husband and wife. Maybe Mai Lin and Ahcho had been a couple all along. As the thought came to Grace, she chuckled to herself.

So little she and the Reverend had ever understood of what transpired around them in this strange land. How had they ever convinced themselves that they were anything but tourists? They were as ignorant as the most ignorant of coolies who eyed the white visitors with curiosity and fear. Grace's amusement at the way her Chinese servants had kept secrets seemed to lighten her heart and even her body. She could feel her limbs becoming less pained and her chest not nearly so burdened by the illness. Yes, it must be true about Mai Lin and Ahcho. There was love there all along.

How remarkable, but no less so, than the rain that finally fell here in this parched and blistered land. She listened for Mai Lin's snores and Ahcho's steady sleeping breath. When she was sure the two elders were asleep, Grace wished them sweet dreams and softly began to shift and move.

She pulled the great wolf hide around her and lifted the animal's jaw up over her head. As she sat up, she felt as small and light as a child under the enormous fur. If only the Reverend had not given it away, he might still be with her today. For Grace understood that the fur did offer true protection, though mostly against one's own fears.

She stood on weak legs and listened again for the rain. It continued to fall, and she was sure it was doing some good. She stepped slowly across the bare floorboards, opened the screen door, and stepped outside onto the porch. She paused before the broken-down railing where her husband had once stood and waxed poetic about the divine and mysterious landscape all around. In so many ways, he had been right. She did not regret for a moment coming to this land. For this rough place, with the help of the wolf hide now, had made her fearless. She was a modern American woman after all, striding into a future of her own making.

Grace stepped down the porch steps and into the rain, which was slowing now to a mere sprinkle. Her feet avoided the shallow puddles. When she looked up again, she saw her husband before her, a donkey trailing at his heels. The Reverend John Wesley Watson held the reins in one hand, an open book in the other. His steps were slow as he came closer, his head bent. His boots, long topcoat, and hat were covered in a thick yellow layer of loess. The Reverend squinted through his gold-rimmed glasses, concern on his face. He stopped and surveyed their cottage, and Grace wanted to tell him not to be upset at the sight. They would make it right again. But he merely pulled out his handkerchief and wiped his glasses of the infernal dust.

The rain stopped altogether, and Grace turned up the dirt road and began to walk. Little Wesley toddled along not far in front of her. He kicked pebbles as he went. His colorful Mongolian robe caught the sun's rays, and she thought she heard the high tinkling of bells accompanying him. Amulets and talismans swung from his neck and around his waist. Grace was glad he wore a thick fur hat upon his golden head, for it would protect him in the desert climate. She picked up her pace to join her son, but the distance between them remained the same no matter how quickly she moved her feet.

Then she saw why the boy was maintaining such a rapid pace. He followed his father, who strode on ahead, his donkey left behind. The Reverend's footsteps struck the hard dirt, his march unfaltering. Here on the road to Yao dao ho, the Reverend seemed at peace, his gaze taking in the landscape that he loved. Grace trailed after her husband and their firstborn child.

As she walked, she vaguely sensed Mai Lin hovering nearby, pressing a loving hand on her chest and applying the most pungent of compresses. Why was she always administering to Grace? She wished to be left alone now. She was trying her best to hear the song that Wesley and the Reverend were singing. A hymn, no doubt, but which one?

The Reverend stopped singing and counted softly to himself, saying the numbers of churches or converts or perhaps only the calculation of successful crops a farmer could hope to garner in a good year. The number of fields ready to cultivate, enumerated with satisfaction. Grace was happy for him that he had forgotten his disappointments and grave mistakes and had returned to what he knew best: the land. He was born of farmers and remained a farmer in his heart. The Reverend seemed contented as he wiped the sweat from his neck with a handkerchief that bore his initials.

Grace watched as he accidentally let it slip from his hand. When he did not stoop to collect it, she hurried to retrieve it from the muddy road, thinking it might be useful on the journey ahead. Little Wesley traipsed right over the flimsy thing, still singing with his head flung back. A carefree boy on his merry way.

When Grace reached the thin white handkerchief, she scooped it up, but it slipped through her fingers and was lifted away again on the wind. A strong breeze off the desert was not unusual in early summer, Grace reminded herself, as she heard soft moaning and weeping nearby. Mai Lin and Ahcho made far too much of things. She wished she could tell them not to worry. She had found her son and her husband, and they were on the right road now.

Grace turned to watch a gust take the pale handkerchief and blow it further up the trail, where it twisted and hung in the air, finally drifting over an ocean, a vast and white-capped sea. There on a steamer stood a proper and upright couple at the prow. They each held the hand of a small girl, a toddler somehow now, although when Grace had last seen her she had been but a babe in arms. Still, the couple kept the girl between them and pointed out at the endless water and squinted. Grace did so, too, and thought she could just make out America on the horizon.

The handkerchief danced in the swift breeze around this new family, but it was the child who spotted it and reached up to catch it in her small hand. She touched the worn, soft fabric to her cheek, and Grace realized that she could turn away now.

She gazed up the dirt road that led west from Shansi Province. On and on the land rolled, eventually arriving in the great Gobi Desert. The Reverend had told her how remarkable it was to come upon a section of the Great Wall, or the famous Ming Tombs, or the extraordinary monoliths known as the Sand Buddhas. Farther beyond those sights lay the tribal provinces where men in woven costumes herded sheep at the edge of steep cliffs. Bent farmers tended verdant crops and orchards on stepped terraces. Nomads, not all of them rogues, roamed the unpaved byways, hopping rides on ferry barges that crossed forgotten rivers.

Her husband had seen all of this and more. Grace wished with all her heart that she had traveled with him on his many journeys. But it was all right now, for soon she would join him in that mysterious land ahead.

Grace set off, knowing well how far she had left to go. She didn't want to delay a moment longer. She marched with purpose in her step, a modern woman on a road less traveled, but no longer frightened because of it. Indeed, she felt quite grand as she walked on, deeper and deeper into the adopted desert of her dreams.

Author's Note

My grandfather, the Reverend Watts O. Pye, was amongst the first missionaries to return to Shanxi Province in northwestern China less than a decade after the Boxer Rebellion of 1900. During his tenure in Fenchow as head of the Carleton College Mission and in conjunction with the Oberlin-Shansi Program, he helped build a hospital, roads, schools, and a library. I gather from Reverend Pye's journals that he was a fervent evangelist who recorded his success by the number of converts he made while roaming the region. He was the first white man to visit many of the villages and wrote with both humor and respect for the peasants he encountered. In romanticized prose, he recorded the stark and eerie beauty of the land. And while riding on donkey back over the rough terrain, he truly did read and recite aloud from the Romantic poets.

Reverend Pye and my grandmother, Gertrude Chaney, had three children in Shanxi. Their two daughters died young. My father, Lucian W. Pye, was the only offspring to survive into adulthood. The Reverend Pye's death occurred when my father was five, the same year he lost a sister. Not long afterward, young Lucian suffered an illness similar to rickets that kept him bedridden with limp bones for a year. Gertrude, a strong Midwesterner, managed these trials and stayed on in the mission compound in Fenchow with my father even under Japanese occupation. A year after Lucian left for college in the United States, Gertrude was finally forced to abandon China on the neutral Swedish ship *Gripsholm*, which left from Shanghai after the attack on Pearl Harbor. She always wanted to return but never did.

My father soon returned to China as a translator for the U.S. Marine Corps, and thanks in part to the G.I. Bill, he studied at Yale and went on to become a prominent sinologist in the field of political science. He authored over twenty books on China and the postwar developing countries of Asia. He always said that political scientists were frustrated novelists, but I think he was just being kind to me—although his scholarly approach did center on hard-to-quantify subjects such as the Chinese political mind and spirit.

Although I have never been to China, I was steeped in its aura. I grew up in a household decorated with Chinese objects, and they carried with them the feeling of an earlier time. My grandmother Gertrude doted on me as the youngest, and together we held tea parties using her finest porcelains from Shanxi. Families pass down wisdom and pain often in equal measure, and I sensed my father and grandmother's losses in China. Like many American families, the earlier generations survived experiences that we can hardly imagine, yet strangely inherit. This book is a fictional expression of that distant, haunted time and place—one that exists in my mind and not precisely on any map.

Acknowledgments

Like many debut novels, *River of Dust* has many generous people behind its creation. I am deeply grateful to Greg Michalson for his insightful and wise editing and for deciding that this story was worthy of Unbridled's excellent name. Much appreciation, too, goes to my agent, Gail Hochman, for taking on this project with enthusiasm. I especially want to thank Nancy Zafris, brilliant author and teacher, for her invaluable help redirecting my energies so that I wrote *this* manuscript in particular, and also for seeing that it was read by the right person at the right moment.

For a number of years, I worked on a previous manuscript set partly in China. While that book did not find its way to publication, many kind friends read part or all of earlier incarnations: Margaret Buchanan, Patty Smith, Nathan Long, Susann Cokal, the late Emyl Jenkins, Rosemary Ahern, James Marcus, Kirk Schroder, Phyllis Theroux, Brian Deleeuw, Meg Medina, Julie Heffernan, Jonathan Kalb, Kate Davis, David Heilbroner, Karl Marlantes, and Robert Goolrick. Additional authors Gigi Amateau, Leslie Pietrzyk, Belle Boggs, James Prosek, Dean King, Suzanne Berne, Sheri Holman, and Arielle Eckstut also generously extended a hand to help me join their ranks.

For many years I have benefited from the encouraging company of writers and publishing professionals through the literary nonprofit organization James River Writers. The Virginia Center for the Creative Arts,

WriterHouse, the Tin House Writer's Workshop, and the Acadia Summer Arts Program have each offered time, fine company, and a place to work.

My siblings, Lyndy and Chris, have offered generous support over decades, as have my in-laws, Carol and Earl Ravenal. I wish that my mother and father were here to enjoy this publication. My mother, Mary Toombs Waddill, was a crackerjack editor and reader, and her wisdom, goodness, and love continue to guide me always. My father wrote prolifically for decades, sometimes with a Red Sox or Celtics game on the TV, and showed me that writing can be both a discipline and a joy.

And, finally, this novel is dedicated to my immediate family: Eva, for her bright spirit and abiding faith in me and herself; Daniel, for his clearheadedness, humor, and solid love; and, most of all, John, who has been at my side for thirty-plus years and has helped us to make a hopeful life together where I could pursue what I wanted most.